HARVEST FEST HOMICIDE

EMERALD BAY MYSTERIES
BOOK 1

KATE ANNIE BROWN

DEDICATION

Hey, brother…Anthony, this one's for you. Thanks for always being supportive and encouraging, and for the many laughs over character backstories. And also for being the one I can count on for ridiculous memes and reels to make me smile on the hard days. Love you, Bub!

PROLOGUE
SAN FRANCISCO

"ARE YOU MAKING HEARTBREAK SOUP?" My roommate Georgia's voice echoed down the hall just before I saw her head pop around the corner of our tiny kitchen. Black curls framed her face wildly and her eyes narrowed behind thick glasses.

I turned back to the pot of creamy tomato basil soup, stirring it slowly to keep from splattering on myself. The sharp, acidic aroma of the tomatoes was cut perfectly by the addition of heavy cream and Italian herbs, with just a bit of sugar for balance. A wedge of parmesan lay on the counter, ready to be finely shredded over the top.

"Uh, it's tomato basil," I answered.

"Exactly." My roommate moved closer, inhaling appreciatively. "Girl, I'm not complaining, but the only time you make this is when one of us has a messy breakup or someone dies."

"That's not true." I rolled my eyes, opening my mouth to argue further, but then Georgia started naming names. She ticked them off with her perfectly manicured fingers, one by one.

"Okay, fine. You win." I hesitated. "I finally ended it with Christopher today." I scowled as I turned off the burner and ladled out two bowls of soup. "Happy now?"

Georgia's eyes turned compassionate, her mouth quirking downward.

"Aw, I'm sorry, Alex. I mean, don't get me wrong. I'm glad you're done with him." Georgia draped her arm over my shoulder. "But are you okay?"

"I'm fine." I returned her hug and then turned away, flipping the sandwiches that were sizzling on the grill pan. "I should have broken up with him sooner. I'm more upset about quitting the restaurant, actually."

"Wait, what? You quit Bloom?" Georgia grabbed my shoulders, spinning me around and forcing me to look into her eyes. "Spill."

The fact that we were both more distressed about my quitting the restaurant than breaking up with a guy said a lot about the quality—or lack thereof—of my former relationship.

I pointed toward our two seats at the bar with the spatula in my hand.

"Food first," I said. "Then I'll tell you everything."

"Deal," she conceded. Georgia grabbed two glasses and poured us drinks while I plated our triple cheese grilled sandwiches—creamy muenster, sharp cheddar, and tangy parmesan. I had added smashed avocado and spicy aioli to round out the flavors. I sliced through the sandwiches with a sharp knife and melted cheese oozed onto the plate.

We sat down and dug in. Georgia closed her eyes in bliss as she took the first bite of creamy soup.

"Mmm. I'll take this over your fancy pants concoctions any day." She had a point there. My current position at the restaurant was sauté chef and I was primarily in charge of sautéing food and preparing the various sauces and gravies that accompanied each dish. While I loved a good espagnole or béarnaise sauce, there was something about down home cooking that hit a little differently.

"Okay, so what was the final straw?" Georgia asked.

"He made one of the junior chefs cry," I said simply. There was more to the story than that, but I didn't want to get into it.

"What a jerk," Georgia said, shaking her head. She knew I had a soft spot for the younger chefs and line cooks just staring out in the culinary industry. They reminded me of myself at that age, with wide eyes and dreams too big for my midwestern hometown.

"I told Christopher I'd finish out the week, but I was done and so were we."

"Good for you, roomie. You deserve better," Georgia said, bumping her shoulder to mine.

Christopher had always been confident, which I had admired when we started dating a few months ago. He was also super talented, so I didn't begrudge him when he was promoted to head chef recently.

Too bad he'd let all that power go to his head. Maybe he thought he was doing his job to run the kitchen efficiently. But there were better ways to accomplish that than belittling and screaming at the staff. Unfortunately, his method was far too common, in my experience.

I'd loved Bloom, with its rich, yet delicate menu, fresh ingredients, and tight-knit kitchen brigade. It was upscale and classy without being too snooty. But I'd had enough of everyone walking on eggshells around Christopher and his toxic managerial style.

It had been a relief to walk out of the restaurant into the bright California sunshine, like a weight had been lifted from me and I could breathe again. Normally, I stayed until closing time and returned home long after midnight, but this was one of the rare days that I was only scheduled for prep and lunch. Even though I had no idea what I would do next, I knew I'd made the right decision.

Now, however, I was starting to come down from the adrenaline rush of such a rash decision, and a weary exhaustion began to settle into my bones. I had turned thirty just a few months ago, but today, I felt far older.

Thank goodness I'd made comfort food. I took another savory, yet sweet, bite of soup.

"What are you going to do now?" Georgia asked.

I sighed. "I'm not sure. I have a little savings, but I need to find a new gig ASAP."

The truth was, even before everything went down at Bloom, I had started to become disillusioned with the restaurant industry in San Francisco. Working the line was merciless, with long hours and meager pay, and there was a disconnect from the customers in the dining room. Having such a narrow focus on sauces had become tedious, and I missed variety. But I was good at my job, and I loved creating beautiful and delicious food.

I'd always dreamed of running my own place, once I'd paid my dues, but it was becoming abundantly clear I'd never be able to afford it in the Bay area. Georgia and I barely scraped by each month.

"You should do this," Georgia said, gesturing to our spread. "Some of your best work," she said, doing a chef's kiss with her hand.

I laughed. In times of stress, I always fell back on the recipes I'd learned in Granny Lu's kitchen. A wave of homesickness washed over me as I took a bite of sandwich.

A familiar prickle of premonition trailed up my spine and down my arm, goosebumps following in its wake. I stopped chewing, startled. I hadn't felt such a sense so keenly in years.

Speak of the devil, I thought. The phone rang, and I jumped up to answer it.

"Granny?"

"Hi, dear. How's my best girl?" My Granny Lu's sultry voice cracked through the phone.

I hesitated. In the blank space of my silence, Granny Lu picked up on the tension that coiled tightly around me.

"What's wrong?"

I paused before answering.

"Alexandria?" she prompted. Oof. She meant business with the use of my full name. Hardly anyone called me that.

"It's just been a long day, Granny."

"Tell me all about it, hon."

I recounted the events of the last few hours, and Granny tsked and offered up support in all the right places.

"But enough about me," I said. "I don't really want to talk about it anymore. How are things at the café?"

Granny owned and operated Lulu's Café, a cute little lakeside restaurant on Main Street in my hometown of Emerald Bay, Missouri. I had learned all my foundational culinary knowledge from her, in the warm, aromatic kitchen at Lulu's.

"You know, I think this phone call is fortuitous," she began slowly. I could practically hear the wheels turning in her mind. She was scheming.

"Word of the day calendar strikes again?" I asked, interrupting her train of thought.

"When you're my age, you have to keep the mind active to keep it young, you know," Granny bristled.

I grinned. Granny had crosswords and sudoku puzzles stashed all over her house and the café, as if she needed any more activity to keep her mind busy.

"*Anyway*," she said pointedly. "Where was I?"

"Fortuitous," I said obediently.

"Exactly. Well, my assistant cook has up and left me."

"Oh, no. What happened?" I asked. I knew she had been counting on her longtime assistant taking over more responsibilities at the café. Granny wasn't getting any younger and it was an enormous job for one person.

"Long story short, she up and decided to move to Texas to be near her grandchildren. But even with plenty of notice, I can't seem to find anyone suitable for the job."

I smiled to myself. Granny Lu had high standards and wouldn't hire just anyone. She'd sooner work herself into the ground doing it all on her own than hire someone with subpar skills.

"That is, there's no one suitable around *here*," she continued, emphasizing the last word. "But it sounds like I have a granddaughter who would be perfect for the job, and lucky for me, she's recently free of employment."

I was silent for a moment. Granny Lu wanted me to come home and work for her?

"What do you say, Alex? You've got the talent and the work ethic. And we miss you around these parts," Granny said.

"Hang on, Gran. I'm not a charity case, you know. I don't need you to bail me out of trouble."

"What do you take me for?" Granny Lu said. "You're one of the only people I'd trust to come cook for my customers. Who knows? You might actually like it. I won't be around forever, you know. And honestly...I could use a little help tightening up my books as well. You'd be doing me a favor, not the other way around."

I felt a lump in my throat. Granny didn't give out praise easily, so the fact that she had asked spoke volumes. Was the café in trouble? Economic times had been hard the past few years and had taken a toll on local businesses. If Granny needed my help, I didn't want to let her down.

But could I really return to Emerald Bay? I had history there, and it wasn't a big secret that I'd had no intention of returning when I'd left town twelve years ago. Weren't some things better kept in the past?

Then again, Granny was getting on in years, and I wasn't one to turn my back if my family needed me. Lulu's Café had been like a second home to me, and I had such warm, fond memories of the place.

Plus, I missed my dad, and even our scheduled weekly video chat didn't seem to be enough these days. I was becoming acutely aware of the passage of time slipping through my fingers. More so than I'd been as a teenager, desperate to leave the confines of small-town life.

Was anything really holding me to San Francisco now? Of course, I had friends, but we were all so busy we rarely saw one another. When you constantly work late into the night, it takes a toll on your social life.

Even the apartment lease was in Georgia's name, and I just paid her my portion of the rent. There was no shortage of singles in our circle of friends looking for a nice place like ours in a safe neighborhood, tiny though it was.

Maybe the timing of my exit from Bloom wasn't a rash decision or coincidence, but an opportunity paving the way for me to go a new direction. At least, until I figured out what I wanted to do with my life.

I cleared my throat.

"You know what, Granny? I'll think about it."

"That's all I ask, hon. You sleep on it and let me know."

"All right. I will."

"Love you, Alex."

"Love you too, Granny."

I ended the call and returned to the kitchen, where Georgia looked at me quizzically.

"What was that all about?" she asked. I realized I still stared at the phone in disbelief, and I set it down on the counter and stirred my cooled soup.

"It was my Granny Lu. She wants me to come home and help at the café."

Georgia swore softly and looked deep into my eyes as though trying to read my thoughts. She knew me well enough to see something there.

"You're leaving, aren't you?"

I didn't really need to think on it, like I'd told Granny Lu. She needed me, and I'd made up my mind before I'd even hung up the phone. Sure, I could be a little impulsive, but I trusted my gut, and my instincts were usually right. I thought about the premonition I'd had just before Granny called me. I hadn't felt my weird sixth sense for years, and I wondered at the significance of its sudden appearance.

I slowly nodded. "I think I am. After promising to never return, I'm finally going home."

CHAPTER 1
SOMETIMES YOU WANT TO GO WHERE EVERYBODY KNOWS YOUR NAME

EMERALD BAY, TWO MONTHS LATER

"YOUR DOG POOPED on my side of the yard again." Deacon Lane's deep voice boomed through my screen door. I jumped mid-coffee pour and sloshed hot liquid all over my left hand.

I gritted my teeth and stepped over to the sink, rinsing my scalded skin under the cool water.

"Be right there," I called, biting back a sarcastic reply. I preferred nobody speak to me before my first cup of coffee, but human interaction looked to be unavoidable this morning. I dried my hands and begrudgingly grabbed a small bag to retrieve the offending waste.

The screen door slammed behind me as I walked into the back yard I shared with my duplex neighbor. The sky was a brilliant blue, sunshine dappled the cool autumn morning, and a gentle breeze ruffled my hair. It would have been a beautiful day, if it weren't for Deacon's stupid, handsome face grinning at me in that self-satisfied way of his.

The mystery mix pooch I'd recently adopted sat at Deacon's feet, on the receiving end of a good scratch behind the ears. I'd named him Captain America in honor of my favorite Avenger. He was part blue heeler, but the rest of his heritage was questionable. Captain had a coarse, multicolored coat of gray, black, brown, and white, with ears that flopped over adorably rather than standing straight up.

His tongue lolled to the side happily and his brown eyes watched me innocently. I swear, it looked like he was smiling.

"Traitor," I muttered at Cap, as I trudged past the two of them.

"Right by the fence over there." Deacon pointed with one hand, the other lazily holding a cup of coffee. *Not* spilled on his hands, I noticed. I quickly scooped up the offending poop and disposed of it in the trash bin.

Sheila Jenkins really did me dirty when she rented out the east side of her duplex to me when I returned home a little over a month ago. As an old family friend, she knew the history I had with Deacon and purposely omitted that he was the "model tenant" living next door.

Sheila isn't exactly known for her discretion, so it must have killed her to keep that little tidbit to herself. And Deacon had been conveniently out of town when I'd seen the place, fallen in love, and promptly moved in.

I hadn't been back home, other than my twice-yearly visits, since we graduated high school. I'd managed to avoid Deacon for twelve years, dividing my time between my family and childhood best friend.

Although I'd been frustrated with Sheila when Deacon turned up on my doorstep to welcome me to the neighborhood, I'd determined to do the mature thing and bury the hatchet. High school was a long time, ago, after all. But it turned out that a grown-up Deacon had come up with new and different ways to get under my skin.

I sighed, admiring the view beyond the backyard fence. Halloween was less than two weeks away, and the trees were beginning to change color, with layers of crimson, gold and orange. Sparkling dewdrops clung to the spiderwebs along the fence, making it appear as though they were hung with tiny jewels.

Despite Deacon, the duplex townhome was a lovely place, and I was happy with my decision to return to Missouri, even if it was only temporary. Granny and I agreed I'd work for her at least six months, and then we'd decide if I should make it permanent or help her find a replacement.

After years of cramped living in San Francisco, having so much space seemed luxurious, almost excessive. Georgia and I had struggled every month to make rent on the tiny one-bedroom place we'd shared in the city. Here, I had two bedrooms, an enclosed garage, and the shared back yard. A bathroom all to myself was the icing on the cake.

Situated at the top of a hill, the property sloped down toward the city park and creek beyond. My upstairs bedroom had a small balcony with an even better view. Past the thick trees of the valley, I could spot a tiny sliver of the lake into which the creek flowed.

I turned back to Deacon and my dog. "Come on, Cap, time for your walk." Cap ran to me at the mention of his favorite word, his mottled gray and black tail wagging.

"Aren't you going to say, 'good morning?'" Deacon asked.

"Morning, Chief," I ground out politely.

"Good morning, Alex." I briefly glanced at Deacon before ducking inside. His warm brown eyes held a bit of mirth, and I got the feeling he was laughing at me.

The irony that he was now the head of the Emerald Bay police force wasn't lost on me. As teens, our citizenship was closer to misdemeanor-adjacent, rather than law-abiding. And Deacon had been the ringleader of it all.

I stepped back into my cozy living room, holding the door open for Cap. He wasted no time trotting over to the set of hooks on which hung his harness and leash. He parked himself in front of it and looked at me pointedly, his white chest puffed out and paws shuffling with anticipation.

"I know, I'm coming," I said. I rushed into the kitchen and took a large swig of what remained of my coffee. Ick. It was plain black, considerably cooled, and remarkably unsatisfying.

Cap whined from the entryway. Promising to make myself a fresh cup with plenty of cream and sugar after our walk, I quickly prepped Cap, slipped on my favorite walking kicks, and headed out the door.

Cap and I rounded the side of the house and cut through the narrow walkway between the neighbor's fence and ours. Wayfinder Trail, a paved jogging and biking path that wound through town, skirted the back end of our property, and soon Cap and I were walking briskly down the hill toward the park.

Apartment living paired with my hectic schedule hadn't allowed me to have a dog the last few years. When my aunt, who is a nearby veterinarian, had called and asked me to foster a homeless dog that had been brought to her practice, I'd made the quick drive to her office.

I'd taken one look into Cap's eyes and felt an instant connection. As weird as it sounds, it was like he knew what I was thinking and feeling, and vice versa. He was a bit of a mess at first, with a dirty, matted coat and trust issues with humans. But once he'd been cleaned up, loved on, and had the ticks removed, the proud and loyal dog he truly was had begun to shine through. Captain had come home to live with me as soon as he'd gotten a clean bill of health, and we'd bonded fiercely over the past few weeks.

Our daily morning walk through town was quickly becoming one of my favorite parts of the day. Back in the city, I'd usually slept late into the morning after working all night. And although I still wouldn't classify myself as a morning person, there was something refreshing about starting the day with a brisk, scenic walk.

The trail left the confines of my neighborhood and entered a thick tunnel of trees. Birds sang overhead and squirrels darted across the path, stopping every so often to search for fallen nuts along the ground.

It had rained last night, and damp yellow leaves clung to the pavement, still wet in the shade of the trees. The pungent, earthy smell of decomposing leaves swirled around me. There was a crisp nip in the October air, perfect for the light hoodie I'd slipped on.

Soon, we had emerged from the wooded area and the trail opened to the city park. Cap picked up the pace eagerly. A few parents and children were out, the toddlers squealing in delight on the baby swings and preschoolers chasing one another through the dewy grass.

Supplies for the Halloween Harvest Festival, which would be opening later in the week, were piled up in the open spaces. A few volunteers worked together organizing decorations and an enormous mound of hay bales.

Cap and I took the trail away from the children's playground, past the picnic area, amphitheater, and through the vast open space that led to the bridge over Hollow Creek. I stopped in the center of the bridge, as had become my habit, and took a deep breath. Cap sat quietly next to me, as though he, too, needed this moment of peace before a busy day.

Clear water bubbled over smooth river stones, its pleasant rushing sound a soothing melody to my ears. The ornamental trees throughout the park were gorgeous, going out in a blaze of colorful glory before their winter sleep.

I hadn't realized how much I'd longed for a true autumn and change of the seasons. Looking out at the midwestern morning almost brought tears to my eyes.

At times I missed San Francisco. The city held such rich heritage, a bevy of culinary delights, and my diverse group of friends. I still mourned the loss of proximity to the ocean and watching the fog roll in off the bay.

However, I did not miss the smog and people living practically on top of one another.

Emerald Bay had a beauty all its own, and the slower pace of life had been the balm I didn't know my soul needed. I took a deep breath, readying myself for whatever this day would bring.

"Mornin', Alex!" a familiar voice called. I turned and waved to Tucker, one of my after-school employees.

"Hey, Tucker! Y'all have a good day at school." I cleared my throat, realizing how quickly my accent had come back after years of hiatus.

Tucker walked hand-in-hand with one of the Miller girls, though I couldn't remember her first name. They both gave me a friendly wave back. She was swimming in his large sweatshirt, and it looked like he was carrying her backpack—unless Tucker had developed a sudden fondness for dusty rose luggage. The high school was just a block past the park, and I turned away as they disappeared down the street.

Cap and I headed in the opposite direction. Across the bridge, the path forked. The left trail led to the downtown district, the quintessential Main Street, USA. The right path led to the lake, with the creek flowing on one side and trees lining the other. A small, sandy beach lay beyond.

At the end of Main Street, Lulu's Café stood proudly, the green and white striped awning shivering in the breeze. Above the awnings, cheerful window boxes were affixed directly under each second-story pane, filled so full of bright red flowers that the blooms spilled over the sides.

I chuckled to myself. Granny Lu lived in the apartment above the café, and her black thumb was legendary. However, she faithfully planted seasonal flowers all year long. Silk ones, of course, that couldn't be killed.

My eyes flitted back down to Lulu's. The red brick exterior was faded, but clean and sturdy, and the south door opened to a small patio that held a few iron café tables.

When the weather was warm, those tables were shaded by large umbrellas that matched the awning, and Lulu's would be hopping with lake rats and beachgoers enjoying the tastiest fare in town, along with homemade ice cream and sorbets.

But on a cold day such as this one, patrons would find a cozy atmosphere and hearty meals inside the café, and locals would linger over hot beverages, pastries, and small-town gossip.

We took the route alongside the lake today, following the creek as it widened and flowed into a peaceful cove. The sandy beach was deserted, which was a shame, as the sunrise was spectacular this morning. The sun peeked over the rim of the lake, scattering golden rivulets along the blue surface.

I kept to the path, which left the beach and followed a rocky shoreline north along the public lake access until it wove into a waterside neighborhood.

I admired the tidy front yards of the quaint lake cottages we passed. Some were permanent residences, but many were vacation rentals catering to a steady stream of visitors looking for a peaceful retreat. A few of the properties had docks stretching out into the lake, holding various watercrafts. A lone fisherman stood on one, casting his line out into the water.

Strains of a melody drifted on the breeze, and I noticed a bearded man sitting on a front porch, strumming a guitar and singing softly. He didn't seem to notice me, lost in his mournful tune of lost love.

As I came to the end of the street, a large dumpster stood out like a sore thumb amongst the pristinely manicured lawns. It was placed in front of one of the older cottages, construction materials littering the front porch. The owner must have been in the middle of a renovation, bringing the property up to date to match the rest of the charming neighborhood.

At the house next door, an elderly woman was out planting a gorgeous batch of yellow and purple mums in front of her porch. Her back was to me, but it looked a lot like Myra Crawford, who had been the mayor's wife when I was a kid.

I wasn't surprised at all to see the local garden club's "Best Bloom" award staked by her mailbox for all to see. Never mind that it was from the Rose Festival back in June. I'd probably leave it up year-round too, if I were her.

The path peaked up a hill past the neighborhood and sloped back down toward the Shady Glen Mobile Park as the trees thickened and encroached on the trail. A collection of jack-o'-lanterns were arranged at the front gate, along with several well-kept shrubs and bushes. Past the rows of homes, there was a small private beach for residents.

Rusty Davenport, the owner and manager of the place, sat in a lawn chair beneath the steps to his trailer, a paper plate balanced on his lap and a hearty breakfast piled high on it. His Pit Viper sunglasses caught the early morning light, reflecting a yellow-tinted rainbow of colors back at us.

"Nice morning, huh?" Rusty called, giving us a friendly wave. He was a bit rough around the edges, but always seemed cheerful enough.

"Sure is," I said, smiling.

"Here you go, Cap," Rusty said, standing and tossing the end of a sausage link toward us. Cap eagerly gobbled it up, tail wagging. I wasn't sure Rusty remembered my name, but of course, Cap made fast friends with everyone he met.

Wayfinder Trail split just ahead, and we took the path that curved back toward town. If we'd continued along the lake, the trail wove through a swath of dense forest before leading to some of the nicer estates in the area, my best friend Cara's house included. She and her family had moved into her childhood home a few years back, when her parents relocated to a retirement community for active seniors on the other side of the lake.

By the time Cap and I crested the hill behind our duplex, I had removed my hoodie, my workout tank having plastered itself to my sweaty body despite the cool temperature. I punched in the four-digit garage code, put out fresh water and food for Cap, and took the stairs two at a time. I was eager for a cool shower.

Half an hour later, I came back downstairs and made a fresh cup of coffee—this time with plenty of salted caramel creamer.

Since I prepared food all day, I generally kept my breakfast a simple affair. I tossed fresh berries and granola over a bowl of yogurt and curled up in my oversized corner chair, a splurge purchase I'd gifted myself when I moved in. Cap curled up contentedly next to the ottoman, the black and gray fur on his back shining in the morning sunlight. I took a satisfying sip of my coffee, savoring the last few peaceful moments before the rush of the day.

―――――

I let myself in the back door of Lulu's Café, the smell of fresh-baked goods wafting over me. Nyla Freeman came in early each morning, taking care of the day's baking. Hot cinnamon rolls, fresh loaves of crusty bread, and bubbling apple pies lined the countertops, cooling on neatly organized racks.

Nyla was busy wiping down the center worktable, her full sleeve of tattoos on display down her bare right arm. Baking kept her perpetually warm, and she sported muscle tanks year-round beneath a flour-dusted apron. She looked up and greeted me as I pulled the door shut behind me.

Granny Lu had her back to me, humming along to the classic country station playing from the ancient radio and filling the coffee pot.

"Granny, I thought we agreed I'd open today," I said, shaking my head at her. Granny turned around and pulled me into a big hug.

Though I was now a head taller than her, Granny's arms still felt like a warm, safe place to be. She'd been training me for a month, but I was still waiting for her to loosen the reins a bit.

Lord knew she needed to slow down, but that was proving easier said than done, especially since she lived in the apartment directly overhead. There was a separate entrance tucked between

Lulu's and the apparel shop next door, but even so, it was far too easy for her to pop downstairs to check on things. I'd quickly learned it was pointless to schedule her to have time off.

"I know, hon," Granny answered. "It's just that I've started my morning with Nyla and a cup of coffee every day for nearly twenty years and it's a hard habit to break. I'm going to get out of your way and drink my coffee. You won't even know I'm here, promise," she said.

I looked skeptically at Nyla, and she winked at me. Granny was right; Nyla was nearly as much a part of Lulu's as Granny Lu herself. She was in her mid-fifties now, but in excellent shape. It seemed contradictory that someone who baked treats for a living could be so fit, but Nyla was an avid runner and weightlifter, the only indication she had aged in the last fifteen years being the gray that liberally streaked her deep red hair.

The best thing about Nyla, though, was her calm, unflappable demeanor. "Cool as a cucumber," Granny Lu always said.

Granny, on the other hand, was a seventy-five-year-old firecracker with plenty of spark left. Although her spirit animal was the Energizer bunny, she didn't have the stamina she demanded of herself anymore. But try telling her that.

"All right, then, why don't you go sit down? I'll bring the coffee when it's done," I said.

Granny ignored me, instead puttering around the large kitchen, cleaning up this and that. She grumbled something about not being a porcelain doll.

I sighed, removing the oversized flannel shirt I'd used as a jacket and hanging it on a hook by the back door. I grabbed a fresh green apron and tied it over my plain black tee. My brown hair was braided away from my face on both sides and secured into a bun at the nape of my neck with bobby pins. No stray hairs in this kitchen. Not today, Satan.

I washed my hands at the enormous sink basin as though preparing for surgery. Granny and I were both sticklers for personal hygiene and food safety. I glanced at today's menu, and then ducked into the pantry and began pulling out the necessary ingredients. We offered a daily soup special, and as it was Tuesday, the offering was county potato soup—a hearty, cheesy concoction filled with veggies and topped with crispy bacon.

I chopped onions, garlic, carrots, and celery, setting a portion aside to add to quiche later. The rest I began sautéing in a huge stockpot drizzled with olive oil. They sizzled satisfyingly, and I quickly tossed the scraps and began peeling potatoes.

Granny and Nyla had exited the kitchen and sat at the bar, chattering away. The kitchen was arranged in a U-shape, with countertops and supplies running along three sides and a large stainless-steel island in the middle.

A half wall ran along the fourth side, creating a large window through which we could see out into the restaurant. Two swinging doors were situated at each end of the wall, one for entering and the other for exiting.

A narrow walkway ran between the half wall and the bar with its smooth, well-worn wooden top. Coffee cups and supplies lined the shelves underneath the bar, within easy reach for our servers. Beyond that, comfortable, jewel-green booths lined the walls of the café. Spotless windows overlooked Main Street to the west and the patio and park to the south.

The café hadn't changed much since Granny opened it when I was eight years old, but she'd cared for it well, and it showed. The walls were decorated with an eclectic lake theme. Funky vintage waterskiing posters mingled with mounted pieces of driftwood, netting, and oars arranged artfully throughout the space. I swallowed past a lump in my throat when my eyes landed on the glass-encased display of my grandpa's fishing lures along the north wall.

Pops had been the only one who'd ever dared called Granny "Lulu," suggesting the name for the café as a joke, but it had stuck.

To everyone else, Granny was Luella Rivers, or most often, simply Lu. A woman beloved by the townsfolk. I hoped that in time, they'd come to accept me as well. I cringed at the memories some of them might have of me. I'd grown up a lot and had a new appreciation for Emerald Bay, but I was still waiting to see what it thought of me as an adult Alexandria Rivers.

Lulu's wasn't in danger of closing, not yet, anyway. Granny had asked me to look over the budget and tighten things up where I could. Her profit margin had grown thin in the past few years, while the cost of supplies and ingredients steadily rose. She'd stubbornly refused to increase prices and had gotten herself into quite the financial pickle as a result.

I'd spent many nights poring over spreadsheets, figuring out what was working well and what needed to go, and then slowly implementing the changes. To her credit, Granny had been willing to listen to my suggestions and take action. Where she saw fit, that is.

The café had never been a fancy place, but the food was always delicious. We offered a daily soup, a handful of signature sandwiches and salads, and a limited menu of other seasonal specialties. Of course, Nyla kept us stocked with plenty of dessert items and baked goods.

By the time I had the potato soup simmering, quiche baking, and bacon cooling on the counter, Nyla and Granny had cleaned up after themselves, and we all readied for opening. At ten o'clock sharp, I crossed the black and white checkered tiles, unlocked the front door, and flipped the sign to open.

A wreath of orange and scarlet leaves graced our front door, coordinating with the floral bouquets affixed to the black lamp-posts along the sidewalk.

Our first customers arrived moments after I'd flipped the sign, like clockwork. I opened the door for them as they shuffled inside.

The Vets, affectionately named, were a retired group of former military members. They came in every Tuesday and Thursday morning to play cards, shoot the breeze, and avoid their wives.

"Good morning, boys." I smiled. Of course, I shouldn't have favorite customers. But if I did, they were top of the list.

"Mornin', Alex." Ike Townsend grinned at me, removing his hat and exposing his shiny bald head. I helped Reggie Newman and Jim Wetherby with their coats, hanging them on the tree next to the front door. Curtis Jones, the last member, rubbed his bare hands together, attempting to warm them, as the foursome slid into chairs at their usual table. They never sat in a booth, claiming booths were not conducive to foursome card games. As it was, they still frequently accused one another of cheating.

"I hope Nyla made cinnamon rolls today," Curtis said.

"She sure did. I'll bring one right out. Anyone else?" I asked. Jim nodded while the other two shook their heads.

"The usual for everyone, or is anyone feeling adventurous today?" I waggled my eyebrows at them. They stuck with the usual three black coffees and one iced tea.

"Wait, what was that fruity iced tea you had me sample last week?" Ike asked, as I turned to walk away.

"That would be our strawberry-peach black tea," I answered. "A Cara specialty."

"Yeah, that one. I'll have that."

I grinned. My best friend Cara made delicious handmade artisan teas, and we had recently started carrying them. Some, like the strawberry-peach, we brewed into iced tea. Others, such as the specialty autumn blends, we served hot.

I slipped into the kitchen, where Jasmine, our head waitress, was already pouring cups of coffee for the guys. Her curly black hair, held away from her face with a scarf, bobbed along to the music.

"Curtis and Jim want cinnamon rolls, too," I said, scooping ice into a glass and filling it with fresh-brewed tea. The sweet scents of tart strawberry and ripe peach wafted up.

"Sure thing, sugar," Jasmine said. She expertly balanced her loaded tray with one hand as she exited the kitchen. She was back in a flash, the empty tray tucked under her arm.

"Reggie says he wants to try, and I quote, 'Alex's egg pie' today," Jasmine said, doing air quotes as she leaned over the half wall. I laughed as I grabbed a potholder and pulled a ham, cheese, and spinach quiche out of the oven.

"Right on time," I said. Since we opened mid-morning, we didn't serve a full breakfast menu, but there were plenty of folks who stopped in before the lunch rush for a hot drink and quiche, or one of Nyla's fresh pastries.

An elderly couple entered and seated themselves. Granny seemed to recognize them, because she left the kitchen to say hello. I saw her gesture in my direction and they turned their attention on me.

The woman gave a tentative smile, but the man scowled at me, his chaotic white eyebrows drawn together so tightly the two had become one. I wracked my brain wondering what I'd done in my wayward youth to warrant his ire. He clearly remembered something about me, and it wasn't good.

He shifted his grip on the cane he'd brought in, and the memories came crashing down on me. I shuddered, recalling the elderly man shaking his cane at me in a threatening manner. Of course. The gnome incident.

The man's name was Dr. Pepper. No, I'm not making that up; it's his honest to goodness name. He was a retired dentist who had been old since I was a child. Years ago, he'd had an impressive collection of garden gnomes.

The night before fall homecoming junior year, Deacon and I had stolen twenty-two of them and placed them as offensive and defensive players on the football field. Cara had refused to participate, because her family went to church with the Peppers, and she had a pesky habit of trying to talk sense into us. It didn't usually work.

Deacon and I had found the prank hilarious, but Dr. Pepper was less than amused. You'd think a man named after a soft drink, with an affinity for garden gnomes, would have a whimsical sense of humor. That was not the case.

I shook my head at the memory. Oh, to be young and sense-less again. Even as I thought this, I tried not to smile at the absurdity of the prank. It was ultimately harmless, and I still found it kind of amusing.

I was literally up to my elbows in raw ingredients but decided to apologize to Dr. Pepper as soon as I had a spare moment. I had found that most of Emerald Bay's residents were willing to give me a second chance when approached in humil-ity, with only a precious few who were not so gracious.

I didn't have long to ruminate on the situation as the café grew busier by the minute. The hours flew by as I prepared for lunch and Jasmine hustled back and forth serving our morning customers.

I did manage to apologize to Dr. Pepper, which was met with a noncommittal grunt. Well, at least I tried. It would take time for people to realize I'd changed, and I tried to shake it off the best I could.

Nyla finished washing up her baking supplies and headed home, while Granny wrapped up her socializing and pitched in with the cooking.

"Can't stop, won't stop." That's the motto of Luella Rivers.

By noon, over half the booths were filled and the café hummed with conversation. The sunny sky had gradually dark-ened all morning, and now a steady rain fell, driving customers indoors. The comforting scents of simmering soup and grilling paninis filled the air.

I heard the jingle of the bells on the door and looked up to see a rail-thin man, with salt and pepper hair, entering. He looked to be a few years older than my dad, but I didn't recog-nize him.

Cara was walking in behind the man, struggling with a large box under one arm and pulling her unwilling toddler along with the other. I wasn't sure if the older man had seen her or not, but he'd certainly let the door slam in her face.

A cold prickle skittered over my forearms, and I shivered.

Since I'd been home, my emotional sensitivity had been on high alert, and the sensations I'd steeled myself against since I was young had returned in full force. An unpleasant discomfort settled over me, and I wondered what it meant.

One of the Vets scowled at the man's retreat and jumped up to hold the door for Cara. As quickly as a man waiting for a hip replacement could, that is.

"Thanks," Cara said. Catching my eye, she called, "Special delivery!"

I stepped out of the kitchen to relieve her of the box. Her daughter, Olive, clung to her tightly, her blond curls covering one eye.

"Why didn't you give me a call? I could have picked these up later," I said, setting the box down at the bar.

"It's okay, I needed to get out of the house," she said, jerking her head toward Olive. I smiled at the little girl.

"Do you have a hug for Auntie Alex today?" I held my arms out. Olive promptly stuck two fingers in her mouth and buried her face in her mom's shoulder.

"It's been one of those days," Cara said, shrugging. Cara was a stay-at-home mom to two-year-old Olive and four-year-old Arthur.

Last year, Cara had started selling her homemade tea blends in an online shop, and after I'd moved back, I'd talked her into letting us sell them at Lulu's.

I opened the box and examined the neatly packed glass jars and cardboard boxes. Each box and jar were stamped with the cursive letters "PT" for "PersnickeTea," Cara's brand.

"What did you make this time?" I asked.

"The usual, plus a few fall blends. Spiced apple, cinnamon orange, and lavender lemon."

"Sounds amazing," I said. I glanced at the kitchen, wishing I had time to sit and have a cup with Cara. Her tea obsession had begun several years earlier, and she made the most delicious blends.

"I know, you've got to get back to work," she said.

"Sorry. Why don't you stay and have a bite?" I lowered my voice. "Maybe Olive would like a sweet treat? I have a little ice cream to top the apple pie."

Cara speared me with a look. *You're not feeding this child dessert for lunch, so don't even think about it.* Message received. How did moms communicate with a single arched brow?

"Right. How about a grilled cheese with applesauce instead?" I suggested.

"Sounds great. And soup for me," she said.

"You got it. Have a seat and I'll bring out a kiddie pack," I said, ducking behind the bar and retrieving a small coloring book, cup of crayons, and a sticker sheet that we kept for our littlest customers.

By the time I got them settled, the lunchtime rush was in full swing and I hustled back to help Granny in the kitchen. We worked side-by-side as Jasmine breezed in and out putting in orders and filling drinks.

I glanced up and saw the thin man from earlier trying to flag Jasmine down, but with a full tray blocking her view, she didn't see him. Another man had finally joined him at table four, and they seemed impatient to order. I sighed, grabbing a notepad and heading over before they could get huffy.

"Welcome to Lulu's," I said, giving my best customer service smile. "Are you ready to order?"

"I'll have the soup of the day," Thin Man said.

"Excellent. That comes with a choice of one of Nyla's fresh hot rolls, half a sandwich, or one of our small salads."

"Just the soup," he said gruffly.

"All right. And you, sir?" I turned to his companion, a portly fellow with rosy cheeks.

"Chicken salad on a croissant for me. With sweet potato fries and a slice of pie."

"You got it. Jasmine will have those out just as soon as they're ready."

"Thanks, sweetheart," Red Face said, handing me the menus with a smarmy smile. I got the feeling if I stuck around, he might try to sell me a used car.

I tried to check my attitude as I re-entered the kitchen. Usually, I wasn't so uncharitable to our customers, but my sixth sense was going haywire about those two.

"Jasmine, I got table four's order," I said, washing my hands again and ladling out soup.

"Thanks, Alex. The less time I have to spend with those two, the better." She swept out of the kitchen with a full tray of drinks before I could ask her what she meant.

"Granny, who are those guys?"

Granny looked up from where she stood plating salads, glancing through the open kitchen and across the café. She shook her head.

"Alan Harvey and Buddy Sikes. Misery loves company, I see."

"What do you mean?"

"Nothing, dear." She waved me off. "I shouldn't speak that way about our clientele, anyway."

Granny Lu hardly ever spoke ill of anyone, which was why her words only added to my curiosity. It would have to wait, though. A party of six had just walked in the door, and we were slammed—at full capacity, in fact.

I hadn't expected the lunch crowd to be so full and hadn't scheduled another waitress, so I felt guilty watching Jasmine run back and forth serving all the tables, but there wasn't much I could do besides get the food ready as quickly as possible.

I looked through the kitchen window and saw Cara making polite conversation with Brenda and Jessica Holliday at the table next to her booth. Jessica was an old classmate of ours—she'd been the resident beauty queen of Emerald Bay High—and more of a frenemy than anything.

I'd once heard her mother, Brenda, self-identify as a trophy wife, so you get the idea of what their family was like. I rolled my eyes as they both tossed their unnaturally platinum hair over their shoulders.

Olive had gained enough confidence to toddle over to the next table, charming all the Vets with her gap-toothed grin.

"Olive, come back, please," Cara said.

Olive looked back with a mischievous smile and ran in the opposite direction of her mother. Cara excused herself from the conversation, hustling to grab her daughter, but not before Olive had made it across the room, bumping into table four before Cara could scoop her up.

Alan Harvey scowled at Cara.

"I'm sorry," Cara said. "She got away from me."

"If you can't control your little brat, you shouldn't bring her here," he spat out.

Cara's eyebrows practically raised off her forehead as she quickly went from apologetic to apoplectic. I was ready to cheer her on as she prepared to go full mama bear on him, but Granny had assessed the situation and rushed over to intervene.

She put an arm around Cara and whispered something to her. Cara calmed, nodding to Granny as she took Olive back to her table. She turned around once to glare at the rude man.

"Now, this is a family place, and we welcome customers of all ages," Granny said, turning to the two men and daring them to argue. "But, I do apologize for the disturbance of your meal, gentlemen. How about a nice dessert on the house?" Granny managed to turn on a charming smile.

She was killing him with kindness. She was definitely a better person than me.

Alan muttered something unintelligible, unable to meet Granny's eyes, but his companion, Buddy, nodded enthusiastically. About the dessert, I presumed.

Granny turned back to the kitchen. The rest of the café suddenly got very busy and loud, pretending we had not been eavesdropping on the whole affair.

As the rush slowed a bit, I made a pass through the café,

checking on the tables to see if anyone needed drinks refilled or dessert brought out. I'd retrieved a coffee carafe from the bar and was pouring beverages for table nine when I noticed those two men at table four again.

When you work in the service industry, you become a master at reading body language. And though these two spoke in quiet tones, they were agitated with one another.

I passed a little closer to their table, noticing that the one named Alan had ordered another bowl of soup after finishing the first one. Buddy's pie sat half-eaten as he pointed an accusing finger at Alan, and his face was even redder than before. Animosity rolled off the two of them in waves, and I had to stop myself from gasping at the intensity of it.

I braced myself with one hand on the edge of a table, pretending to straighten the condiment caddy in the center of it with the other. My chest tightened and I felt my pulse speed up as hot anger overwhelmed me—theirs, not my own.

I took several calming breaths, my eyes darting around the café for a new focus. I spotted Cara and Olive, now happily eating lunch. Blocking out all the noise around me, I watched Cara make silly faces at her daughter, Olive giggling in return.

That was better. At least, I felt stable enough to edge closer to the two men. Despite my discomfort, I was curious to hear what they were saying. Just as I walked by, Alan flung his arms out angrily, before slamming them down on the table. Unfortunately, the full bowl of county potato was in his way. Creamy soup flew through the air, splattering the carafe, my arms, and the front of my apron. The bowl wobbled and crashed to the floor.

"Whoa!" I jumped back a moment too late. A hush fell over the restaurant as Alan leaped to his feet. He looked around at the customers staring at us in surprise, embarrassed red blotches mottling his thin neck.

"I…uh…sorry. I have to go. Buddy, when you come to your senses, you know where to find me." Alan dug some cash out of his back pocket and threw it on the table. He hurried past me, bumping my shoulder in his rush to make a quick getaway.

Buddy handed me a stack of napkins.

"Here you go, sweetheart. Apologies. Business. You know how it is," he said.

I didn't, but I took the napkins anyway and wiped the dripping soup from my arms.

"It's all right. Accidents happen," I said, a tremor in my voice. "I'll just go wash up and then I'll bring your check," I said.

"Could you box me up another piece of pie to go? And I believe I'll take a set of the spiced apple tea. The wife loves that kind of thing."

"Of course," I said.

Buddy Sikes was soon on his way, and the lunch crowd trickled out. I tried to focus on our afternoon clean up, but something about my interaction with the two men didn't set well at all.

CHAPTER 2
UNPLEASANTVILLE

THE NEXT MORNING DAWNED DREARY, and I yawned and stretched as I readied Cap for his walk. There had been nothing but blissful silence from the other side of the duplex, and I thanked my lucky stars for the peaceful morning.

As we left the house, I noticed Deacon's police car was still in the driveway. His personal vehicle, a gray pickup truck, was missing from its normal spot by the curb. The garage had been open when I'd come home the other day, and his extensive home gym setup didn't allow for any parking inside.

He'd been kicking the stuffing out of a punching bag when I'd slipped by, unnoticed, and peeked inside. A weight bench and squat bar took up a large portion of the space, plus the mountain bike I'd seen him riding out on Wayfinder occasionally.

The man loved to work out, and it showed on his muscled frame. Meanwhile, I had to force myself outside each morning to make sure Cap got his exercise.

I didn't like to take the same walking route every day, so we headed in the opposite direction on Wayfinder. This portion of the path wound through the neighborhoods of town, forking in multiple directions before meeting up with the lakeside paths.

Halloween decorations gave the neighborhood a festive air, ranging from friendly jack-o-lanterns to downright creepy grave-yards. Wizard's hats danced in the breeze along a front porch, and skeletal hands jutted up from the earth near crooked tomb-stones, as though escaping a freshly dug grave. A yard with every square inch covered in blow-up pumpkins and cartoonish monsters made me smile.

I was looking forward to having trick-or-treaters next week. We'd rarely had any kids come to the apartment, and I missed the tradition.

Lost in my thoughts, I ran through an actual spider web hanging from a low-lying branch above the sidewalk. Immedi-ately, I dropped Cap's leash and did some embarrassing ninja moves trying to get it off my face and arms. Cap stared at me in disapproval, wondering why we'd stopped, but he was obedient enough to wait for my outburst to subside.

I really, really hate spiders. It's the legs for me. Anything more than four legs just feels excessive.

I glanced around sheepishly, hoping nobody had witnessed my sudden jerky movements, but the street appeared to be empty.

"All right, Cap, show's over," I said, adjusting my shirt and picking up my bruised dignity. The trail met up with the down-town path as we left the neighborhood, and we headed up Main Street. It was still quiet as most businesses hadn't opened for the day, but I could see the back light on at Lulu's.

Nyla was up at the crack of dawn every day, churning out baked treats. She had promised a pumpkin roll today, and my mouth watered as I anticipated the sweet and spicy treat. This was why I needed the morning walk just as much as Cap. Prob-ably more so, actually.

Main Street was not a through road. To my left, Lulu's patio stood, leading to the public beach and park beyond. Straight ahead was a parking area for both places, and to the right, the road curved ninety degrees onto Oak Street. It led to the elementary and high schools, along with the town's grocery store. Taking another right led to Cherry Street, which held a few more downtown businesses, including the fire department behind the police station.

At the junction of Main and Oak, I left the downtown area and headed toward the park. Crossing the footbridge over the creek, I saw the entire area bustling with activity as volunteers were out early setting up for the festival. Opening night was tomorrow, and people scrambled to make sure everything was ready.

The pile of hay bales I had passed yesterday had been transformed into a cool maze, the entrance decorated with scarecrows, pumpkins, and corn stalks. By day it would be open for the little kids, but at night it turned truly creepy with strobe lights, fog, and monsters.

Hammers slammed rhythmically against wood as vendor booths were constructed to sell crafts, hot food, and drinks.

That reminded me, Lulu's was planning to have a booth selling chili, cornbread and desserts Saturday afternoon. I was representing the café in the chili cook-off, while Nyla was contributing pies in the bake-off.

I needed to make sure our supply order was set to be delivered by Friday morning. I mentally added it to my to-do list for the day.

I spotted Deacon unloading a truck bed full of pumpkins with Ravi Kumar, one of our friends from high school. Like me, Ravi had lit out of town as quickly as possible but had found his way back again a few years ago. I hadn't seen him since my return, but I'd heard he was teaching and coaching at the high school.

Deacon and Ravi carried large crates, stacking them on the ground next to a roped-off area that would hold the pumpkin launching competition. Entrants would compete to see which homemade contraption could hurl a pumpkin the furthest.

Deacon and Ravi added to an already enormous pile of

deformed gourds—apparently the rejects from all the local farms and grocery stores. I was too far away to hear their conversation, but Deacon laughed at something Ravi said, his face splitting into an easy grin.

I quickly turned away, intending to take the path that would lead up the hill toward home. I wasn't in the mood to talk or reminisce about our shared history.

At the same time, Cap jerked his leash in the opposite direction, and the thin strap slipped from my hand. In an uncharacteristic act of defiance, he bounded back toward the hay maze and disappeared through the entrance.

"Captain America Rivers! Come back right now!" I hissed, trying not to draw attention our way as I ran after him. I ducked under the orange and black bunting and followed him into the maze.

Though I was annoyed at my wayward dog, I had to admit that whoever had assembled the maze had done a great job. Giant spiderwebs covered the hay bales, and the intersections were decorated with skulls, headstones, and wide-mouthed jack-o-lanterns. Every so often a silhouette cut-out, made of black painted plywood, loomed over the path. Under the cover of darkness, it would be super creepy.

The walkway was wide enough for a few single hay bales to be scattered here and there, creating perfect hiding places for actors from the high school drama club. In the nighttime version of the maze, ghouls, monsters, and zombies would jump out and chase whoever dared enter. It was going to be a hit.

Where was my dog? The maze was more complicated than it appeared from the outside.

"Come here, boy," I called, trying to find the right path through the maze. I kept having to turn around and retrace my steps.

I stopped and listened. I could hear Cap whining, and I followed the sound.

Around the corner, I found Cap sniffing a large scarecrow

that had slumped from its perch over a bale of hay. I picked up his leash, looped it around my wrist, and bent down to rub his soft head.

"You know better than to run off like that," I scolded gently. Cap looked at me and whimpered.

"What is it?" I asked. He nosed the scarecrow again.

"You want me to fix it?" I asked. "Fine, we'll put the scarecrow back where it goes, and then we need to get home."

I tugged at the flannel fabric covering the back of the scarecrow, but something felt wrong. It was far too heavy to be stuffed with mere straw. Cold dread trickled down my spine.

My hand hovered above the thing, unsure what to do. I slowly reached down, over the back of the hay bale, and picked up an arm. A shock of terror slammed through my body. Lifeless, pale fingers dangled limply from the sleeve opening. Human ones.

I dropped the arm, wiping my suddenly sweaty palm against my leggings.

My heart pounded, a few steps ahead of my mind as I processed the scene before me. I reached for the floppy hat that had obscured the head and neck. I had to know for sure, and I peeled back the loose brim slowly before working up enough courage to remove it entirely.

Shaggy, salt and pepper hair covered the neck and ears. And as I bent down next to the body, I could see the dull, vacant eyes of Alan Harvey staring at the ground.

I was almost certain he was dead, but I had to be sure. Hands shaking, I gulped and felt along his wrist with two fingers. No pulse. His skin was sickeningly cool to the touch, but I jerked my hand back as if I'd been burned.

At the same time, I felt a bevy of turbulent emotions rolling off him in waves. I could sense confusion, anger and raw fear as he fought for life.

I couldn't sense the last moments of a corpse...could I?

I jumped back as a bloodcurdling scream pierced the air. It

took me a moment to realize the scream was coming from my own mouth, and once I did, I snapped it shut, backing away quickly. The hat slipped from my fingers and fell to the dirt.

I tried to retrace my steps, but the shock of finding a dead body had completely disoriented me. Each wall of hay looked like the one before, and I felt myself getting more and more lost within the maze. It didn't help that I was dragging poor Cap along with me as he resisted my every turn.

I heard a commotion, no doubt brought about by my horror-movie scream, and I began running toward the sound. I rounded a turn and ran smack into a solid wall. Of chest, that is.

Firm hands gripped my shoulders, and I looked up into the dark eyes of Deacon Lane. Instead of his usual smirk, his brows were knit together in concern. I couldn't imagine the terror he must have seen in my eyes to warrant any reaction to me besides mocking disdain.

"What's wrong, Alex? I heard you scream."

I gasped to catch my breath, vaguely aware that his hands clasped my upper arms tightly.

"There—there's a man in here. I…I think he's dead." I pointed shakily at the corner from which I'd emerged.

"What? Where?"

Cap pulled on his leash, and I let him take the lead. All too quickly, we were back at the nightmarish scene. I kept my distance this time as Deacon carefully approached the body of Mr. Harvey. He knelt and checked for a pulse, then shook his head.

"Body's cold—must have happened last night. Poor old guy." I was vaguely aware that Ravi hovered somewhere behind me. He must have followed Deacon in, but the whole thing felt like a fever dream.

"What do you think happened?" I asked.

Deacon stood up, surveying the scene. It looked like Alan had stumbled and fallen over the bale of hay. An insulated mug lay on the ground beside him, the top still screwed on tightly. A mint-green paper tea tag was tucked between the lid and inside of the cup, and I could just make out the black letters *PT* stamped on it. PersnickeTea. Cara's tea.

"It's hard to say. Could be a stroke, heart attack, or something like that. I'm going to call it in and secure the area. Nobody touch anything, got it?"

We nodded, but something in my face must have given me away. Deacon rolled his eyes.

"You touched something already, didn't you?" he asked.

"I thought he was a scarecrow. I was going to put him back up," I said.

"Ohhh-kay," he said slowly. "Tell me exactly what you did."

I walked him through it, giving the body a wide berth this time.

"What were you doing in here, anyway?" Deacon sighed, scrubbing his hands over his face and through his hair.

"Cap got away from me and ran in here. He was whining and nosing at—at Mr. Harvey here." I gestured.

He nodded, absently patting Cap's head.

"Good boy. All right, I better make some calls. Why don't you wait outside? Only police or the medical team should be in here." Ravi nodded and we headed back out. He put a friendly arm around me until we were out of the maze.

I slumped onto a hay bale near the entrance, exhaustion washing over me after the adrenaline rush of the past twenty minutes. Cap hopped up next to me and put his head in my lap, sensing my need for comfort, and I stroked the soft fur between his ears.

"Boy, when you come back to town, you do it with a bang, huh?" Ravi said, trying to lighten the mood. I gave a mirthless laugh.

"Apparently," I said.

"Are you all right? Can I get you anything?" Ravi asked, still standing and shifting from foot to foot. He removed his thick-framed, black glasses and cleaned them with the edge of his shirt before returning them the bridge of his nose. He had always been a little squirrely, and it didn't look like time had changed that much.

I shook my head. "I don't think so."

A few people had gathered around, and Ravi filled them in while we waited.

Soon, two police cars and the county coroner arrived, and Deacon came out to brief them. Someone put a blanket around my shoulders, and I realized I was shaking. Whether it was from sitting in the cold or simply my nerves, I couldn't be sure.

I'd never seen a dead body before, not even at a funeral. Viewing Mr. Harvey like that, with all the life drained out of him, left me disturbed and filled my limbs with a nervous energy. Not to mention the weird vibes I'd picked up from his corpse. I stood up suddenly, wanting nothing more than to walk —or run—Captain home.

I was just about to ask Deacon if I was needed for anything else, when I noticed a familiar white pickup truck pull up next to the park. The words *JR Electrical* were painted on the side in black and cherry red. I groaned inwardly, not because I didn't want to be with him. I did. I just hated seeing the worried look he reserved solely for me, and I tried my best to keep it at bay.

"Alex, I called your dad to come get you."

My head whipped around at Deacon's sudden voice next to me.

"I can see that. What am I, five?" I asked.

"I figured you'd want a ride home," he said. "I was trying to be helpful."

I clenched and released my jaw.

"Cap and I are perfectly capable of walking, or getting our own ride," I replied, sighing.

I loved my dad, but he got particularly anxious about his only daughter. I would have called later and downplayed the whole affair, but no. Deacon had to butt in where it was none of his business.

"Really, you want to walk home by yourself after discovering a dead man?" The chief frowned at me, crossing his arms.

"I'm not alone," I insisted, pulling Cap's leash closer to me. "And I'm a big girl."

The confident air of my words deflated like a punctured balloon as my dad pushed his way through the crowd, running the last few steps and pulling me into a bone-crushing hug. Instinctively, I sagged against him, drinking in the comforting scent of his worn Carhartt jacket and spearmint gum.

"Are you okay, sweetheart?" he asked, pulling back to examine me as if for injuries.

"Dad, I'm fine. Really." His hazel eyes, just a shade darker than my own, held my gaze for a moment. Satisfied, he nodded.

"Good." Dad turned slightly away from me.

"Thanks for the call, Chief." He reached out and gave Deacon a firm handshake.

"No problem, Joe. Just wanted to make sure she got home safely," Deacon replied.

I resisted the urge to roll my eyes and stamp my foot while they discussed my wellbeing as if I wasn't *right there*.

"Hello?" I said loudly, and they both turned back to me. "Am I free to go?" I asked, placing my hands on my hips as I faced Deacon.

"Yes. But I'll need you to come by the station later today and give an official statement," Deacon said. "No rush; we'll be tied up here for a while."

I nodded. "Okay."

I said goodbye to Ravi and walked with Dad, away from the gossiping crowd. Cap trotted along beside us. I glanced back at the maze, the scene of my nightmarish morning, and found Deacon's eyes still on me. I caught a concerned expression on his face before he quickly looked away, walking back toward the two cops talking with the coroner.

"So, what happened, kiddo?" Dad asked, once we were settled in his truck and headed toward my house. Cap was tucked in the backseat, between Dad's work tools and the window, eagerly watching the neighborhood whizz by. He was going to need a good nap when we got home after his eventful morning. Maybe we both would.

I watched the little tree air freshener dangling from the rearview mirror as I relayed the story again for Dad.

"I hate that you had to be the one to find him, Alex. Good thing Deacon was nearby." Dad's work-roughened hand slid over mine.

"Yeah, about that...since when are you two all buddy-buddy?" I couldn't think of any reason Deacon would have Dad's cell phone number on him.

"Oh, we volunteer at the food bank together. Didn't I tell you? And I did some work at the station last year updating the old wiring."

Dad relaxed in his seat, taking the curve slowly as we pulled onto my street.

"You might not realize this, but I didn't like him much back when you two were friends. He was always getting you into trouble."

I snorted. Dad was not at all subtle about his feelings for Deacon back then. He'd loved me too much to realize that I instigated things just as much as Deacon had.

Dad looked at me, his mouth quirked into a half-grin. "Okay, maybe you *did* know. But he's changed, really turned out to be a good kid. This town is lucky to have him."

I flicked my eyes back to the road. Funny that this was coming from the man who'd had to pick us up at the police station more than once when we were teens. And now it seemed Dad was Deacon's number one fan. Darn that stupid Lane charm.

"I think I should stay," Dad said, pulling up to the duplex. "You shouldn't be alone right now. I'll just call—"

"I'll be fine, Dad. You go on to work," I said, leaning over for a hug.

"Are you sure?" Dad asked.

"Positive. Cap and I are just going to nap, anyway." He hesitated, and I knew he wanted to ignore my words and come inside anyway.

"Please, Dad. I need to be alone right now."

"All right. But I'm coming by to check on you later."

"Deal." I opened the door, and Cap hopped out. "And Dad?" I asked.

"Yeah?"

"Thanks for coming to get me."

"I'll always get you, kid, no matter how grown up you are. Text me if you want a ride to the station later, or just some company."

"Okay," I said. "Love you."

"Love you, too."

He waited until I was safely inside before backing out of the driveway. I locked the door behind me and waved from the narrow front window as his truck pulled away. Then I turned around, sagged against the front door, and let the tears fall.

———

After I had cried out all the stress from the morning, I called Granny Lu and let her know what was going on. Then I took a long shower, trying to scrub away the memory of Alan's lifeless eyes from my mind. When the water ran cold, I turned off the tap and changed into a pair of oversized sweats.

I made myself a cup of hot tea and heated up two of yesterday's cinnamon rolls—no light breakfast for me today. If there was ever a morning to eat my feelings, this was it. I felt zero guilt.

I wrapped myself in the thickest fleece blanket I owned and settled into the couch. I couldn't seem to get warm, and Cap hopped up next to me, laying his head in my lap. He had stayed close to me all morning, even waiting right outside the shower while I got ready. Now he seemed content beside me, his thick tail thumping the couch cushion.

The wind had picked up outside, and I watched the bright red leaves from the backyard maple trees swirling violently on the small patio.

Of course, the experience of finding a dead body, especially of someone who'd been very much alive yesterday, was upsetting. But I couldn't shake the feeling that something else was amiss.

I wondered why Alan Harvey had been in the maze. I'd noticed the comfortable walking shoes he'd been wearing, so perhaps he'd just been curious on his evening stroll. But it seemed out of character, from the little I knew of him, that he'd be interested in something as quaint as a harvest maze.

I tried to nap, but I felt too keyed up to really sleep. I puttered around the house for a while, but finally, after letting Cap out to do his business, I hopped into my car to head to the station.

The red brick building faced directly across the street from Lulu's, where it looked like the midmorning crowd was picking up. Granny Lu had said not to worry about coming in today, but I planned to check in with her after giving my statement.

A mechanical beep sounded as I pulled open the heavy glass door, but the station was otherwise quiet and deserted.

"Hello?" I called out.

There was a shuffling and then Donny Swanson emerged from a room in the back. I stifled a grin at the half-eaten donut in his hand. In his early forties, with a paunchy middle and an easy smile, Donny was a big ol' teddy bear and one of Emerald Bay's deputies.

"Oh, hey Alex. Sorry to hear about what happened," Donny said, shoving the last of the donut into his mouth as he made his way toward me. He wiped his hands on his pants, leaving a smear of white glaze on the black fabric.

"Thanks. It's been a…strange morning, for sure."

"Everyone else is still at the park, or on patrol. They left me in charge here," Donny said.

"Deac—I mean, Chief Lane—said I should come here and give a statement," I said.

"Sure, I can take that for you," he said, opening the half-door that separated the lobby from the rest of the station.

"Step into my office," he chuckled, leading me to one of six desks in the open space. There were two open doors at the back of the room and one closed. I assumed Donny had come from the breakroom, and the other was a secluded office with a neatly arranged desk. Deacon's office. The closed door led to a couple of holding cells, while a lone door to the right connected the police station with City Hall.

The metal chair scraped against the white speckled linoleum floor as I sat down across from Donny. A half-empty cup of coffee balanced precariously atop a stack of files, and Donny moved it to the desk behind him before pulling out paperwork and a notebook from his desk drawer.

"So, how do we do this?" I asked. I'd never given a police statement before, at least, not as a witness. I'd been on the other side of it a time or two.

The passage of time really made a girl think. I mean, one minute you're a teen stealing traffic signs on a dare, the next you're a full-grown adult happening upon a dead body. Weird.

"Just walk me through what happened this morning, and I'll ask a few questions and take some notes."

I nodded. I could do that. After I'd rehashed the experience yet again, Deputy Swanson handed me the notebook to provide a written statement.

I was just finishing up and looking over the paper before I signed it, when the door beeped, and Deacon strolled in. He was still wearing his jeans and dark green hoodie from this morning. A pair of work gloves dangled out of his back pocket, forgotten.

I wondered if he was supposed to have the day off today. He was carrying several sealed plastic bags, and I recognized Mr. Harvey's drinking mug inside one.

Deacon nodded when he saw me. His eyes looked tired and lacked their usual spark of humor.

"Alex," he said. "Is that your statement?"

I nodded.

"Thanks for coming in. I know you probably don't want to think about it anymore than you have to."

I nodded again. Understatement of the year.

"You're welcome," I said. Look at us, being professional and civil to one another.

Deacon passed me and went on into his office, and I hastily handed my signed statement to Donny before standing up to follow him.

Deacon set the evidence bags down on his desk and rolled his shoulders, his back to me.

"Is this standard procedure?" I asked from the doorway. Deacon jumped.

"Geez, Alex. Give me a heart attack, why don't you."

"Sorry," I said.

"Is what standard procedure?" he asked, sitting down in his desk chair. I took that as an invitation and sat down in the seat opposite him.

"Securing the scene, witness statements, and all that? When the death was most likely from natural causes?"

"With any unexpected, unattended death, we have to make sure we go by the book, just in case. An autopsy and toxicology screen will be done, and then we'll know for sure. But based on Harvey's age and health history, it's most likely a sudden medical event."

I nodded. That made sense. My eyes fell to the mug again, and the little tea tag, which was bagged separately.

"He was drinking Cara's tea," I said.

"I noticed that."

"He's never bought any from the café."

"Maybe he did when you weren't around," Deacon suggested.

"I guess so," I said, even though I'd been at Lulu's from open to close nearly every day since I'd come back to town, and I didn't remember ever seeing Mr. Harvey until yesterday.

"He could have ordered it online," I mused.

Something shiny caught my eye, and I picked up the plastic bag to get a closer look inside.

"Hey, evidence!" Deacon said, reaching to grab the bag, but I pulled it out of his reach. Unless he wanted to jump over the desk, I was going to finish my inspection.

"Chill. I'm not going to open it. I just need to get a closer look." I narrowed my eyes at the little tea bag and the silver staple that held it together.

"Cara doesn't staple her tea bags shut," I said.

"What do you mean?" Deacon asked, coming around the desk and snatching the evidence bag from my hand.

"She orders all these little disposable tea bags in bulk, and they come with a tiny drawstring closure. Look here—it's ripped out and stapled shut instead."

"Huh." Deacon inspected the tea bag.

"You don't think...I mean, surely someone didn't hurt Mr. Harvey on purpose?"

Deacon raised his eyebrows at me. "That's quite a stretch. I'm sure there's a perfectly logical reason why its stapled shut instead. Maybe Cara broke it herself and didn't want to waste the bag. Or Mr. Harvey did it."

"Maybe," I said.

"Alex?"

"Yeah?"

"I'm good at my job, and I'll be thorough. Now, if you'll

excuse me, I've got a lot of work to do. Phone calls to make." He waved his hand at me, as if to shoo me out of the office.

"Okay," I said, feeling a little dismissed. I glanced at the evidence bag again. "See you later."

I went and gathered my things from Donny's desk and said goodbye to him.

CHAPTER 3
WON'T YOU BE MY NEIGHBOR?

I WALKED over to the café to check on things, and Granny Lu assured me that she had everything under control. Our second server was back today to assist Jasmine, and Nyla planned to stay and help Granny with the lunch rush. The four of them nearly pushed me out the door with instructions to rest like a flock of mother hens.

After promising to return for the afternoon cleanup and dinner prep, I crossed the street back to my car. While I waited for it to warm up against the chill, I sent Cara a text.

Me: Can I swing by?

I didn't feel like sitting idly at home, and that darn stapled teabag was bugging me. Cara responded almost immediately.

Cara: Are you off work today? PLEASE COME OVER.

Her reply came through, and I grinned despite myself. Cara loved her kids, but sometimes she was starved for adult conversation.

Me: Long story…I'll explain in person. On my way.

I reversed out of my parking space and headed down Main, away from the park and the festival preparations. At the edge of town, I took Lakeside Drive, the road winding into densely packed trees as we neared the water. The houses along this road were spread out, each one boasting a few acres and secluded lake access.

Cara's house had been the party spot when we were younger, and we had spent long summer days swimming off the dock and taking her parents' boat out on the lake.

When her folks had decided to move to a retirement community, Cara and her husband had quickly settled into the home. Lake properties were hard to come by and prices were at a premium, especially ones located so conveniently close to town. The old house was a bit dated, but they'd worked hard to spruce up the place.

In less than five minutes I was pulling into the driveway, the fine gravel crunching under my tires before I rolled to a stop in front of the garage and hopped out. The two-story house greeted me like an old friend. The exterior of stone, combined with freshly painted navy-blue siding, gave just the right air of rustic yet sophisticated.

Cara's porch was decked out with pumpkins, yellow potted flowers, and a large, leafy autumn wreath on the front door. Black witch's hats were strung with fishing line along the porch roof, giving the illusion that they floated in midair. I wiped my feet on the door mat, which read *Wizards Welcome, Muggles Tolerated.* Cara was an unabashed Potterhead.

I rapped on the front door with my knuckles, and, hearing a muffled greeting from somewhere inside, I pushed through the unlocked door. I hoped Cara had just unlatched it because she saw me pull up. Years of city living had made me more cautious than your average Emerald Bay resident, who stubbornly insisted it "wasn't the kind of place" where one needed to lock doors.

I made my way into the empty foyer, through the formal dining room that was rarely used, and into the bright kitchen. Cara was hunched at the sink overflowing with dishes, while Arthur and Olive sat at the breakfast nook having lunch. Olive banged a spoon at her highchair, and Arthur jumped up to greet me.

He had Cara's blue eyes and the orneriest smile you've ever seen, and unlike his sister, he was always happy to see me. I had just enough time to brace myself before the sturdy boy launched himself into my arms.

"Hey, buddy!" I said.

"We made cookies, Aunt Alex!" I looked as he pointed, and sure enough, chocolate chip cookies were scattered haphazardly on two wire cooling racks by the oven. Cara turned around, blowing her curly blond hair off her forehead.

"I don't know why I let myself get talked into these things," she said, giving the stink eye to the mixing bowls, baking sheets, and sticky batter that littered the speckled countertops.

"Because you're a good mom," I said, swiping a cookie and carrying Arthur back over to his place at the table. I took a big bite, making a big show over how delicious it was, and he giggled.

"If you say so," Cara said. "You hungry? I was just about to make a sandwich. Or there's a little macaroni and cheese left," she said, pointing at the pot on the table.

"More mack and roni!" Olive said, lifting her empty plate.

"Sure," I said, moving to the fridge to start pulling out meats, cheese, and condiments like I owned the place. "You take care of her, and I'll get the sandwiches."

Cara went to refill Olive's plate of pasta and fruit, while I assembled two sandwiches for us. I wasn't particularly hungry, but I rarely turned down a good sandwich, and Cara always had excellent bakery bread. She sank into an empty chair while I stacked ham and provolone on wheat for her, and turkey and cheddar on sourdough for me.

"Thanks, friend," Cara said as I plunked down our plates at the table.

"No problem," I replied.

"So, what are you up to today? Did Granny Lu make you take a day off?"

"Sort of," I said, nibbling the edge of my sandwich. "It's been a weird morning. Cap and I stumbled onto something…unexpected…on our morning walk."

I eyed Arthur, who had finished eating and had wandered off to play with his cars in the adjoining living room. He didn't appear to be paying any attention to us.

"What was it?" Cara asked, taking a sip of water from an enormous pink hydration jug.

"Alan Harvey's body. He's dead, Cara," I whispered.

Cara choked on her drink, coughing loudly. I waited for her to recover, slapping her on the back for good measure.

"What happened to him? That's crazy. Are you all right?" Once she found her voice, Cara fired questions at me without waiting for a reply.

"I'm okay. Deacon thinks a heart attack or something like that, but he's looking into it. I had to go down to the station and give a statement and everything."

"Wow. And to think we just saw him yesterday, and he was fine. Well, rude, but fine." Cara wrinkled her nose at the memory.

"I know. I still can't believe it," I agreed.

Olive yawned and rubbed her eyes, smearing cheese sauce on her face. Cara shook her head, wetting a cloth to wipe down the little girl's face.

"I'm going to have to get her down for a nap. Can you stay a while?"

"Sure," I said. "I told Granny I'd be back at three, so I've got time."

"Okay. I'll be back as soon as I can, and then I want to hear everything."

Cara gathered up Olive and told a reluctant Arthur it was time for a rest, and the three of them trooped upstairs.

I cleared the table and loaded the dishwasher while I waited for Cara, and then wiped down the counters, removing all traces of cookie dough. If I was here, I might as well do something useful.

A familiar meowing reached my ears, and a moment later the Wheeler family cat prowled into the kitchen, looking around suspiciously. Satisfied that I was alone, she came forward and wound herself around my legs, rubbing up against them.

"Hey, Magellan," I said, reaching down to stroke the soft gray and black striped tabby. She didn't care much for Cap, but was friendly otherwise.

I picked up Magellan, snagged another cookie, and carried her to the sofa, snuggling down with her while she purred like a little motorboat. I gazed at the tranquil scene out the living room window.

The Wheelers had a killer view of Windfall Lake. The property was flanked by dense forest on either side of the secure childproof fence, while the grassy lawn sloped gently toward the open water. A tidy railed gangway stretched over the rocky shoreline, connecting to a covered dock that bobbed in the wind, gray lake water splashing gently against the sides.

"She's finally asleep," Cara said, coming down the stairs. "Victory!" She pumped her fist into the air.

Cara made her way straight to the kettle and began pulling out my favorite tea while thanking me for cleaning up the kitchen mess.

A loud thump sounded above the living room, and Magellan darted off my lap to the safety of a secluded corner.

"Does Arthur still take a nap?" I asked, eyeing the ceiling and wondering how sturdy it was. Arthur's bedroom was directly overhead.

"No," Cara replied. "But he's supposed to play 'quietly' in his room until his timer goes off." She grabbed a video monitor and rolled her eyes. "He's body-slamming all his stuffed animals."

I laughed. Gosh, I loved that kid.

Cara handed me a steaming cup of cinnamon-orange black tea, with a dash of milk and brown sugar, and joined me with her own mug on the opposite end of the sofa.

"Thanks," I said, taking a careful sip. "This is perfect."

"Okay, start at the beginning. How did you find Mr. Harvey?" Cara asked.

I relayed the events of the morning, while Cara listened with rapt attention. It felt like days ago, rather than hours.

"That is craziness," she said.

"That's not the strangest part. It looked like he had been on a walk, and he was drinking your tea in one of those insulated travel mugs."

"Really?"

"Yep. Has he ever bought tea from your online shop?" Cara squinted her eyes, trying to recall.

"Not that I remember. Most people that wanted to buy locally came to me personally, until you started carrying it," she said.

"That's what I thought. And I haven't seen him buy it at the café. Anyway, Deacon put it in one of those evidence bags, and I noticed that the tea bag was stapled shut."

"But I don't use staples," Cara said, frowning.

"Exactly. So, who gave Mr. Harvey the tea, and why had it been messed with?"

Cara wrinkled her forehead. "I thought you said they were thinking it was a heart attack."

"That's the assumption. But they can't know for sure until an autopsy. And with the way Alan and Buddy Sikes were arguing..." I let the sentence trail off, putting two and two together. "Wait. Buddy bought your tea for his wife yesterday. At least, that's what he told me."

"Hmm," Cara said, taking another sip of her tea. "It's just that..." she trailed off.

"What?" I prompted.

"Well, it's just a little far fetched, is all. Say someone gave Alan the tea. Maybe he broke the string himself accidentally and stapled it shut so it didn't go to waste." She shrugged. "It's far more likely than a murderer running around town offing people."

Spoken like a true Emerald Bay lifer. Trusting to a fault.

"Not people. One person," I corrected. "But what about Buddy?"

Cara scrunched her nose up in distaste.

"He's kind of sleazy, sure. But I'm not sure he has it in him to physically hurt someone else. And from what I've seen, Alan didn't really get along with most people. It's no surprise that they were arguing. Brenda Holliday even personally apologized for his behavior yesterday."

"What? Why?" I asked. This was the first I'd heard of that. After the two men had left the café yesterday, I'd rushed to clean up and get back to work, and Cara and I hadn't had a chance to talk before she had to get Olive home for a nap.

"Alan was Brenda's uncle. There was a lot of family drama," Cara said.

I hadn't realized they were related, so that was certainly interesting. I thought about Granny Lu's and Jasmine's reactions to the men yesterday. Maybe I was reading into the situation too much, and Alan had just been a miserable old man who'd met a tragic end.

By the time Lulu's opened the next morning, all anyone could talk about was Alan's death. The café was abuzz with the news, each patron overly curious about my role in it. I hid out in the kitchen as much as possible, already weary of reliving yesterday's events and riding the waves of my turbulent emotions.

It wasn't surprising that I wasn't coping well, the scene far too fresh in my mind to cast aside. I had slept fitfully, with nightmarish dreams of Alan Harvey's dead eyes staring at me, and the terror I'd sensed upon seeing him roiling through my body over and over.

The café was too loud, the emotions too sharp. I sucked in a breath, stepping into the supply closet and closing the door behind me. Crouching on the floor, I tucked my knees to my chest and wrapped my arms around them, interlacing my fingers. Voices were muffled in here, and I concentrated on the quiet and took deep, steadying breaths.

That was how Granny found me five minutes later.

"Land sakes, Alexandria. What on earth are you doing?"

"Hiding," I replied, my voice muffled as my face pressed against my jeans.

"Oh, dear. Well, at least go somewhere more comfortable." Granny looked around, her sharp gaze coming to rest on me sitting on the concrete floor surrounded by mops and cleaning supplies.

Her eyes softened. "Go up to my house and take a break, clear your head. I can manage for an hour on my own."

"But it's the lunch rush."

"And who do you think handled the lunch rush before you came along, smarty pants?" Granny put her hands on her hips. "Now scoot. You're no good to me in this state, anyway."

Granny shooed me out of the supply closet, handing me her housekeys. I glanced out at the full dining room. I might never make it outside it if I went through the eating area. Grabbing my heavy flannel jacket, I slipped out the back door and into the alley.

The entrance to Granny's loft was around the front, next to Lulu's main doors. But the fire escape was out in the alley, so I grabbed the metal ladder and climbed to the second story landing.

Once inside, I marveled at how much hadn't changed over the years. Sure, Granny had redecorated here and there, but the overall vibe remained the same.

Cozily cluttered, the apartment was the kind of place that

invited you to sit in the corner chair with an oversized throw and stay awhile. The air smelled like baking spices, lavender, and the many half-burned candles that littered the coffee table. A stack of books and puzzles balanced precariously on an end table.

Granny Lu's cat was curled up in a ball on top of a cozy pet bed. He opened one eye, but seeing that it was only me and not Granny, he promptly went back to sleep. She was the only human he didn't completely ignore.

I bypassed the living room and kitchen, the only part of the place that was spotless, striding straight to Granny's closet. Shrugging out of my jacket and kicking off my shoes, I found what I was looking for: an oversized, cozy blue robe that had belonged to Pops. It still smelled a little like him, and a lot like Granny.

Wrapping myself in the robe, I went back to the kitchen to make myself a cup of tea: chamomile and peppermint, with a drizzle of honey.

Sighing, I collapsed into the recliner and pulled a thick blanket over my lap. I blew across the surface of the tea, sending the rising steam dancing into the air in little swirls.

I finally felt like I could breathe.

Since I had returned home, my body had become hyper-aware of the emotions and energies of the people surrounding me. It was surprising, but manageable. But after I'd found Alan Harvey's body, my whole system had gotten overwhelmed. A stress response, obviously.

I wasn't accustomed to stepping away or taking breaks from work. In the city, there didn't ever seem to be enough time or space in which to do so. Sitting in a cozy chair, in the quiet peacefulness of Granny's apartment, with a cup of tea was an unexpected luxury. I closed my eyes, reveling in the moment.

Even if the old gal was a tad pushy when she insisted on my going upstairs, I was glad of it now.

Half an hour later, I felt a lot more grounded as I locked up and walked back downstairs. Pops' robe was back where it belonged, waiting in its place until one of the Rivers women needed it again.

Back in the kitchen, I washed up and donned my apron for the last part of the lunch rush. Granny winked at me, and I mouthed, "Thanks." Of all people, she understood, and there weren't many words necessary.

As the crowd finally trickled out, I let my mind wander over our new business plan while we began our afternoon cleanup. Dinner preparations would be next, and that looked different now than when I'd arrived in town.

Just a few months ago, Granny had kept the café open six nights a week, only closing on Sunday. She'd spend that morning in church and the afternoon visiting friends or relatives. Granny was adamant that a day of rest was healthy for every-one, regardless of their belief system.

After reviewing her books, I'd convinced her to only open and keep staff for the busiest nights, which were Friday and Saturday.

Times had changed in recent years, and families were busier than ever. People were less likely to eat out at a restaurant on weeknights, but many folks still wanted the convenience of a ready-made meal. For the past month, we'd been trying out having a nightly special for call in orders. Customers could then pick up their orders, or we would deliver for a nominal fee. It cut down on our operating costs while maximizing profit.

Granny had pushed back at first, as had a handful of customers, but after just a few weeks, I could already see a difference in the books. The model had also allowed us to reach new customer demographics.

This evening's meal was Mexican themed, and the quiet of the restaurant coupled with the sizzle of onions, peppers and chicken on the grill soothed my soul and made my mouth water. Just as good home cooking should.

———

I carefully set the piping hot tray of chicken enchiladas in my passenger seat, followed by the container of spicy black beans, house made salsa and bag of tortilla chips. It was cold in the alley behind the café, and I hurried around the car into the warm interior of the driver's side.

Tucker was on delivery duty tonight, but Rusty Davenport had called in a last-minute order. Since I had just enough ingredients left over, I made an exception for his missing the deadline to order, whipping up one more batch of the special and promising to deliver it myself.

Granny Lu was closing, so after I made the delivery to Rusty, I would be heading home for the night. It had been a long day, and I was looking forward to a nice soak in the bathtub after eating my own dinner. The small foil container of enchiladas and beans I'd prepared for myself set in the back seat, sliding a bit as I turned towards Shady Glen.

Light from the police station spilled out onto the dim sidewalk, and I wondered if they had the results of the autopsy report yet. Doubtful. The nearest hospital was twenty miles away, and it was rather small. I imagined Alan's remains had to be sent off to one of the bigger cities to be examined.

I shivered, remembering his lifeless eyes and the strange sensations I'd had when I found his body. I hadn't enjoyed my brief interaction with the man while he was alive, but in death, I had only pity for him.

The last remnants of daylight were fading quickly, replaced by a riot of color to the west as the sun dipped below the horizon. It was a beautiful evening, and if I hadn't been so tired, I might be tempted to enjoy the crisp night air on my back patio. As it was, I had a date with my pajamas and a good book.

As I cruised through the residential area beside the lake, I noticed police cars parked in front of one of the cottages at the end of the lane, two houses down from the one that was mid-renovation. Myra Crawford's house, with its bountiful gardens, was set in between the two.

I recognized Deacon's cruiser as one of the cop cars, and I slowed down almost to a stop, craning my neck to see what they were doing. Lights were on in the cottage, and I could make out two officers through a front window.

Daylight was fading fast, but movement along the right side of the house shifted my attention. A dark, hooded figure hopped the short picket fence, darting across Mrs. Crawford's lawn. I lost sight of the person behind her house, but he, or she, reappeared past the renovation house. The trees grew more thickly together there, and although there were several more lake cottages along the street, I lost sight of the figure.

The sound of a horn blaring behind me nearly made me jump out of my skin. Headlights in my rearview mirror blinded me, and I reluctantly resumed driving. My heart pounded, wondering what, or rather, who, I'd just seen. Why was someone skulking around that house, and what was Deacon doing there?

Of course, Wayfinder Trail wound through the neighborhood, but anyone out for a walk should have been on the paved sidewalk in front of the houses, not behind them and through back yards.

The impatient driver behind me turned at the end of the street, and moments later, I had exited the neighborhood and was pulling into the Shady Glen Mobile Park. Unlike the sedate neighborhood through which I'd just driven, the trailer park was alive with activity.

Several bonfires roared, illuminating the growing darkness. Folks sat around in lawn chairs or stood with drinks in hand, talking amongst themselves. Music drifted through the air along with the smoke, and a group of kids and dogs ran circles around the adults.

I parked in a vacant spot near Rusty's home and carefully lifted a tray out of the passenger side of the car. I made my way to his front door, but a woman's voice interrupted.

"You lookin' for Rusty?"

"Yes, ma'am," I replied. "Delivery from Lulu's."

"Oh, good. Over here, darlin'," the woman drawled. She gestured to a folding table that had been set up near one of the fires, framed by tiki torches. S'mores fixings were already laid out to one side, along with a collection of potluck dishes and paper plates.

"I'm Lori, by the way. Rusty's wife."

"Nice to meet you," I said, carefully setting down the hot tray. "Alex Rivers."

"I'll run inside and get your cash," Lori said, gesturing to the mobile home.

"Sure," I said. "I'll get the rest of the order from the car."

A few moments later, we met back at the tables. Rusty trailed his wife, pulling several bills from a wallet.

"Thanks for the last-minute order. Smells great," Rusty said, handing me the payment along with a generous tip. "Keep the change." My opinion of him went up a notch.

You'd think rich folks would be the best tippers, but I'd found sometimes they were the stingiest of all. And then you had people like Rusty, exceeding your (admittedly biased) expectations.

"Thank you," I said. "Hope y'all enjoy it." I paused. "Are you celebrating something?"

Lori and Rusty glanced at one another.

"Not celebrating, exactly…" Rusty trailed off, a wicked grin splitting his face. Lori smacked his arm, as though shocked he'd say such a thing. He laughed and winked at me.

"Rusty, have some respect." Lori turned back to me. "Of course, we're not celebrating…I mean, it's terrible what happened to him. But you see, we haven't been able to enjoy a nice night around a campfire with our friends for a long time, and the weather's absolutely perfect tonight," Lori said.

I must've looked confused, and Lori seemed to be the kind of person who felt the need to fill any silence with chatter.

"It's just that he wasn't a good neighbor, always complaining about noise and making trouble for Rusty and I. Shady Glen is more than a business, and these people are more than tenants. We're practically family."

"Lori," Rusty said, shaking his head.

"I'm sorry, who wasn't a good neighbor?" I asked Lori, ignoring Rusty. I suspected I already knew.

"Alan Harvey," she replied. His house is just though the trees that way." She gestured at the neighborhood I'd just left. Of course.

I thought about the police cars I'd seen parked in front of the cottage. It was the last house before the road curved back into the charming lakeside neighborhood, and it was separated from the trailer park by a steep hill covered in thick trees and under-brush, with only Wayfinder making a clear path between the two properties. The road took the long way around, further from the lake and skirting around the forestry.

"That's too bad," I said, looking around at the obvious cama-raderie and friendship surrounding the fires.

"It wasn't like we made racket to all hours of the night," Lori rushed to explain again. "Most of us have kids, you know."

"Oh Lori, don't get started on that now. It's all behind us," Rusty said. Lori shook her head and launched into a diatribe.

"That man took every opportunity to pick on my son. Even confiscated his bike for a while, when my son leaned it on his fence while exploring the woods. I've never met such a crotchety old man in my life. It was like he made it his mission to get rid of us."

"What do you mean?" I asked.

"Nothing," Rusty cut her off. "He just never liked living next to a 'low-class trailer park.'" He grimaced. "His words, not mine. Even offered to buy me out a couple of times."

"Oh? Were you planning to sell?"

"Shoot, no. This is our home, and we deserve to be here just as much as he did. We might not be fancy, but these are good people. Salt of the earth," Rusty said. "He'd have evicted every last one of them."

A man came up behind Rusty, putting a friendly arm around his shoulder.

"Time to eat yet, man?"

"Sure, Ken. Round everyone up and we'll start filling plates."

"Sorry, I'll let you get back to it. Have a nice evening," I said, backing toward my car. Lori said goodbye, while Rusty merely waved as he turned to open a cooler and started passing drinks to eager hands.

As I pulled away, careful of the dogs and kids, I wondered if there was anyone in town who didn't have a bone to pick with Alan Harvey. And I was more curious than ever about the hooded figure that seemed to be spying on his house while the police searched it.

CHAPTER 4
SINCERELY, THE BREAKFAST CLUB

THE SKY WAS JUST BEGINNING to lighten in the east as I knocked on the high school cafeteria door early Thursday morning. The principal, Anita Fletcher, held the heavy door open and ushered me into the warm, expansive space.

"Good morning," she said cheerfully. "Let me help you with those." Mrs. Fletcher took one of the trays I had balanced in my arms, her heels clacking across the linoleum floor as she carried the load of cinnamon rolls to an empty table. I followed her with my own tray of cherry Danish pastries.

I hadn't been back to the high school since graduation, and it amazed me how much it hadn't changed. The curious aroma of school lunch, gym socks, and low-quality air freshener permeated the air, accented with a hint of bleach. By all accounts it should have been off-putting, but I found the smell oddly endearing.

"Thank you for coming so early. I find these morning meetings go better if I provide treats. Teachers aren't so different from teenagers in that way," she said, chucking at her own joke.

"You're welcome," I said. I set my tray next to hers. As I looked down, I saw sticky cherry filling had bubbled over one side and, lucky me, it was smeared across the front of my white shirt.

"Oops," I muttered, pulling at the clingy fabric. I was feeling the Halloween spirit this morning and had dressed more nicely than usual in jeans, boots, and a white top paired with an oversized, chunky cardigan in a deep orange color.

"Oh, dear," Mrs. Fletcher said, eyeing the red stain on my shirt. "Why don't you head to the restroom before that sets?"

"I think I will, thanks," I replied. A few teachers had begun to trickle in, eyeing the breakfast treats with delight. I scooted past them and walked quickly to the nearest bathroom, just down the hall and across from the science lab.

Bright green lockers stood sentry between classroom doors, and homemade signs with the words, "Go, Cougars!" in sparkling gold and emerald littered the walls. I glanced at the name plates beside each door, recognizing a few teachers' names, but most were unfamiliar.

Mr. Kumar was posted next to the science lab, and I realized Ravi must have replaced our ancient biology teacher when she retired. It was strange to see his name written as an authority figure. I pushed the bathroom door open and slipped inside.

After I'd done my best to clean the cherry stain from my shirt and washed my hands, I propped the door open with my foot while I tossed the paper towel into the open trash can.

"I could use your help, man," a familiar voice echoed down the empty hall, and I paused with the door cracked.

I peeked out, wondering if I'd been spotted. Deacon stood at the entrance to the science lab, his back to me. Ravi was with him, and he motioned for Deacon to follow him into the classroom. As far as I could tell, neither had noticed me.

I waited until they disappeared, and then slipped back into the hallway, careful to keep my boots from tapping loudly. I felt ridiculous tiptoeing down the hallway, but I preferred to avoid Deacon this early in the morning. Muffled voices filtered out into the hallway as I passed the door.

"It's not official police business yet, but I just need to know if it's possible or if I'm chasing a rabbit trail. I wish they'd hurry up with the toxicology report, but I don't expect it until next week," Deacon said.

Were they talking about Mr. Harvey? I chastised myself for eavesdropping, yet I crept closer to the door anyway. Had Deacon found something suspicious last night? I leaned as close as I could to the doorway while staying out of their line of sight. My hands pressed up against a poster, its glittery embellishments digging into my palms.

"I can get the samples for you to examine," Ravi said. "It's not outside the realm of possibility, but someone would have to know what to look for and where to find it," he said, pausing for a moment. "It wouldn't be an accident."

"That's what I'm afraid of," Deacon said, scrubbing his hands over his face. He looked like he hadn't slept much the night before, and if he was concerned about a potential murder, I could understand why.

My thoughts flitted once again to the sensations I'd experienced when I'd come in contact with the body. Terror, dread, the inescapable certainty that death was coming. I shuddered.

"I keep anything dangerous locked in the closet," Ravi said, fiddling with a set of keys. He unlocked the door and disappeared inside, propping the door open with a stopper. After a bit of shuffling, Ravi returned with a collection of bottles and jars in a plastic tub, which he placed on a lab table. Deacon picked up the nearest bottle, examining the contents.

Ravi made two more trips into the closet, the last time with a large rolled-up poster in hand. I couldn't quite see what the jars contained, and I leaned forward, squinting.

Just then, the poster on which I was leaning gave way with a loud rip, sliding down the wall along with my hand. I pitched forward, my head colliding against the edge of the door jamb with a loud thud.

An embarrassing yelp burst out of my mouth as pain radiated from my forehead through the back of my skull. Two pairs of eyes snapped toward the doorway as I groaned in a rather undignified manner.

"Lex?" My high school nickname slipped from Deacon's lips. His eyes narrowed at me, while Ravi's rounded with surprise. He looked like he was trying not to laugh.

I straightened, pressing my hand to my throbbing head. It came away wet, and I frowned, distracted by the trickle of blood dripping down my wrist.

Just what I needed. I stared at the red liquid for a moment, wondering how I was going to explain myself. I didn't particularly want to look at either of them, but Deacon's voice forced my eyes upward.

"Come here," he sighed, shaking his head at me. He had already moved to the back of the classroom where the sink and paper towels were located.

"Do you have a first aid kit?" he asked, and Ravi nodded.

"Dude. I give teenagers scalpels to dissect frogs. Of course I do." Ravi rummaged in his desk while Deacon gently pushed me onto a stool and held a paper towel to the cut, applying firm pressure.

"Ow," I said, scowling at him.

"Need to get the bleeding stopped," he muttered, his lips pressing together in a thin line.

I held still, noticing that my white shirt now had a few nice drops of blood to go along with the cherry stain I'd scrubbed at unsuccessfully. Awesome. This was why my personal uniform was usually a black tee and jeans.

Deacon carefully pulled back the towel to examine the cut as Ravi plopped the emergency kit on the lab table beside us.

"You okay, Alex?" Ravi asked.

"Yeah, I'm fine," I said weakly. The cut was no big deal, but my pride had a taken a hit.

"It's not deep," Deacon said, glancing from my eyes to the

wound, and back again. There were an awful lot of questions in his eyes.

I squirmed under his scrutiny, finally reaching my hand out for the first aid kid.

"Great, so I'll just head over to the bathroom to clean up," I began.

"It's all right, I've got it," Deacon said, cutting me off. Ravi handed him an alcohol wipe and he tore it open, gently cleaning the side of my face where I'd smeared the blood. He tossed it into the trash and took another one.

"I can do that myself," I said.

"Don't you faint at the sight of blood?" Deacon asked. Ravi barked out a laugh, and then not-so-subtly tried to cover it with a cough.

I huffed out a breath.

"That was one time, and I'm pretty sure it had more to do with the concussion than the blood," I said. Sighing, I focused my attention on a brightly colored bulletin board explaining the scientific method.

I was never going to live down the bike ramp fiasco of eighth grade. The only consolation was that I, in fact, *had* ramped higher than Deacon. And since I had to go to the hospital afterward, it had put a stop to anyone else trying to outdo me. So, technically, I was *still* the reigning champion.

"I beat you, anyway," I couldn't resist adding.

The corner of Deacon's lip quirked up, while a stinging pain shot through my head as he dabbed a little too hard at the cut with an alcohol prep pad. I sucked in a breath.

"Whoops," he said. He didn't look one bit repentant.

I stuck my tongue out at him. Something about the classroom was really bringing out our maturity.

"What are you doing here, anyway?" Ravi asked, bringing my attention back to the reason I was there in the first place.

"Delivering breakfast to Mrs. Fletcher. Speaking of, don't you have a staff meeting to go to?" I asked him.

Ravi glanced at his watch and groaned. "In five minutes, and I can't be late again," he said, jumping up. He went back to his messy desk, shuffling some papers around until he located a dark green binder and a pen, which he tucked behind one ear.

"Well, I'm off to another staff meeting that could probably be condensed into an email. Except Fletcher always includes 'team building exercises.' Is the food good, at least?"

"What do you take me for?" I asked. "Cinnamon rolls and cherry Danish. Nothing but the best from Lulu's."

"Okay, fine, I'll go. Gotta keep up my physique." He grinned, patting his stomach. "Will you two be all right here?"

"Yes," Deacon and I said at the same time.

"I've got to get going soon, anyway," I said.

"Me too," Deacon added. "Thanks for the help, Ravi."

"Anytime. Look, I'll leave the closet door propped open, just return the samples and make sure the door closes behind you. It'll lock automatically."

Deacon nodded, and Ravi rushed out of the room, with only about a minute to spare before his meeting was due to start. Mrs. Fletcher might not be as stern as our old principal, but judging from the way Ravi jogged out of the room without a backward glance, she seemed to run a tight ship.

The silence that suddenly enveloped us felt deafening, with Deacon close enough I could smell his favorite gum. Cinnamon.

Warm fingers brushed a stray hair away from my forehead as he applied antiseptic ointment and a butterfly bandage. I felt my face flush. Why was it so hot in here?

"So, what exactly is Ravi helping you with?" I asked, looking pointedly at the lab table next to the closet.

Deacon cleared his throat. "Research." He moved to the sink, washing his hands before putting the first aid kit back together and placing it on Ravi's desk.

"What kind of research? Does it have to do with Mr. Harvey?"

"I can't discuss details of the case, you know."

"So, you're saying there *is* a case?" I asked.

Deacon sighed and rolled his eyes at me. "Let's just say there are a few things that don't add up yet, okay? And until I get the autopsy report, I'm dealing with hunches and a solo investigation. Happy now?"

I grinned. "I knew it."

"You don't know anything."

"I know I saw something suspicious last night," I said.

"What are you talking about?" Deacon narrowed his eyes but leaned forward with interest.

"Last night, I was delivering an order to Shady Glen and I happened to drive by Alan Harvey's house, though I didn't know it was his at the time. Anyway, there was this dark, hooded figure lurking around the house. I couldn't tell who it was, but then the person ran off, cutting through backyards until I lost sight of him."

Deacon frowned, crossing his arms. "A shadowy figure, huh? Could you be more cliché?"

I huffed out a breath. "I'm not making this up. Don't you think it's odd that someone was prowling around Alan's house last night while you were searching it?"

"Actually, I do. But I don't know what to make of it, and 'dark, hooded figure' isn't enough to go on. Which direction did the guy go?"

"Toward the other cottages, in the direction of town, not the trailer park," I answered. "You should talk to Mr. Harvey's neighbors, and also find out who's renting lake cottages this week for the festival."

Deacon made a noncommittal grunt.

"Just trying to be helpful," I muttered.

"If a shadowy figure answers, you'll be the first to know," Deacon said. I sighed and scowled at him. Fine.

I sidled over to the table with its curious collection of samples that Ravi had fetched from the closet. Dried flowers and plants. Interesting. I checked the label on the nearest one, written in the stereotypical loopy style of a teenage girl. *Nerium Oleander.* The next jar was marked *Atropa Belladonna (deadly nightshade).*

Even if I hadn't spent much of my childhood hiking the many wooded trails of the Ozarks with my dad, it wouldn't take much to figure out that these were poisonous plants. But since I had, I knew these specific ones grew native in our area. Moreover, the poster Ravi had brought from the closet was covered with photographs and descriptions of the plants.

"The tea?" I asked Deacon, who was examining a small jar with tiny white petals and dry green leaves.

He bit his lip, hesitating. "I don't know for sure. I just needed to see if it was possible."

"And is it?"

"Maybe." He shrugged, but his brows knit together in concern. I checked the label of the jar in his hands. *Ageratina Altissima (white snakeroot).* Interesting.

"Well, I should be going," I said brightly. Deacon eyed me warily, no doubt wondering at my abrupt change in tone. *Be cool.*

I backed toward the door. "No need to see me out. I can see you've got lots of work to do, and school will be starting in half an hour."

"All right. See you around, Lex." Deacon held my eyes a moment more, until I bumped into the lab stool I'd forgotten to push under the table.

I let out an awkward laugh and gave him a little wave. "Bye, Deacon." I exited the classroom but watched from the hallway for a few moments as he turned away.

Deacon picked up the first jar again, reaching for his phone and beginning to snap a few pictures. *Jackpot.* He was onto something. And now, so was I.

I let myself into the duplex Thursday evening, balancing a small container of baked ziti in one hand and a package of garlic rolls in the other. When I reached the kitchen, I relieved myself of the awkward load. The day had flown by, but my feet were aching, and I collapsed onto the sofa with a sigh, kicking my shoes off and stretching across the cushions.

I debated lying there for the rest of the night, but my stomach growled loudly. I groaned and rolled to my side, willing my stomach to fill itself so I could remain in a blissful, catatonic state.

Eventually my hunger won out and I stood up, reluctantly moving back to the kitchen. The smell of garlic, cheese and tomatoes wafted up as I fixed a small plate for myself and put the rest into the refrigerator. I let Cap inside and he danced around my feet while I poured a glass of water and turned on some music.

"Hey, fella. Who's a good boy?" I said, bending down to give him a lengthy rub behind the ears. "We didn't get our walk this morning, did we? I'm sorry about that." Cap sniffed at my hand appreciatively and tried to get a good lick. I laughed.

"You just want me for the snacks, is that it? Sorry, buddy. No pasta for you." I reached for one of his doggie treats on top of the refrigerator, making him sit before tossing him one and settling down with my dinner.

The early breakfast run to the school had cut into our morning routine, and Cap had had to settle with playing fetch in the yard for a few spare minutes before I'd gone to work that morning.

I looked out the window and down the hill toward the park, which was aglow with lights. Opening night of the Halloween Harvest Fest.

I hadn't planned on going, but Cap was restless. I looked longingly at the sofa and oversized pillows.

With the way he was prowling around the house, a walk before bed might do him some good. Down to the park and back wouldn't take long, and I was more than a little curious to scope out the festival.

Half an hour later, Cap and I left the house, taking the path that skirted the back yard and down the hill. Moonlight glinted off the yellowed grass but was swallowed up by darkness as we entered the wooded portion of the trail. My heavy flashlight bobbed along the path, illuminating only a few feet ahead before darkness swallowed up the remaining light.

Palms suddenly slicked with sweat, I checked that my pepper spray was still looped around my wrist with a stretchy band while contemplating the wisdom of walking this forested path alone. A quick sweep of the flashlight left and right revealed nothing but a small animal skittering away from the sudden brightness.

Cap pulled on the leash, and we continued a few moments more before breaking out into the open. A low hum of voices wafted up from the park, punctuated with an occasional shriek of delight. I felt myself relax, loosening my white-knuckled grip on Cap's leash as we neared the park.

The distinct aroma of funnel cakes filled the air, and I made a mental note to skip dinner next time so I could get my fill of carnival food. Never mind the calories.

I strolled through the festivities, spotting some familiar faces and waving to a few café regulars in greeting. Lots of kids were out playing games, while harried parents trailed behind. A few teens gathered around a picnic table, and I caught a couple of them glancing toward the maze forlornly. A sign posted next to the police tape warned that it was closed until further notice.

"Hey, Alex. How's your head?" I turned toward Ravi's voice. He was grinning at me.

"It's fine," I said, wincing at the memory from the morning. I was surprised to see the blond at his side was none other than Jessica Holliday, high school mean girl, all grown up. However, not as surprised as I had been to spot her at the staff meeting when I'd left the school this morning.

Cara had confirmed that she was now the school guidance

counselor. I wondered if she counseled kids to be nicer than she had been back in the day.

I tried to shake off my contempt. We were all different people than we'd been in the past, after all. Weren't we? Or did a leopard never change its spots?

"Hi, Jessica. How are you?" I asked tentatively. I reminded myself that Alan had been her great-uncle, and she deserved some sympathy for his sudden passing, if nothing else.

"As well as can be expected, I suppose," she said, an unsteady smile on her face.

"I'm sorry about your uncle. I'm sure it was a shock."

"Thank you. We weren't close, but still, he was family. And— I hope this doesn't make me sound callous—but it's put me in something of a pickle. Ravi was just helping me figure out what to do." Jessica picked at the sleeve of her sweater, her brow furrowed.

"About what?" I asked.

"Jessica is the faculty sponsor for the drama club," Ravi explained.

I fought the urge to roll my eyes, because *of course she was.*

"Her students' big project this semester was the hay maze," he continued. "Now that it's closed, they're trying to replace it on short notice."

"They've been working so hard. I hate to see it all go to waste," Jessica said, her big blue eyes rounded with sincerity.

"I see. I'm sure they're disappointed." I paused. "I'll be thinking on it and let you know if I have any ideas," I said. Tucker had been bummed that he wouldn't be able to go with his friends, and he'd bemoaned the fact all afternoon.

"Thanks," Jessica said, flipping her long hair over her shoulder. "I'm sure I'll come up with something, with Ravi's help. He's really good with the kids." She placed a hand on his arm.

Ravi smiled at her, the tips of his ears turning red, but Jessica stared past him. *Uh-oh. Friend zoned.*

"Well, I'd better be going," I said, tugging on Cap's leash.

He'd found a discarded nacho and was sniffing at it. "See you guys later."

I turned and headed back toward home. I wondered if the case would wrap up soon enough for the drama club kids to reopen the maze, or if they'd need to find another outlet for their project. Nearly every square inch of the park was already filled, so there were few options, unless they decided to do something off-site. However, then they wouldn't be able to capitalize on the park's foot traffic.

I glanced back at the maze one last time. Its dark corner of the park stood in gloomy contrast to the lively lights and noise of the rest of the area. I tried not to shudder as I left the festival behind and entered the quiet woods on the trail home.

Jessica hadn't seemed all that broken up by her uncle's death, but with Alan's reputation, perhaps it wasn't surprising that they hadn't been close. I wondered about his other family members, recalling that her mother, Brenda, had indicated there had been some familial drama.

As I approached the duplex and noted that Deacon's side of the house was still dark, I wondered if he was having as hard of a time as I was unraveling the web that was the Alan Harvey case.

———

Friday nights at Lulu's Café were a raucous affair, with friends young and old and families alike celebrating the beginning of the weekend. The town's loyalties were split on this particular evening, with half the crowd preparing for an evening at the festival and the other half loyal to the Emerald Bay Cougars and their home football game.

Either way, the two events were good for business, and I applauded myself for hiring Tucker's girlfriend (I'd finally discovered her name was Ava) as an extra waitress to work weekends. She'd come in the day before with a professional, typed resume and I'd hired her on the spot.

I hoped there would be minimal drama between the two teens, but as Ava was working tables and Tucker was our cleaning and delivery boy, there wouldn't be much opportunity for hormonal interaction. Plus, Ava had a peaceful energy about her. My gut told me that she'd fit in with our team nicely.

After a crash course in our procedures earlier in the day, I'd sent Ava to sink or swim in our small party room. Jasmine said she would back her up if she got too swamped.

Situated at the back of the café on the left side, the small room was used for overflow seating but could also be rented out for private parties. Every other Friday night the book club ladies had a standing date to rent the room. They set up shop at six pm sharp and gabbed until we closed the place down at ten.

The book club, or as they called themselves, the Silver Vixens, was far more likely to gossip about the goings-on of the town than to discuss literature. Ranging in age from about fifty to eighty, the ladies came in all varieties of sweet and sauciness.

During a lull in the kitchen, I popped in to check on the group. They could be a bit demanding at times, and as they practically ran the town, I was determined to keep them as loyal customers.

"How is everyone's food tasting?"

"Delicious, Alex," Sheila Jenkins, my traitorous landlord and real estate agent, said.

Murmurs of agreement sounded around the table. Ava had only delivered one wrong side order, and that had already been remedied, so I was happy everything else appeared to be going smoothly.

"Great. Can I get anyone drink refills?" I carried a pitcher of sweet tea in one hand and water in the other. A few of the women nodded, and I began refilling the glasses that were running low.

Janet Oakes, the book club's leader, drew the group's attention back to the hardcover novel in her hand.

"I thought the character development of the heroine was particularly strong," she began.

"Alex, are you still serving Cara's tea?" Marta Lopez asked me, cutting off Janet.

"Yes, of course," I answered.

"We heard Alan Harvey was drinking a cup of her tea when he passed," Phyllis Goat said. Her nose wrinkled. "I wouldn't keep selling it, if I were you. It could be bad for business if word gets out."

I stiffened slightly. Phyllis was a pot-stirrer if there ever was one. Plus, I don't think she'd ever forgiven me for accidentally kicking a soccer ball into her prized petunias and crushing them when I was seven.

"Cara had nothing to do with what happened to Mr. Harvey, I can assure you of that. It's my understanding that they're still waiting on the autopsy report to find out the cause of death, anyway," I replied, gathering up two glasses for soda refills.

I wondered where they'd heard about the tea. My eyes skittered across the table and landed on Diane Frasier, who was fidgeting with her napkin. Bingo. Receptionist at city hall, which adjoined the police station. Well-meaning, but very chatty.

Marta rolled her eyes. "Of course, the tea had nothing to do with it. I'd like to try the ginger peach, by the way," she said to me. I nodded.

"Besides, Alan had a heart condition," Brenda Holliday piped up. "And he wasn't the best at taking his meds regularly."

I strained to listen, but as I was already walking away to fetch the soda refills and tea, I couldn't very well stop without being obvious.

When I returned, Marta and Phyllis were still arguing about tea, while Myra Crawford dabbed at her eyes with a napkin. She sniffled, and I wondered what had upset her so much.

Alarmed at the tension hovering over the party room, I asked if anyone would like to put in a dessert order yet.

"Not quite," Janet answered for the group. "But we do need to get back on task." She tapped the book with a long, burgundy fingernail. "As I was saying," she began.

I tuned her out as I set Diane's soda in front of her. "Hon, I'm not one to agree with Phyllis, but you actually might want to think about suspending your tea sales, for a while, anyway," Diane whispered to me. "Chief Lane is looking into possible poisoning, and people are starting to talk."

"Hmm," I said, not committing one way or another. I glanced down the table at Myra, who was dabbing at her eyes while Marta put a comforting arm around her.

"Do you know why Myra's so upset?" I asked quietly.

"Her husband passed of a heart attack a couple years ago, and she still has a rough time when it's brought up. I guess thinking Alan may have died the same way brought back the memories. He was her next-door neighbor."

"Poor Myra," I murmured. Her husband, Gerald, had been the town mayor when I was younger. I vaguely remembered Granny Lu telling me that he'd died suddenly a few years back.

I cleared away a few dishes that were empty and made my way back to the kitchen. I'd left Granny Lu alone for too long and needed to get back to work.

As the evening wore on, Jasmine reported that several customers had asked about Cara's tea, worried that it had been contaminated somehow and was the cause of Alan's unfortunate end.

Darn Diane and her gossiping ways. There were only a handful of people who knew about Deacon following that lead, and we all knew Cara would never do such a thing.

But the town rumor mill had latched onto this particularly juicy morsel, and more than once I overheard someone retelling the story of Alan yelling at Cara and her daughter the day before he died. The unspoken insinuation *"What if she tried to get even?"* lingered in the air.

It was ludicrous, and anyone who'd ever met Cara would say so, but I couldn't stand to see my best friend's name dragged through the mud. It looked like I was going to have to do something about it.

CHAPTER 5
PARANORMAL ACTIVITY

I ROLLED out of bed early Saturday morning, settling down with my laptop and a notepad to do some research before getting together with Cara.

I'd texted her after I arrived home last night, and she'd agreed to meet up for a morning walk. If we happened to stroll past Alan Harvey's house, so be it.

I wanted to get a feel for who the man was, and who possibly could have wanted to hurt him. Sure, he had been unpleasant, but it was a big leap from passing dislike to murderous intent. And my gut was screaming that this had been no accident.

A handful of internet searches and a call to Granny Lu later, I had half a page of notes and a better picture of the man's life. It was a little depressing, really. Mr. Harvey had been married once and had a messy divorce and two estranged children to show for it. I was sure Deacon would investigate them, but they all lived out of state.

Alan had one social media account, but it appeared to be mostly used for political rants. However, I did find records that showed that he'd worked in construction as a young man and as the county assessor in his later years, before retiring.

I stretched, glancing at the clock. Time to get moving. I brushed my teeth, dressed, and headed to the car.

Cap and I cruised through the October sunshine to Cara's house. I even rolled down the back window so he could stick his head out. His tongue lolled happily in the breeze.

Saturday morning domestic sounds wafted into the entryway as I opened Cara's front door. Bacon sizzled in the kitchen, children chattered, and cartoons played from the television.

"Stay," I said to Cap, and he made himself comfortable on the porch with only a small whine. He loved Magellan, but she didn't love him back.

"Hey, Lex," Tim, Cara's husband, greeted me. He held a spatula in one hand and an obnoxiously large cup of coffee in the other. Tim was always dressed like a beach party might spontaneously happen, and even on this brisk morning, he wore a hoodie, board shorts, and flip flops.

"Morning," I replied.

"She's still getting ready," he said, jerking his head toward their bedroom door off the kitchen. "Breakfast?"

"Sounds great," I said, helping myself to a cup of coffee and reaching for the creamer in the fridge. I'd been too preoccupied with my research to eat anything earlier.

"Come on, monsters! Time to eat," Tim said, sticking his head into the living room.

Once Arthur and Olive were settled at the table, Tim and I sat down with our own plates and chatted while we waited for Cara.

I'd always liked Tim, and though he hadn't been a part of my life quite as long as Cara, he might as well have been. She'd been smitten with him since the summer we'd been fifteen, when Tim had come to Emerald Bay to work for his grandpa at the marina.

He'd become ingrained in our friend group ever since. Tim spent three more summers working on the lake, and after graduation, he and Cara went to the same university. They eloped on Spring Break of their junior year and graduated the following

May, she with a degree in fine arts, and he with one in engineering.

These days, Tim still kept a tiny office at the marina, working his dream job—designing boats for a watercraft company. I glanced out the window toward the covered dock that concealed Tim's other baby. On weekdays, Tim's morning commute consisted of a short cruise across the lake on a shiny red speedboat he'd designed himself.

"You and Deacon kiss and make up yet?" Tim asked, swallowing a mouthful of pancake.

I rolled my eyes. "We're…tolerating each other," I said.

"The sooner you do, the better. Cara and I are tired of picking sides." Deacon and Tim had become fast friends when he and Cara started dating, and they were still thick as thieves.

"Find a new dream, Timmy," I said, violently piercing a strawberry with my fork.

"Don't you think it's kind of petty—" Whatever Tim was about to say was cut off by Cara breezing into the room in and planting a kiss on his lips.

"Breakfast made and I got to sleep in," she said. "My hero."

"I heard you up in the night with Olive," Tim said, using the softer tone he reserved solely for Cara. He dropped his fork and kissed her thoroughly, his hands cradling her head gently.

I made a yuck face at Arthur and he made one back. I cleared my throat loudly.

"Get a room, you two," I said.

"Yeah, get a woom!" Arthur echoed.

Cara came up for air and wrinkled her nose at me. "Oh, nice. Thanks for teaching him that."

"Sorry," I said, grinning. "Eat up. We've got a busy morning before I have to get back for the chili cook-off."

"What time is that?"

"The contest starts at three o'clock, but I need to be back by one to haul everything over from the café and get set up."

I was entering two kinds of chili on behalf of Lulu's, one a traditional red chili with beef and beans, and the other a spicy green chili with shredded pork. I'd spent a good portion of Friday afternoon making huge pots of both, and they only needed to be heated this afternoon.

Chili is always better the second day anyway, after the flavors have had the chance to marinate overnight. I'd heard there were lots of other entrants, but I felt we had a pretty good shot at winning.

Regardless, after the contest there would be a chili feed for the crowd, with the winning entry generally being the most popular. Since I would be working all afternoon and evening, Granny Lu had taken the morning shift at the café and planned to close after lunch to encourage people to attend the festival.

It would be a busy day, with the pie bake-off taking place after the chili contest. The bounce houses and carnival rides would be open in addition to the food vendors and craft stalls.

"Ready to go?" Cara asked, finishing up her breakfast and clearing plates.

"Yep. I definitely need that walk now," I said, patting my stomach. "Thanks, Tim."

"Think about what I said about Deacon," he called after me.

"Fat chance!" I hollered over my shoulder.

Cara and I headed outside, where Cap was waiting. He jumped up eagerly and I fastened his harness to the leash. Wayfinder Trail meandered near Cara's house, and after a quick jaunt through the trees surrounding her property, we were on the paved path and headed toward town.

"So, what's the story?" Cara asked. She had been eager to get out of the house, but she had an inkling I was after more than simply exercise.

I sighed. "Everyone was talking last night, in the café, about Deacon investigating possible poisoning. By the guilty look on her face, I'm guessing Diane's been chatting up every person she's encountered this week."

Cara nodded and blew out a breath. "Well," she said, hesitating. She bit her lip. "Deacon did drop by yesterday."

"He did?"

Cara nodded. "He wanted to see my workspace and my teas. I'm probably not supposed to say anything, but he took samples. He kept it casual, tried to downplay it, but I know him well enough that I could see the case is weighing heavily on him."

"Yeah, I've noticed that, too. You should have heard the gossip last night, Cara." I hesitated. "Some of it was about you."

"About me?"

I nodded. "You know, the run-in you had with Alan the morning before he died."

"That's ridiculous." Cara scoffed.

"I mean, not *that* many people think you're a murderer. Some just speculated you might be negligent, and your tea got contaminated somehow," I said.

"Gee, thanks," Cara said drily. "That makes me feel so much better."

"Sorry, that came out wrong," I said. "But it really makes me want to dig to the bottom of this and find the truth."

"What's that saying, about the simplest answer usually being the truth? So isn't it far more likely that Alan died of a heart attack, like they initially thought, than some sicko's running around town poisoning tea?"

When she put it like that, it did sound a bit crazy.

"Yes, but I feel like Deacon's onto something. And…there's more." I was struggling with this part. It was hard enough to be honest with myself, let alone my closest friend. I hadn't faced this part of myself in about twelve years, and I wasn't keen to do so now, but it was getting to the point I couldn't ignore it anymore.

Cara watched me carefully, her eyebrows raised in question.

"Remember when we were kids, and I thought I was psychic?" I blurted out. Cara's face registered surprise, but she nodded slowly.

"Sure. Your sixth sense. Granny Lu said you got it from her," Cara said. The trees thinned enough for us to catch a glimpse of the lake a short distance away. The water looked calm as glass this morning, a stark contrast to the inner turmoil I felt.

"Right. She wanted me to embrace my 'gift' and I just wanted to feel normal." Cara had never questioned my weird premonitions and the overwhelming emotions I felt around people. Children don't balk at the impossible the way adults do.

Granny Lu had explained that we were "highly sensitive empaths." I certainly hadn't welcomed perceiving others' emotions, pushing the unpleasant feelings away the best I could. By the time I was a teenager, I hadn't been successful, but I had developed coping mechanisms to appear normal, even if I didn't feel that way on the inside.

I did my best to steel myself against the emotions of others, like a mental shield, of sorts. If that failed, I perfected hiding the extreme feelings that would slam through me whenever I was in close contact with someone experiencing deep emotions.

After I'd left town, my gift had finally seemed to weaken, which suited me just fine. The more I ignored it and the further life took me from Emerald Bay, the less intense my gift became, until it had all but disappeared. But since my return to town, or rather, since Granny called me that day I'd quit Bloom, the emotions had returned with a vengeance. I couldn't *stop* feeling, it seemed. And it was exhausting.

Cara waited, the birds chirping around us, until I spoke.

"I pushed the sense away and ignored it for as long as I could. And it worked, for a time. But since I came home, there have been instances in which I've found myself intensely feeling what those around me are feeling. Stronger than I ever did when I was a kid. It's the reason I'm so sure that Alan Harvey was murdered. I could sense it, surrounding his body that day I found him. It's almost as if whatever he was feeling before he died lingered somehow. Anger, terror, dread, all rolled up into one and leaching off his body in waves. There was a moment right before he died, and he *knew*. I felt it. Someone did this to him. But it's not like I can access his memories, I only have his emotions. Every time I think I'm onto something, it slips through my fingertips."

Cara had stopped on the path, staring at me.

"Are you for real, Lex?"

I nodded miserably.

"You're not messing with me? Because I'm so sleep-deprived that what you're saying is actually starting to make sense."

"You don't think I'm crazy?"

Cara laughed. "Oh, I know you're crazy." She looped her arm through mine and began to walk again. "But not because of this."

"How can you believe me, just like that?"

"Have you forgotten all the weird stuff I witnessed with you growing up?"

She was right. We had simply stopped speaking of it as we got older.

"Besides," she continued. "I've learned the older I get, the less I truly understand about the world."

"You've become so wise in your golden years."

Cara side-eyed me. "I still wish our experiment to communicate telepathically had gone better."

A giggle escaped me. I felt so much lighter speaking to someone besides Granny Lu about my gift.

"It's like you have a superpower. But how to you plan to use it?" Cara asked. "I know we're not walking aimlessly toward Alan Harvey's house."

"I don't know if I *can* use it. My sixth sense is…glitchy," I admitted.

"What do you mean?"

"I can't control it. It's like it has a mind of its own, slamming me with energy one moment and vanishing the next. I just wanted to get close to Alan's house, see if I could sense anything. What I wouldn't give to get inside the place and take a look around…" I trailed off.

"No. No way. No B and E for me this morning." Cara shook her head. "I can't go to jail with you; I'm supposed to bring the snacks to Arthur's soccer game this afternoon."

"Priorities," I said, nodding. "Of course, I wouldn't break into his house."

Would I? I'd been acting a tad out of character since discovering a dead body. The whole situation had me in an existential…kerfuffle. There was no other word for it.

The Shady Glen Mobile Park came into view, and we took the path down the hill toward Alan's neighborhood. All was quiet, and I wondered if there had been another late-night party. I was disappointed to note that no police cars were parked in front of Alan's house. If Deacon had been there, perhaps we could have knocked on the door and been invited inside. *Lol, Lex.*

No, I couldn't see him welcoming us into a murder victim's home during an active investigation, but wouldn't that be nice and easy? It would save me a lot of trouble, anyway.

As we passed Alan's house, I noticed Myra Crawford stooped in front of her mailbox. A neat square of earth was exposed around it, and on closer inspection I saw that her knees rested on a cushioned garden kneeler. She was carefully planting delicate-looking purple and golden blooms, gently covering them with dirt before firmly patting firmly around the stems.

"Good morning, Mrs. Crawford," I said, smiling.

"Hello, girls," she said, looking up at us from her wide-brimmed hat.

"Beautiful flowers," Cara said. "It seems that every time I drive by there's something new to admire in your gardens."

"Thank you. You know what they say about idle hands. I like to keep mine busy."

"What are you planting?" I asked.

"Pansies," Myra said, lightly touching the thin petals. "It's really getting too late in the year for planting, but these beauties can stand a little frost."

I studied Myra as she examined the flowers. A faint sadness floated around her like a cloud, and I remembered her tears from the night before.

"I'm sorry about your neighbor," I blurted out, before I could think better of it. I looked back at Alan's house, sitting quiet and empty. Past Myra's house stood the one with the large dumpster in front. I felt nothing looking at Alan's place, so I shifted my focus to the elderly woman in front of me.

Mrs. Crawford shakily got to her feet. "Yes, it was quite a shock. Although, when you get to be my age, these kinds of things happen more often than one would like."

"Are you all right, Mrs. Crawford? You look a little pale," I said. I was worried the woman would faint right in front of me.

"I'll be fine," she said, fanning herself with one of those paper flower cards used to identify plants, holding it by one thin point. I wasn't sure the tiny rectangle was moving any air at all. "Once things are more settled with Alan's will."

"His will?" Cara asked.

"Yes. I'd like to know who my new landlord will be, and what they plan to do with the properties." Myra gestured to the three houses.

"He was your landlord? I didn't realize," I said.

"Yes, and he was in the process of renovating that cottage. I do hope whoever takes over doesn't mind having a renter. Some people don't want the hassle. And then I'd be out of my home." Her lip trembled, and she pressed her mouth firmly closed.

"I'm sure they'd see you're a reliable tenant," I said. "But, I'm curious. How was he? As a landlord, I mean," I said.

Myra looked at me, her brown eyes turning sharp beneath her hat. "You've met him before, correct?" she asked. I nodded.

"He was, as in everything, difficult. But after my husband passed, I didn't want to stay in that big house in town. Our children are all grown and gone, and the upkeep of the place was too much for me."

In my childhood, Mrs. Crawford and her husband Gerald, then the mayor, had lived in a beautiful two-story house near downtown. Its white columns had presided regally over the expansive front porch, inviting folks to sit and sip iced tea on a hot afternoon.

If I recalled correctly, there had been a pool and a koi pond in the back yard, and they'd added a conservatory to the back of the house after Mr. Crawford retired. I could see how an elderly widow would have wanted to simplify things, no matter how beautiful the home had been.

Myra glanced back at her little yellow painted cottage, which looked like it could have come straight out of a fairy tale with the white gingerbread trim along the front, next to the peach climbing roses on a trellis. "This little house fits my needs perfectly, plus, I'm not responsible for any maintenance."

"Did Mr. Harvey ever mention anything about his will?" I asked.

Myra shook her head. "He has children, but I don't think they're on good terms. They lived with his ex-wife when they were growing up, but they're both adults now."

"I'm sure everything will work out, Mrs. Crawford. Maybe you ought to take a break and have something to drink? We could lend a hand, if you like," Cara said.

Myra waved her away, the sunlight making the age spots on her pale skin more pronounced.

"No, no, I'm sturdier than I look. Although a glass of lemonade on the porch sounds like just the ticket. Have a nice walk, girls."

She turned and collected the sectioned plastic container that had held her plants and a small garden spade before walking toward the cottage. Cara and I made sure Mrs. Crawford made it up the three steps to the porch, then we backtracked to Alan's house. I wanted to get a good look at it, as well as the one he was renovating. The blinds were open, but it's not as if I could just go peeking into the windows without attracting the wrong kind of attention.

Alan's house stood in stark contrast to Myra's. The siding of his cottage was painted a deep sage green. Where she had cultivated flowerbeds in every spare corner of her lot, his garden beds were filled with smooth river rock. I concentrated on the front window, framed in black, but I didn't feel anything.

"Do you think he had money trouble?" Cara asked suddenly.

"Anything's possible, I suppose. Why do you ask?"

"It's just that I drive by here a lot. Up until the end of the summer, there were people out here working every day on that cottage." She gestured to the one that was under construction, a simple house in the same style as the rest of the neighborhood, except with peeling paint in an unfortunate shade of eighties brown. We approached the renovated house.

"And then one day, it just stopped. Like maybe he ran out of money and couldn't pay to finish it," Cara continued.

"Hmm," I said, peeking over the edge of the large dumpster. A roll-off, my dad would call it, used at a lot of demolition sites. It was filled with crumbling drywall, busted cabinets, and piles of musty carpet.

"If I were Mr. Harvey and I ran out of money, what would I do to get my dirty hands on some? How desperate do you think I'd be?" I mused.

Cara shrugged. It was an intriguing theory, one that deserved further exploration. Perhaps Alan had squeezed the wrong person, expecting a loan, and they'd simply decided he was a problem they needed to be rid of instead.

———

The festival was in full swing by the time I got to the park early in the afternoon. The weather was gorgeous and sunny, but just cool enough to don my brown leather jacket over the dark green tee I wore. My straight brown hair was contained in a claw clip paired with my favorite gold hoop earrings, and I completed the outfit with ripped jeans and hiking boots. If I was going to be on my feet all day, better go with durability and comfort. Behind me, I pulled a heavy duty wagon loaded with all my supplies for the contest.

Lots of vendor booths were set up and busy with customers, along with civic organizations giving away swag bags. The Emerald Bay Garden Club was selling potted plants and flowers, golden and orange blooms shining in the sunlight. Lori Davenport from the trailer park and Marta from book club sat together, running the booth. Lori handed change to a customer while Marta gave me a friendly wave from her seat.

I finally reached our assigned place in the cook-off area, where everyone bustled about like busy bees in a hive. I got right to work setting up the stall and getting the vats of chili on the warmers, and then organizing paper goods and disposable utensils for the meal to come after the contest. Jasmine had hand-lettered a chalkboard that read *Lulu's Café*, which I proudly displayed at the front of my table.

A few of the stalls, like ours, advertised local establishments, while some of the others were manned by individuals looking to show off their culinary prowess.

I sized up the competition, noting that Betty from the diner along the highway was present. Mr. Duncan, a neighbor of my dad's and the reigning champion three times over, puttered around his booth. He noticed me staring and gave a friendly wave. I grinned and slowly pointed at my eyes with two fingers and then back at him. He laughed and shook a wooden spoon at me.

I wasn't sure what exactly qualified one to judge a chili contest and a pie bake-off, but a group had gathered in the center of the food stalls. They each wore name tags with "Judge" written in bold black ink. I recognized Sheila Jenkins and Deputy

Donny Swanson, along with two men and another woman I didn't know.

I stirred the lightly simmering green chili, sniffing the air appreciatively. The rich, spicy scent mingled with cotton candy and corn dogs, and shrieks of delight echoed from the nearby carnival rides.

"How about sneaking your old man a taste?" a voice at my ear said suddenly, and I jumped. My dad grinned, setting the two large trays he'd been carrying on the table. Nyla was behind him, and she relieved herself of a similar load. Sixteen wrapped pies completed her contribution to our booth.

I eyed a large brown stain on the front of his shirt. "Looks like you've been sampling already," I observed.

"You know I can't resist Nyla's famous pecan pie," he winked. "Had to make sure it was fit to enter the contest."

"Please," Nyla said, rolling her eyes. "He demanded payment for helping me haul these over from the café."

"Very chivalrous," I said.

Dad shrugged. "Can you blame me?" he asked. Dad has always been notorious for his sweet tooth, but Nyla didn't appear to mind. They'd been friends for years, and anytime he snuck into the kitchen at the café, he snagged one or two of her baked goods.

I replaced the lid on the pot and set down the huge ladle on a spoon rest, moving to the front of the booth to check out the pie selection. Nyla had baked gooey pecan pies, bubbling apple pies, spiced pumpkin pies, and her specialty, an out-of-this-world triple berry concoction.

"Nyla, these look amazing. I can't wait to try them." I said eagerly.

"See? Like father, like daughter," Dad said, slinging his arm over my shoulder.

The sound of a clanging gong echoed through the booth and I winced at the loud noise. I looked around to see Phyllis Goat calling the chili contest to order, rubber mallet in hand.

A gong seemed excessive when her penetrating voice would have done the trick, but I kept my mouth shut while she lined out the rules and regulations. Before long, the judges were making their rounds to the various booths, and I ladled out samples when they approached our table.

"Mmm, this is amazing," Sheila said, her eyes rolling back in her head after she took a bite of green chili.

"Yes, very nice," her fellow judge, said, sampling his own bowl of red chili. He wore glasses and a tweed blazer over his button-up shirt. He reminded me of a professor who spent his days in a dusty library with a cup of tea.

"Respectable traditional recipe," he continued. It wasn't exactly glowing praise, but I'd take it. He produced a small notepad and pen from his pocket, jotting down a few notes before sampling the green chili and moving on. The other judges had already tried my chilis but had been tight-lipped with their reactions.

"How are you holding up, hon?" Sheila asked, lingering as she took another bite. "What a terrible week you've had, first finding Alan's body and then Phyllis practically running a smear campaign against you and Cara last night."

"I'm doing all right, all things considered," I said.

"That's the spirit," Sheila said. "Don't let the old goat get you down." She gestured toward Phyllis behind her with a plastic spoon. I had just taken a sip of bottled water, and I felt it catch in my throat hearing at Sheila's pet name for Phyllis.

"Cough it out," Sheila said, giving me a good smack on the back and chuckling to herself. She leaned in close to me and lowered her voice.

"Life's full of unpleasant people, like Phyllis and Alan. But it's also too short to let them get the best of you."

"Did you know Alan well?" I asked.

"Well enough," she said, taking another bite. "Our paths crossed many times back when I first got my real estate license, and he was the county assessor. Sneaky one, that man. I made sure to keep my nose clean and steered clear of him as much as I could, which was darn near impossible."

"Sneaky how?"

"Oh, he was always trying to get the dirt on everyone. Liked people to owe him favors, you know." She shrugged. "I wasn't sorry to see him retire; I'll say that much. Made my job, and the experience of my clients, a lot more pleasant."

"Shei-la!" Phyllis's voice singsonged the name. "We're waiting on you. This is a serious contest, not social hour." Phyllis turned her gaze on me, placing her hands on her hips. "Any attempt to influence the judges in your favor will get you disqualified immediately."

"Calm down, Phyllis, we're just having a little chat. You know, for this *friendly* competition." Sheila winked at me before heading to the next table.

A few moments later, the judges had finished their rounds and gathered to deliberate. I mopped up the table where a smear of chili marred the pumpkin-printed tablecloth Granny had sent.

While I waited for the judges to deliberate, I people-watched the growing crowd. I spotted Jessica leading Ravi and a group of teens, their arms filled with an assortment of boxes and large tubs. She walked backwards, looking positively smug and calling out instructions. She certainly appeared happier than when I'd seen her at opening night.

"Hey, Ravi!" I called as they passed. "Jessica," I said, nodding as she turned to me. I had completely forgotten about the drama club's quandary with the maze being closed until further notice.

"Where are you headed with all that stuff?" I asked.

"We got approval to relocate to a section of Wayfinder Trail, just over there as it disappears into the woods," Ravi said.

"We're going to call it the Forest of Fear, isn't that the cutest? Ravi-roo here came up with it." Jessica bent down to brush a leaf off her heeled ankle boots.

"Ravi-roo?" I mouthed to my friend in disbelief. She could not be serious. Ravi shrugged, a goofy grin on his face.

I unfurled my brow as Jessica straightened. "That's great. I'll have to check it out," I said.

"For sure," Jessica replied. "Well, better get a move on, crew, if we're going to open tonight. We've got a lot of work to do." She flipped her hair over one shoulder and headed in the direction of the woods.

"Good luck," I called. Ravi and the group of teens trailed after her like a brood of ducklings following their mother.

"The results are in!" Phyllis shouted. She banged the gong twice for good measure, even though all the competitors came forward eagerly to hear how we'd fared.

In the end, after an unnecessarily lengthy speech by Phyllis, I didn't win first place. Mr. Duncan kept his title for the fourth year running, leaving me eager to get my hands on a bowl of his famous five-alarm chili that everyone was raving about.

However, all was not lost, because both my entrants came in right behind Mr. Duncan's. The green chili took second place, and my red chili was awarded third.

Although I was disappointed, claiming the next two spots didn't feel like small potatoes. The crowd didn't seem to think so, either, and poor Betty shot daggers at me as she packed up her supplies.

I smiled at Betty, but she turned her back to me. I made a mental note to reach out to her, maybe take her a slice of Nyla's pie, which was currently being sampled by the judges. We might be competitors, but Granny Lu always said that small businesses needed to support one another, and I certainly didn't need to make any more enemies.

Once the competition was over and my booth boasted both the red and white ribbons, plus a blue one for Nyla, hungry customers formed an eager line. They kept us busy for the rest of the afternoon.

———

"All work and no play?" Deacon asked. I wiggled myself out of my car's backseat where I'd placed the last of the soup warmers, now empty.

"It's been a long day," I said. "Good, but long. You?"

"Yeah, been at the station most of the day following up with next of kin," he said, shoving his hands in his pockets and bouncing on his toes.

"Oh? What did you find out?"

"Mr. Harvey's kids are in Chicago and the St. Louis area. His ex-wife, too. All have alibis though, so don't get any ideas."

I shut the car door and leaned against the side of it, crossing my arms. "Who, me?" I asked, widening my eyes innocently.

Deacon shook his head. "Anyway, I promised Ravi I'd come check out the Forest of Fear."

I glanced toward the darkened trail at the edge of the festival. If the bloodcurdling screams I'd been hearing since dusk were any indication, the change of venue wasn't hurting the theater kids at all.

Memories of being young washed over me, and suddenly I felt like a teenager again, with the anticipation of being deliciously afraid. The spook walk looked enticing.

"You want to come?" Deacon asked. "With me?" He looked uncertain.

"Me? Why?" I asked. I couldn't think of a legitimate reason Deacon would invite me to anything. Not anymore, at least.

"I don't know, for old time's sake, maybe?" he said, shoving his hands into the pockets of his jeans. Exasperation laced his tone.

"No, I better be going." I needed to drop my equipment by Lulu's and wash it before I headed home for the night. My feet were aching, and my throat was dry and scratchy from talking to customers all day.

Or perhaps it was all just an excuse to avoid being alone with Deacon. For reasons I couldn't explain, the thought made my stomach churn.

"Fine," he said, turning to walk away. He muttered something else, but I couldn't hear it.

"What was that?" I asked.

"Nothing. Just not surprising, is all." He continued down the sidewalk, tension squaring his shoulders and piercing into me.

I clenched and unclenched my fists. Maybe Tim was right. Maybe I was being petty. It had been twelve years. Shouldn't I be over it by now?

I huffed out a breath, hit the lock button on my key fob, and hurried to catch up.

"Deacon, wait," I said. He paused on the sidewalk, his posture stiff, until I stopped beside him.

"I...I know I need to let it go. But it's not easy," I said. I stared at my feet, but Deacon remained quiet. When I finally looked up, he was watching me. The anger that had been roiling off him just moments ago had abated and was replaced by something gentler. Remorse.

"For what it's worth, I'm sorry. If I could go back, I'd have done everything differently," he said.

I nodded, biting my lip. "Me, too."

"Can...can we please call a truce? We're adults, we're neighbors, and neither one of us is going away anytime soon." Deacon took a deep breath. "I'm not your enemy, Lex."

"We'll see," I said, striding toward the Forest of Fear.

"That's not a no," he said, matching my pace. His errant, crooked grin was back in place.

I rolled my eyes and joined the back of the line snaking up the path. We stood together in the awkward silence of two people who used to be friends but weren't sure how to act around one another anymore.

When it was our group's turn to enter, I took a deep breath. What had I been thinking? Normally, I loved this kind of stuff, but the whole 'finding a dead body' thing had put a slight damper on my Halloween spirit.

"Are you coming?" Deacon asked, pausing a few steps ahead of me to turn around.

"Yeah," I said, taking a big gulp of air and willing my feet to move. We entered the forest together, our group having moved on ahead without us, and rushed to catch up.

I had to admit, Jessica, Ravi, and their team of students had done an exceptional job with the limited time they had. Yellow caution tape marked off the path, and creepy spiderwebs clung to the trees. Thanks to some handy extension cords, eerie green lighting reflected off the fog machines that churned out smoky air. Teens in ghostly makeup wandered the woods.

Soon, I found myself shrieking along with everyone else as various monsters and zombies jumped out of the darkness at us. Once or twice, I reflexively clutched Deacon's arm, before quickly pulling away.

As we neared the end of the walk, a man in a mask with a chainsaw burst out of the trees, its small engine revving up as he ran toward us.

The group took its cue and ran toward the exit. A makeshift bridge had been constructed over a narrow ravine, and just after we skittered over it, a sudden softness made my knees buckle beneath me. I fell to the ground, Deacon crashing right beside me. Dry earth and leaves stuck to my palms, my knees squishing into something pliable underneath them.

Classic. The old "mattress covered with dirt" trick.

"Come on!" Deacon grabbed my hand and pulled me to my feet. The chainsaw revved behind my head, and we ran, hand in hand, toward the sounds and lights of the festival.

My scream was filled with laughter and a side of hysteria, and I caught Deacon's grin as strobe lights flashed around us. We burst out of the exit, the noise of the forest and the chainsaw fading into the background along with the screams of the next group.

I stopped to catch my breath, pressing my hand against my

chest, and Deacon dropped the one he held. He rested his hands on his knees and grinned up at me, breathing hard.

"Not bad for a group of kids, huh?" he said.

"Michael Myers back there about gave me a heart attack," I admitted. "Or was that supposed to be Jason?" I was getting my villains confused.

"I think it was the guy from *Texas Chainsaw Massacre*," Deacon said.

"Whatever. You know I don't like slasher movies," I said, waving my hand in dismissal. "Anyway, he was good. Scary good."

"Hey guys, what did you think?" A creepy mad scientist suddenly appeared at my elbow. He had dark circles under his eyes, and blood splatter covered his white lab coat.

"Gahh! Ravi, don't do that." I punched his arm for good measure.

"Easy, killer," Deacon said. He turned to Ravi.

"Man, that was awesome! The kids did a great job." They did that weird bro hug, slapping one another's back while shaking hands.

"They really did," I said, leaning against a tree trunk. "It's going to take a minute for my heart rate to get back to normal."

"Glad you guys came," he said. "Jess has been amazing pulling it all together." He turned his puppy dog eyes toward an undead beauty queen who was emerging from the woods and speaking into a handheld radio. A shiny tiara balanced over perfectly coiffed hair. She motioned to someone manning the ticket line and headed, thankfully, away from us.

I recognized the pink prom gown and felt more than a little jealous that Jessica could still fit into it after all these years. Mine was probably gathering dust in one of Dad's closets, to never again to see the light of day. Kind of like how I'd never see a size six again. Job hazard, you know.

"Ravi!" Jessica's garbled voice came over the handheld radio at Ravi's hip.

"Better go," he said, practically sprinting away from us. Deacon and I walked quietly away from the crowd.

"He's got it bad. Does Jessica have any clue? Or does she just use him to do whatever she wants?" I asked.

"She's not like that," Deacon said. I shot him a withering look. "Okay, maybe she's a little vain still, but she's much nicer than she used to be. And she loves her students. But no, I don't think she's aware of Ravi's feelings. I keep urging him to man up and tell her, but it's not working."

"I can't believe she's wearing her prom dress," I smirked. "Talk about trying to relive your glory days."

Yes, I was being mean and petty. Not my finest moment.

"She's not the only one stuck on the past," Deacon muttered. Okay, so it was going to be like that.

He walked faster, and I had to jog to catch up. Sighing angrily, I grabbed at his arm to get his attention.

"What?" he said, stopping to face me. The dim glow of the park lights cast harsh shadows across his face.

"Do you even know *why* I got so upset that night?" I demanded, planting my feet and crossing my arms.

"Care to enlighten me? It was just a prank, like we'd done a thousand times before. And you completely overreacted. Why did you let it ruin our friendship?" Deacon asked.

"Because you ruined everything!" I yelled, pushing against his dumb rock-hard pecs. He barely budged, glaring at me.

"Deacon, that was our last night. The last *big* night with all of us together. Just a few more weeks of classes, and then graduation, and I was leaving. And you took it all away from me."

We stood there in a face off, both of us breathing hard, our emotions such a swirl of contempt and regret that I couldn't tell mine from his. My mind drifted back to that night. Prom night, senior year.

It had started off so innocently. Our friend group was in the midst of an intense prank war, boys against girls, and had been since Christmas break. It had started out small and simple. But with the arrival of spring and the end of the school year fast approaching, the pranks had been ratcheting up in intensity, each group trying to outdo the other and have the last laugh.

The girls and I thought we had victory in the bag. Our most recent prank had been tricky to pull off, but we managed to successfully dye the guys' white baseball uniforms a heinous bubblegum pink. The true victory in that particular case was that we managed to keep it under wraps until they were already at our rival school's locker room. Boy, were they in for a surprise when they opened their gym bags to change.

It was epic. Sure, we got Saturday detention and had to soak and hand scrub fourteen uniforms with stain remover for hours, but the bragging rights were *so* worth it.

We rode our high into the week of prom. Cara and I were on the decorating committee and had worked countless hours planning a memorable night.

It was bittersweet for me, because I planned to leave right after graduation for a three-month long job at a summer camp in upstate New York. I was going to see the world. At least, a wider version of it than I'd been exposed to before. Camp counselors were allowed to visit New York City on the few weekends we had off. And at the end of my summer adventure, I planned to pack up and leave Emerald Bay for good.

Everything was going great the night of prom. Deacon and I had even gone together, as friends, since neither of us were dating anyone at the time. We were all dancing and laughing, and then he'd disappeared to get us some punch. And that's when he enacted his revenge.

Deacon and the guys had snuck in an industrial-sized box of laundry detergent and dumped it into the bubbling fountain in the middle of the gym. This was before low-sudsing, high efficiency formulas were the standard. Soon, bubbles began to form in the churning water.

Before we knew it, a soapy mass was overflowing onto the gym floor. People were falling left and right in the slippery solution, some directly *into* the fountain. Including a faculty chaperone.

Sure, it sounds funny now, but it wasn't a laughing matter at all that night. The principal was furious, as he'd been dealing with our antics all semester. In fact, we were probably the reason he retired that year.

Prom was canceled, and everyone was forced to go home. All those hours and hours of work, and we didn't even get to enjoy it. Worse, somehow, *I* got wrapped up in the blame for it.

Deacon and I had to clean up the entire gym ourselves, and we were banned from the after party. This was a big deal, as it was a lock-in style party the parents hosted, with tons of games, food, and cash prizes. A lot of the kids looked forward to it more than the prom itself.

"Bubblegate," as it came to be known, went down in Emerald Bay High history as one of the greatest pranks ever played, but at the time all I could dwell on was the fact that I'd missed out on this last moment with all my friends, one I could never get back, all because of Deacon's stupid idea.

"Why did you do it?" I asked, pulling myself back to the present. Deacon kicked at the ground with his boot.

"You were in such a hurry to blow out of town. Maybe I wanted to make sure you didn't forget us." He lifted his brown eyes to meet mine, his normally confident mask slipping away, and I saw it—the pain over all our lost years. I'd been angry—rightfully so—but he'd been hurt, too.

"You didn't even say goodbye," Deacon whispered gruffly.

He was right. After the gym emptied and he and I were left to clean up the mess, I'd yelled at him for a while. He'd tried to explain, but I wasn't interested in anything he had to say. And then I punished him with silence.

I hadn't spoken a word to Deacon Lane until that day he showed up on my doorstep last month. He'd called and texted, but I'd never answered, and he finally gave up.

"I…I'm sorry, Deacon. Losing your friendship…it was the worst. And it was my fault."

"I'm sorry, too. You have no idea how many times I wished I could undo it all."

I sighed. "We are such idiots," I said.

"Were," he corrected. "We *were* idiots. We've grown up a little since then. Right?"

"I have. Jury's still out on you." I couldn't resist. Agitating him was my default setting.

He pointed a thumb at his chest. "Chief of police, remember?"

I groaned. "You sold out."

He shook his head, a grin peeking out.

"So, what do you say? Friends again?" Deacon asked, holding his hand out.

"I'm willing…to consider it," I conceded, reaching forward. His warm hand enveloped mine, and we shook on it.

Fighting against Deacon was getting exhausting, and it's not like I could keep avoiding him in a town this small. Or in my own home, for that matter. Maybe clearing the air and starting fresh was what we both needed.

"Just don't be a doofus this time, okay?" I said, pulling my hand away.

A real, genuine grin split his face, and for a moment the years melted away. He looked like his eighteen-year-old self again. I fought against the corners of my mouth turning up but found myself losing the battle. I smiled back at him, and in that moment, felt a weight lift off my chest.

"No promises," he said, winking, as we walked the last few steps to the parking lot.

CHAPTER 6
ELEMENTARY, MY DEAR WATSON

I SHOVED the car door closed with my backside, balancing two covered dishes in one hand and Cap's leash in the other. One held my specialty of jalapeño popper deviled eggs, and the other held a giant pan of "funeral potatoes."

I could smell the cheesy goodness of the hash brown casserole, a staple of Emerald Bay potlucks, smothered in sour cream and topped with corn flakes drenched in butter. It might sound strange, but I promise it's a winning combination. Unless you have cholesterol issues.

It was just before noon on Sunday, and I had arrived at Tim and Cara's house early for their annual pre-pumpkin carving barbecue. They both entered the competition every year. From what I'd heard, their trash talk was as entertaining as the pumpkin carving itself.

It was a gorgeous day, unseasonably warm, and I'd traded in my ordinary, plain outfit for my favorite rust-colored skirt, a knotted black top, and a denim jacket for the slight chill in the air. The breeze twirled the loose skirt around my legs, the hem brushing against my lace up boots. I'd even styled my dark hair into waves that fell past my shoulders, instead of my customary ponytail or braids.

I bypassed the front door and walked around to the open side gate, where I found Deacon and Tim setting up folding tables and Cara checking the smoker.

"Brisket's just about perfect," she said.

"Hey, guys," I said, setting the potatoes down on an empty table.

"Hey, Lex," Deacon called.

Cara's head snapped up, and she wrinkled her brow at me. I pretended not to notice. Tim had come over and was trying to peek under the lid of my dish, but I swatted his hand away with a serving spoon.

"Leave that alone. Nobody wants cold potatoes," I said.

"But it smells so gooood," Tim said dramatically, trying to skirt around me and sniff at the steam that escaped the edge.

"It is good. But hands off. D, keep an eye on him." I pointed my spoon at Tim.

Deacon saluted me, and I linked arms with Cara and headed inside to put the eggs in the refrigerator. The kitchen table was covered with packages of buns and condiments, and I began to load up a tray to fill the tables outside.

Childish voices drifted in from the living room, where Olive and Arthur played at a train table. Arthur was busy constructing an elaborate track, while Olive piled colorful wooden blocks into a tower, shouting with delight when it became too tall and toppled over.

"So. Are we just not going to talk about it?" Cara asked.

"Talk about what?" I pulled my attention from the kids.

Cara put both hands on the table across from me and leaned forward, narrowing her eyes.

"'Hey, Lex.' 'Keep an eye on him, D,'" she mimicked in a high-pitched voice. "Since when are you two so buddy-buddy and using your old nicknames? And why don't I know about it?"

"Okay." I blew out a breath. "You don't know because it *just* happened. We may have taken some steps toward reconciliation.

I mean, we can't just snap our fingers and be over everything, but we talked last night at the festival. And it was...nice."

"Nice?" Cara asked. "Nice? Explain."

I relayed the events of the previous evening, and Cara leaned back, whistling slowly.

"This is huge!" she said. "And more importantly, I just won twenty bucks from Tim, and he's on dish duty for a month."

Cara's grin was positively triumphant. She picked up Olive, who had toddled over, and did a little victory dance around the kitchen. Their matching blond curls twirled in the air, and the little girl squealed in delight.

"Um, what are you taking about?" I asked.

Cara stopped twirling long enough to answer. "Just a friendly wager between my husband and me. I bet him you'd forgive Deacon before Halloween. He upped the stakes after talking to you yesterday morning. Oh, boy, I can't wait to see the look on his face."

"You bet on when Deacon and I would make up?"

"That's right, lady. And you just made my day. You know, it's such a relief that we don't have to plan everything separately anymore."

"You invited both of us today," I pointed out.

"Well, yeah, that was some strategic planning on my part." Cara grinned, plopping Olive down on her little toddler couch. "I thought you two could use a little nudge."

I laughed, and the two of us stopped gabbing long enough to pack all the supplies out to the back yard.

"Pay up, Timmy! The divorce is over," Cara yelled gleefully.

Tim groaned, knocking his head back and closing his eyes against the bright sunshine. "One more week, Alex. You couldn't hold a grudge one more week?"

"Yesterday you were telling me to get over it," I said.

"Reverse psychology," Tim shrugged.

"What are you talking about?" Deacon asked, chopping up smoked brisket in an enormous foil pan.

"Don't ask," I said. "These two are twisted."

Before Deacon could inquire further, the first guests arrived, armed with lawn chairs and side dishes. Soon we were all filling plates and stuffing our faces with delicious food.

Talk turned to the festival, and before long Cara and Tim were arguing about who would win the pumpkin carving contest. It was slated to start at four, and several others in attendance planned to compete.

"You're both wrong," my dad said, around a mouthful of deviled eggs. "This is my year to shine. I can feel it."

Cara had invited her parents and my dad, and they were gathered around a folding table.

Everyone had a good laugh at Dad's expense. I don't know why he entered every year. Dad was one of the worst pumpkin carvers Emerald Bay had ever seen. His jack-o-lanterns looked like something a child would create, if someone were ignorant enough to give a kid a carving knife. I know because even after I moved, he would send me a selfie with that year's pumpkin. He always did like to make people laugh, and this was his seasonal running joke.

After everyone ate and played a few rounds of corn hole, people began to trickle out, some bound for the festival and others for home. I gathered up empty trays and took them inside to help clean up.

As I turned to dump an empty stack of plates into the trash can, Ravi came skidding around the corner and nearly smacked right into me.

"Geez, where's the fire?" I asked.

"Sorry, Alex. I was running late and hoping I'd make it in time."

"You can chill; there's still plenty of food." I gestured to the leftovers we'd placed on the kitchen table to be dished into smaller containers. "You missed all the trash talk, though."

"Bummer," Ravi said, heaping a plate with pasta salad, potatoes, baked beans, and smoked meats. Two kinds of bread balanced precariously on top of his food mountain, and he fidgeted with a bottle of barbecue sauce. A nervous energy pulsated around him.

"Is everything okay?" I asked. Ravi looked more twitchy than usual, his dark eyes troubled.

"I don't know. I've been working in my classroom, and I noticed some things missing from the storage closet. You or Deacon didn't take anything last week, did you?"

"I didn't, and I'm sure Deacon would have mentioned it to you if he did."

"What about me?" Deacon asked, coming in through the open screen door. I ignored his question to ask another.

"What's missing?" I asked.

"The big jar of white snakeroot," Ravi said. "There were two jars of each sample—a large one with whole dried plants, and a small one with plucked leaves or petals."

Deacon and I looked at one another. His brow scrunched up with concern.

"There was only the small jar of snakeroot when we were there," Deacon said. I nodded in agreement.

"It must have been missing before," I said. "Does anyone else have access to your closet?"

Ravi shrugged. "The janitor has a master set of keys, and I think Principal Fletcher does, too. Sometimes I leave the door propped open during class if the kids are in and out for supplies."

"So, basically anyone at the school could slip in or out when you're not paying attention?" I asked.

Ravi frowned at me. "It's possible."

Deacon groaned. "So now we've got *actual* missing poison— the very kind I suspected was put into Alan's tea?"

"Wait, what?" I put my hand up. "You found white snakeroot in his tea?"

Deacon crossed his arms. "No, I found tiny petals and leaves *resembling* the snakeroot sample in his tea. The spiced apple sample I got from Cara did not have those, only the tea found at the scene did. I'm hoping to get the toxicology and autopsy reports tomorrow."

"Well, Chief, looks like you've got a case on your hands," I said.

"Not a word out of either of you, okay?" Deacon pointed his index finger at both of us. "We don't need rumors getting out just yet. Ravi, you're going to have to take me back to the school so I can have a look around."

"Can I finish my food, at least?" Ravi asked. He looked forlornly at his plate.

"Bring it with you," Deacon said, grabbing his keys from the counter.

"I'll come too," I said, wiping my hands on a dish towel and tossing it onto the counter.

"No," Deacon said. "Stay out of it, Lex. I'll handle it."

The two of them headed to the front door, Ravi only stopping to grab a drink from the cooler on the floor.

"Don't tell Diane anything if you don't want the whole town to know!" I called after them, and Deacon gave a little wave over his shoulder.

I glared at their retreating backs. Forgiven or not, Deacon Lane was still annoyingly bossy.

"Something interestin' over there?" Granny Lu whispered in my ear. I was standing at the front windows of the café, arms crossed, boring a hole into the police station with my eyes. We were in the pre-lunch lull, and I hadn't been able to keep my attention on work all morning.

I was dying to know if Deacon had received the autopsy and toxicology reports. His police cruiser had been parked in the same spot since I'd arrived at work.

"Nothing, Granny," I said, straightening the salt and pepper shakers at the nearest table.

"Mmm-hmm," she said, raising her eyebrows at me. I didn't take the bait.

I was saved from Granny Lu's prying eyes by the chattering of four women entering the café. Granny greeted them, taking them to an empty booth while I hoofed it back to the kitchen.

Southwestern chicken soup simmered on the stove, and I lifted the lid, breathing in the sharp scent of garlic and onions mingled with the spice of cumin and jalapeño, swimming in a tomato and broth base with chicken, corn and black beans. I took out a new spoon and cautiously sampled a taste. If those ladies wanted the soup of the day, it was absolute perfection, if I did say so myself.

I grated a large block of cheese—so much better than prepackaged shredded cheese coated with that weird anti-caking agent—and checked to make sure I had plenty of ripe avocados for topping. Jasmine poured drinks and put in the order: two soups of the day, one turkey panini and one Cobb salad.

Granny Lu assembled the salad while I grilled the sandwich, ladling out the soup just before the panini was finished. I garnished the plates with avocado slices, cheese, sour cream and cilantro. Normally I would finish off the soup with a side of corn chips and salsa, but the ladies had ordered small salads instead, and Granny had those waiting.

Shrill laughter pierced the air and I looked over the half wall out to the dining room, noticing Brenda Holliday was among the group. She looked to be having a good time with her friends, and I saw several shopping bags tucked at the end of the booth.

Jasmine was busy with another couple who'd just been seated, so I delivered the order myself.

"You ladies doing well today?" I asked politely, carefully setting the steaming bowls on the table.

"Oh, definitely," one of them said. Her burgundy hair bobbed up and down as she nodded her head. "Especially since we have an heiress among us!"

"Oh, let's not make a fuss over it," Brenda said, unrolling her napkin and placing it in her lap.

"Sole beneficiaries, Bren. That should set you and Jessica up for quite some time," the woman continued.

Brenda smiled uncomfortably, and I sensed that she'd rather not be discussing her financial situation in front of me. I finished delivering their food and tucked the large tray under my arm, returning to the kitchen.

So, Alan Harvey had left all his worldly possessions to Brenda and Jessica Holliday. Thanks to Myra, I knew he owned rental properties, but I was somewhat in the dark about the rest of his finances. It seemed a little strange that everything was left to his niece and great-niece, but nothing for his own children. Although, several folks had mentioned they were not close.

I thought about the missing snakeroot from Ravi's classroom. Jessica worked at the school, and from what I'd observed, had Ravi completely under her spell. Could it be possible that she'd taken the poison and knocked off her uncle?

Jessica wasn't my favorite person, but even I wasn't convinced she'd be capable of such a thing. She certainly could access Ravi's supply closet if she wished, though. Money could be a powerful motivator, if someone were desperate enough.

Would she do it for her mother? I knew her stepdad had passed away a few years before, and her mom didn't work. Maybe the two of them had hatched a plan—

"Alexandria!" Granny barked in my ear, and I jumped.

"You're burning the sandwich, hon," she said, taking a gentler tone. I looked down at the sandwich press I was supposed to be watching, seeing the smoke rise and getting a whiff of the acrid smell.

"Ugh, sorry," I said, flipping the lid open and removing the blackened bread. "I got distracted. I'll start over." Granny opened the back door, and I tossed the charred sandwich out into the alley while letting the fresh breeze in to clear the offending smoke. I kicked the exhaust fan up to high and prayed the diners hadn't noticed.

The rest of the lunch rush passed without incident, but my head was still a muddle as I pondered the new information I'd learned. By midafternoon, Granny practically shoved me out the door to take a break. Before I could second-guess myself, I grabbed a portable container and threw a few of Nyla's leftover baked goods into it.

Instead of walking down to the park, as Granny had suggested, I turned at the end of the street and took the crosswalk to the opposite side of Main. It had rained earlier, but now the sky was merely overcast. A strong, cool breeze blew the scent of dried grass and leaves, and I tried to burrow further into the oversized hoodie I'd thrown on over my jeans and tee.

The bell dinged as I entered the police station. One officer sat at his desk, hunched over paperwork, while another made copies at the machine in the back of the room.

"Back so soon?" Donny Swanson asked, his ever-present grin in its usual place. "I hope you're not needing to give another statement."

"Hi, Donny. No, thankfully this is a nicer errand." I held out the box, cracking the lid open. "Apple turnover? We had extra today."

Donny's eyes lit up, and the wax paper I'd wrapped them in crinkled as he selected the biggest, gooiest piece. I pressed my lips together to keep from smiling and offered the same to the other officers, who politely declined.

"Is Dea—I mean, Chief Lane—around?" I asked Donny. He swallowed and took a big gulp from the black coffee cup in his hand, stamped with an Emerald Bay logo and the outline of a sailboat.

"He just stepped over to City Hall for a minute, but he'll be back soon. You can wait in his office, if you like."

"Thanks, I think I will."

Deacon's office door was closed but unlocked, and I let myself in, settling into the extra chair across from his desk. A computer monitor took up one side of the desk, and a stack of files stood on the other. A lone folder rested on the desk right under the screen, and I felt the tingling of my forearm before the goosebumps popped up on my skin.

I glanced behind me, realizing that the angles of the doorway and desk blocked the rest of the cops from seeing me. I strained my ears for the sound of footsteps or Deacon's voice, but I heard neither.

Setting the box of treats on the chair, I tiptoed around Deacon's desk. My heart pounded against my chest. *Is this illegal?* I wondered as I glanced at the file but didn't touch it. HARVEY, ALAN was printed on the label in bold ink. My fingers itched to open it, but I resisted and simply glanced at the computer screen. Unfortunately, the lock screen stared back at me, waiting for a password.

I wasn't brazen enough to hack into Deacon's computer (nor did I have the skill, to be honest) and I turned, disappointed, back to my chair. And then I heard the unmistakable sound of an incoming fax on the machine next to the desk.

Ha! Loophole. A few moments later, several pages waited face-up in the tray.

Do people still use fax machines? I wondered. I had never been the type of girl to work in an office setting, so I wouldn't know. But I supposed it wasn't too surprising that a small town, underfunded police force used semi-outdated technology.

I stopped to scan the top page, keeping my fingers off it. It was Alan's autopsy report. I scanned past his name, age, and other identifying details until I reached the bold CAUSE OF DEATH printed about halfway down the page. HEART FAILURE.

Huh. So, after all that, he really did die of natural causes? Something like disappointment, or unease, settled around me. I was so sure that other forces had been at work here. Maybe my instincts were slipping.

I examined the rest of the document. A selection of boxes was listed under the cause of death line: ACCIDENT, HOMICIDE, NATURAL, SUICIDE and UNDETERMINED. I was surprised to find the last one, UNDETERMINED, ticked off instead of NATURAL.

Hmm, curious. Wasn't heart failure classified as a "natural" cause of death?

At the bottom of the page, the toxicology report was printed. It looked like Mr. Harvey had no drugs or alcohol in his system, but on the very last line was written TOXIN: TREMETOL, POSITIVE.

What is Tremetol? I wondered. Science had never been my strong suit, but even if it had been, I didn't think I'd recognize that word.

A shuffling outside the door startled me, and the handle turned. I straightened up and moved quickly, trying to make it back to my seat, but my foot hooked on the wheel of Deacon's desk chair, and I crashed to the floor, landing on my hands and knees. Super graceful.

A pair of regulation black, lace-up boots appeared under my nose, and I looked up, attempting to put on my best innocent face.

"Lex? Find what you're looking for down there?" Deacon asked. His arms were crossed, and his face scrunched oddly, like it was warring between giving me a good scolding or laughing at me.

"Hey, Deacon. Chief." I attempted a casual smile.

Just one friend visiting another; nothing to see here, folks. The box of apple turnovers was just about a foot away from me, and I reached for it.

"I was just bringing you guys a midafternoon pick-me-up," I said.

"Uh-huh," Deacon said, but he held his hand out to help me to my feet.

"Nyla's apple turnovers," I said, opening the box and setting it on his desk. I could see he was tempted, but not enough to ignore how he'd discovered me sprawled on the floor of his office.

"And?" he asked.

"And what?" I said.

"The real reason you're here? It's not to butt that cute little nose of yours into my case files, is it?"

I held my hands up. "I didn't touch anything. Scout's honor."

"You hated Girl Scouts," he muttered, moving past me to take his seat. I sat down in the chair opposite and waited for him to notice the fax. It took about half a second and he snatched the papers out of the tray, his brow wrinkling as his eyes rapidly scanned the report.

I waited. The ticking of a wall clock was the only sound in the room. He heaved a big sigh as he finished, tucking the papers into Alan's file.

"Did you read this?" he asked.

I bit my lip and didn't answer. Silence was my friend, right? At least it wouldn't incriminate me.

Deacon shook his head at me.

"We're not sixteen anymore, Lex," he said. "You can't just go poking around in police business."

"I didn't touch anything," I repeated, holding up my hands.

Deacon pressed his lips together and looked past me, out into the station. I waited for him to say something, and when he didn't, my curiosity got the better of me.

"What's Tremetol?" I asked quietly.

Deacon sighed. "It's a toxin. According to Ravi, the very one found in individuals with white snakeroot poisoning. Usually, it's caused by livestock accidentally ingesting the plant, tainting their milk, which is then passed on to whoever drinks it. But in this case...I believe it was given to him directly."

"Holy crap," I said. "But the report says he died of heart fail-ure. How can that be?"

Deacon scrubbed his hands over his face in frustration.

"I need to read the entire report thoroughly, but the medical examiner included some notes about that." Deacon picked up the papers again and turned to the second page, his eyes skim-ming the document. After a few moments, he looked up again.

"Tremetol is generally not lethal, at least, not in small quanti-ties. But Alan had a heart condition, which likely exacerbated his reaction to the toxin."

"Someone really did do this to him, then." I said. "On purpose."

"Yeah. It's unlikely that he poisoned himself. Either someone wanted Alan Harvey dead, or they were trying to make him sick and accidentally killed him. Regardless, someone either reckless or dangerous is out there. And it's *my* job to find out who." Deacon speared me with a look. "Not yours. Got it?"

I nodded, swallowing hard. For some reason, even though I had suspected as much, hearing it officially stated by the chief had my stomach in knots. A murderer was loose in Emerald Bay, and we had no idea who it was.

———

As I left Deacon's office, I glanced behind me to see he was already absorbed in rereading the autopsy report. I know I promised to butt out, but on second thought, I decided to make a quick stop through the open door to city hall.

I had it on good authority that Diane, chatty receptionist extraordinaire, loved Nyla's turnovers. It probably wouldn't take much to loosen those already slack lips of hers.

I walked down the short hallway to reception, where Diane stood on a step stool looking into the top drawer of a filing cabi-net. Her tiny frame was angular, her sharp nose accentuated by cropped, dark hair, but her smile was genuine when she noticed me.

"Well, hey there, Alex," she said, turning as she heard me approach. "What are you up to, sugar?"

"Not much," I said. "I made a quick delivery over to the station and wanted to see if you'd like one of these extra turnovers."

"Aren't you sweet? I'd never turn one of those down." Diane stepped off the stool, her short heels clacking against the linoleum as she approached the desk.

I handed her a carefully wrapped turnover, which she placed next to her neatly arranged stack of files.

"Looks delicious. I'm going to enjoy that with my afternoon coffee," she said, her dark eyes flitting to the back break room.

"I keep seeing Silver Vixens today," I mused, gauging her reaction when I mentioned the book club.

"Oh?" Diane asked.

"Yes, Brenda Holliday was just in the café with a few friends. They seemed to be celebrating," I said.

"That's right; the reading of Alan's will was today, wasn't it?" I wasn't surprised Diane was privy to this information—she didn't miss much. "Did the old codger leave it all to Bren?"

"And Jessica too, I believe," I said.

"Well, good for them," Diane said sincerely. "I do hope he left them more than a pile of debts and enemies."

"Why do you say that?"

Diane glanced around, but the surrounding space was empty. "I had a few run-ins with Alan years ago," Diane said. "Let's just say that the man knew how to get what he wanted, and he wasn't afraid to get his hands dirty in order to do so."

"You're the second person who's mentioned that," I said, remembering what Sheila Jenkins had said.

"Last I heard, he was in too much debt to finish the remodel on that cottage of his. Knowing Alan, he probably had plans to buy up all that property along the lake and build himself a nice little kingdom of holiday rentals, so the little snag of running out of money probably made him a little desperate. And a desperate Alan did dangerous things," Diane said ominously.

"What kind of things?" I whispered.

Diane blinked, her eyes clearing of whatever memory had pulled her away. "Nothing, dear. Nothing for you to worry about. I wish Brenda and Jessica the best, though I imagine that 'inheritance' is a bit of a disappointment to them."

I thought about the uncomfortable way Brenda had tried to hush her friend when she'd called her an heiress. Perhaps the woman had put on a front for her posh friends, when in reality, she wasn't a penny richer than she'd been yesterday.

"Well, I'll get out of your hair," I said to Diane. "I'd better get back to the café to help Granny, anyway."

"Sure thing, hon," Diane said, scooting around the desk to give me a little side hug. "Thanks for the treat and tell your grandmother hello."

I left city hall, my mind going over the details I'd learned in the past hour. Alan had been poisoned, but who had the motive? If Alan had been as sneaky as Diane and Sheila had said, could he have a secret stack of money stashed somewhere, or had he died in debt? I was no closer to an answer as I entered the café to prepare for our evening takeout orders.

CHAPTER 7
DO YOU LIKE SCARY MOVIES?

THE BELL chimed at the back door as Tucker and Ava, our resident teens, arrived for work after school. It was nearly four o'clock, and I was up to my elbows in lasagna noodles.

"Hi, guys," I said.

"Hey, boss," Tucker said, his easy grin in place. Ava greeted me while she tied an apron over her clothes and turned to wash up at the sink.

"Where's Mrs. R.?" Tucker asked, helping himself to a stray noodle. He was too intimidated by Granny Lu to call her by her given name. I swatted his hand away.

"I sent her home for the night, since Ava's here to help me," I said. I'd hired the petite girl to help waitress on the weekends, but when she'd expressed an interest in cooking, I'd given her a few extra shifts to work with me. It never hurt to have an extra pair of hands in the kitchen, and Ava was a quick study.

"My girl's the best," Tucker said, slinging his arm over Ava and giving her a quick kiss on the cheek. Her face flamed as she looked to me with alarm, but I just laughed.

"Okay, enough P.D.A., Tuck. Get out of here and let us work," I said.

"You got it." Tucker saluted me and headed for the supply

closet and was soon cleaning tables and mopping the floors of the empty café. He usually cleaned for an hour or two while orders were coming in, and then would take over delivering the takeout meals.

Ava and I fell into easy conversation as we assembled pan after pan of pasta, cheese, and sauce. Once they were in the oven, Ava chopped vegetables for salads while I retrieved the garlic bread dough that had been rising in covered bowls. I divided the dough, rolling each into a long breadstick to rise once more on a pan before baking.

"Have y'all been to the Forest of Fear yet?" I asked Ava, as Tucker entered the kitchen and began washing the dishes we'd used.

"We went opening night," Ava said.

"And we're going again this weekend. They're adding a few new elements and it's going to be lit," Tucker said. "We saw you and the chief there," he added, drying his hands with a towel and leaning against the counter.

"Yeah, we're both good friends with Ravi. I mean, Mr. Kumar," I said. "I thought the forest was really cool, especially having to change everything last minute. Do…um…either of you know Ms. Holliday very well?" I was more than a little curious what the kids thought of Jessica.

"Yeah, she's really nice," Tucker said. "And kind of hot, in a cougar sort of way," he added.

"Ew, Tucker!" Ava shrieked. "Don't be gross."

"But I only have eyes for you, babe," he said quickly.

I shook my head. Clueless male teen, check.

"You know we're the same age, right?" I asked.

"Sorry, Alex. Um, you're a hot cougar, too?" Tucker added.

Ava chucked a carrot stick at his head with surprising ferocity. He ducked and it bounced off the wall before dropping to the floor.

"Oh my gosh, STOP," I said loudly, slapping my palms against the island.

"What?" Tucker asked, while Ava looked at me with wide eyes. I suppose that's what I got for asking teenagers' opinions.

"Try both in appropriate *and* insulting," I said, shaking my head. "Do better, kid."

"Sorry, boss." To his credit, Tucker looked contritely at his shoes.

"Anyway," Ava said quietly, turning back to the cutting board. "I'm the office aide second period, so I see Ms. Holliday all the time. She's really great. Sometimes she covers our classes when they can't find a substitute."

"Really?" I asked. "You didn't notice anything...different... about her today, did you?"

Ava eyed me curiously. "Not really. She left for a meeting while I was working in the office. I didn't see her again until lunch, but she was across the cafeteria."

The meeting must have been the reading of the will, but then, I already knew about that.

"She stopped to talk to Mr. Kumar when I was in bio, and they both seemed really excited about something," Tucker said. "I thought maybe he'd finally asked her out or something."

"Oh, yeah, he's *so* in love with her," Ava said, giggling, and Tucker joined her.

Poor Ravi; the guy couldn't catch a break. But at least I knew who I needed to talk to next.

———

Sounds from the festival drifted down the empty alley as I locked up the café. I bypassed my car and walked the short distance across the bridge and into the park. It wasn't as busy as it had been over the weekend, but all the food and craft stalls were open, and a small crowd was gathered in front of the open amphitheater. The aroma of cinnamon and caramel apples hung in the air, and whimsical, spooky music emanated from speakers throughout the park.

I'd texted Ravi earlier to see if he was free, and when he'd mentioned that he was helping his family at their booth, I'd quickly replied that I'd meet him there after work.

I spotted Ravi standing at the booth, leaning his elbows casually across the countertop. He was in an intense conversation with his niece, her bottom perched on top of the booth and her little feet swinging back and forth.

"Alex, I was hoping you'd come to see us." Dr. Suma Kumar, Ravi's mother, greeted me warmly. She'd been our family physician for as long as I could remember, but if you were to ask me, she worked her real magic in the kitchen. Which was saying something, as she was an excellent doctor.

Once, as teens, we'd bet her a week's worth of Ravi's chores that we could handle her spiciest vindaloo recipe, without taking a sip of milk to cool off. We lost, and my mouth still burned at the memory. And my muscles from the heavy yard work she'd made us do. We learned not to mess with her after that.

"Hey, doc. You know I can't pass up your masala chai. Don't tell Cara," I said, grinning, as she passed a steaming cup of tea into my hands. I sipped contentedly, the milk and brown sugar perfectly offsetting the spiciness of cardamom, cinnamon, and star anise.

Cara had been chasing the perfect chai blend, and to date, it had eluded her, much to her chagrin. And Ravi's mom refused to give up her secret recipe.

"Do you want Gulab jamun too?" Dr. Kumar asked. "They're fresh."

"Mm, yes please," I said, as I swallowed too quickly. The chai burned my throat all the way down. I handed my cash to the doc while Ravi's sister filled a small paper sack with the sweet and sticky dessert.

Ravi took his own cup of chai, and after we said goodbye to his family, we made our way to an empty picnic table near the Ferris wheel. The spooky music had cut off while we'd been at the booth, and now live bluegrass drifted out from the amphitheater.

As we walked, I made a few mental notes of food stalls to try over the next few days. Ordinarily, Emerald Bay didn't offer much in the way of flavor diversity, but the festival brought lots of variety to the area. A treat for a foodie such as myself.

"Who is that guy?" I asked Ravi, gesturing to the musician alternating between his fiddle, harmonica, and vocals. "He looks kind of familiar." The guy wore jeans, a flannel shirt with a vest, and a fedora. He was talented, and I found my foot tapping along to the lively music.

"I'm not sure," Ravi said. "I feel like I've seen him before, too. He looks a few years older than us; maybe he's a local who came back for the festival?"

I shrugged. He was probably right.

"Cheers to the hero of the Forest of Fear," I said, changing the subject and clinking my paper cup with Ravi's. His white teeth flashed in the darkness with a smile.

"Thanks, Lex," he said. "Jess has some ideas how to improve it before this weekend, so we've still got a lot of work to do."

"That's what Tucker and Ava said. They're planning to attend again, and it's going to be, quote, 'lit.'" I grinned.

"That's what we're going for," Ravi said.

"Deacon and I loved it," I said.

"About time you two made up," Ravi said, the paper bag rustling as he snagged a piece of my dessert.

"I know, I know, bygones." I shrugged.

Ravi popped the lid off his chai to cool it down. "I like to think Jess and I played a small part in bringing you two together again." He took a little bow. "You know, you could get over your grudge against Jessica, too," he said quietly.

"I'm not holding a grudge," I insisted. "I've been perfectly polite."

"Polite, maybe. But not friendly," he replied. "She tries to hide it, but I think it hurts her feelings."

"It's not like we were ever friends," I said, sighing. "Besides, you more than make up for it."

"What's that supposed to mean?"

Ugh, this conversation was not going the way I'd planned. I took a deep breath. I'd already stepped in it; might as well fully commit.

"I'm sorry, Ravi, but you're my friend and I don't want to see you get hurt. Have you asked her out, told her how you feel?"

Ravi sighed, his shoulders sagging as he exhaled. "No, I haven't. We started teaching at the same time a few years ago and got along so well. She's different than she used to be and I just…don't want to ruin a good thing."

I wondered if Jessica really had changed, and if she knew how lucky she was. Ravi was a great guy, and a total catch, but I could understand his trepidation.

"I can see what a good friend you've been to her," I said.

"It hasn't been easy for her and her mom, since her stepdad died. Jess has had to be strong for both of them. But, hopefully things are turning around now," Ravi said.

"Turning around how?" I asked.

"Well, I don't know if I should say anything, but Jess told me her uncle left them some money. Enough to get her mom out of that tiny apartment and into a nice place. Jess has been doing her best to support herself and her mom, but you know public education doesn't pay much. She was so happy today," Ravi said, his smile genuine. "Like all her worries just disappeared." He snapped his fingers.

"Oh, that's…nice for them," I murmured. Goosebumps popped up on my forearm and my brain buzzed with this new information that had been dropped into my lap. And I didn't even have to dig for it this time.

"Well, I'd better head home," Ravi said, draining the last of his tea. "I still have papers to grade."

"Did the missing snakeroot ever turn up?" I asked. I'd almost forgotten about it.

"No, not yet." Worry creased his forehead. "I'm kind of in hot water with the administrators over it."

I frowned, pressing my lips together.

"Do you know something?" Ravi asked, studying my face. "Deacon mentioned you nosing around his case. His words, not mine." Ravi held his hands up in mock surrender.

I wondered how much I should say. Technically, I shouldn't know any more than your average citizen, and though I trusted Ravi, I wasn't sure how far his loyalty to Jessica went. Especially considering that there *was* an inheritance, after all.

"Deacon hasn't spoken to you today?" I chewed on my bottom lip.

"No, why?"

"You should probably talk to him. I wouldn't want to be accused of 'butting in' again," I said.

"Okay," Ravi said, shrugging. He didn't press me. I wondered if he'd feel the same way when he found out that Alan Harvey had been poisoned, likely with his own missing snakeroot samples.

———

After Ravi left, I moseyed slowly through the festival. It was winding down for the evening, but a few stragglers still played games and bought the last of the treats before the stalls began to close.

I stopped to listen to the musician. On closer inspection, I realized I'd seen him playing his guitar on the porch of one of the lake cottages. That's why he'd looked so familiar. Soon he finished his set and packed up, with a promise to return for another show over the weekend.

The fun, spooky music had resumed once the concert had ended, setting the mood for the last few carnival goers. I decided to come back another night for street tacos, jambalaya and beignets (On second thought, I should probably plan to spread those out over a few nights. I needed a hot date, but not one with antacids.).

As I reached the footbridge to head back downtown and to my car, someone abruptly cut off the music to the loudspeakers. The sudden silence was eerie. I turned back to the park and glanced around, but nothing seemed amiss. Vendors and festival volunteers busied themselves locking up supplies for the night and prepping for the next day.

The evening was windy, and as I walked, I adjusted a knit cap over my hair to keep it from blowing in my eyes. I could hear the faint sound of lake waves lapping at the shore, and dry, fallen leaves skittered around my feet. Up ahead, the downtown businesses were all dark and deserted.

I wished Cap were with me, but he was safe and warm at home, and suddenly all I wanted was to be there with him. I glanced at the police station, the only building that showed any signs of life. A couple of vehicles remained, but neither of them were Deacon's cruiser. I found myself slightly bereft not seeing his familiar car.

I reluctantly turned away from the street, walking around our patio dining and into the alley. It was even darker back here. The lone streetlight at the end burned out weeks ago and had yet to be replaced. Why hadn't I moved my car out front earlier?

Something rustled in the darkness behind me, but when I whipped around, I didn't see anything. Garbage cans lined the alley, creating tall, looming shadows. We were always fighting the raccoons looking for food scraps, and I'm sure that's all it was. Probably.

I actively fought to keep the image of the hooded figure from Alan's neighborhood from my mind. Somehow, I had completely forgotten about that.

Glancing up, I saw that Granny's apartment windows were all dark. She was an early to bed, early to rise woman. Not that I could have reached her door any quicker than my car. The main entrance was around the front of the building, and the fire escape was slick with rainwater from earlier.

I'd spoken truthfully when I'd mentioned hating slasher films, but that didn't mean I'd never watched any. With my senses on high alert, I felt like a dumb movie character—the kind of girl who cluelessly walks alone into the darkness while the killer is still at large. I glanced down at my sneakers. At least I wasn't wearing high heels.

My keys were already clutched tightly in my hand, slightly dampened from my clammy palms. A soft scraping sounded against the fence. I froze, logic quickly being eclipsed by my fight or flight instincts.

It's just the wind in the trees, I thought. *The branches are brushing up against the fence.*

I fiddled with the little vial of pepper spray attached to the keyring, fumbling until I felt the switch turn to the "on" position. It was at this point I truly began to question my own sanity, parking alone in a dark alley with a murderer on the loose. Yet, here I was.

There was nothing to do but move forward until I reached my car.

Trying not to imagine eyes following me in the darkness, I picked up the pace. Just a few more yards, and I'd be there. A twig snapped nearby, but this time I didn't look back. I unlocked my car remotely and ran the last few steps. Jerking the door open, I leaped into the driver's seat, immediately locking the doors behind me.

My breath came in shallow gasps and my hands shook as I started the car, the headlights illuminating the empty alley ahead. *It's just your imagination,* I told myself as I threw the car in drive. I wasn't waiting around to find out.

I pulled around the corner and slowed in front of the police station, pulling into an empty space. Yellow light bathed the sidewalk in front of me, giving a modicum of comfort, but not enough to slow my pulse. I needed to calm down before operating heavy machinery.

Feeling like a big baby, I grabbed my phone and called my dad. He picked up on the second ring.

"Hey kiddo, what's up?"

"Oh, nothing much," I said, my voice coming out in an unnatural pitch. I cleared my throat.

"What's wrong?" Like I was going to fool him.

"Well, I was leaving the festival, and I got a little…freaked out. Like someone was following me, but I couldn't see them. I don't know, I was probably just imagining it."

I heard a shuffling in the background.

"Where are you now?" Dad asked.

"Parked in front of the station."

"Good, stay put. Lock your doors, and I'll be right there."

"Oh, you don't have to—" I was cut off as I heard the slam of a truck door through the phone. An engine roared to life, and then the connection cut off. I glanced behind my car, but the street was empty. I mentally scolded myself for overreacting, but it was nice to know my dad had my back. I concentrated on slowing my heart rate and deep breathing.

I could see Deputy Swanson and another officer through the glass doors. I knew I could go inside if I wanted, but if I was going to have a nervous breakdown in front of anyone, I'd rather it be my dad.

Sixty seconds later, bright headlights shone into my windows as Dad's big truck pulled next to my much smaller car. That was fast. Dad lived a few blocks away from my place…closer to downtown than I lived, but not close enough to get to me that quickly.

I hopped out of the car as Dad reached the sidewalk, and he pulled me into a bear hug. My face pressed against the buttons of his flannel shirt, but I didn't care.

"Thanks for coming," I mumbled against his chest. He released me and looked me up and down.

"You scared me. Are you all right?" he asked.

"Yeah, I'm fine. I feel kind of stupid now, but back there..." I gestured vaguely toward the alley and shuddered. "I just got really creeped out."

"It's not stupid. I'm glad you called. You need to be more careful...no more parking in the alley and walking alone at night, okay?"

I bit my lip to keep from reminding him that I'd lived on my own for years now, and had walked alone at night plenty, but he had a point. At least until Alan's killer was caught. I nodded.

"Deal," I said.

"Good," he said. "I'm going to follow you home, okay?"

"Okay. Thanks."

Dad's headlights shone in my rearview mirror all the way back to the duplex. When I pulled into the garage, he insisted on coming inside and checking out the whole house, just to make sure no one was hiding in the closet or under the bed.

It felt a little excessive, but I humored him and put the kettle on. Cap circled around my feet until I bent down and gave him big cuddles.

"Hey, buddy. I missed you today." Cap licked my hand in response. He must have missed me, too...either that, or he still smelled dessert on my hands. I washed them at the sink and refilled his food and water bowls.

I picked up my phone and sent a text to Granny to make sure she was okay. Early to bed or not, I had to check in.

Granny: All good here. You know I keep Pops' .38 handy anyway. Now let an old woman sleep. LOL!

Granny was pretty tech savvy for an old woman, but she thought "LOL" meant "lots of love." I chuckled to myself and pocketed my phone. Luella Rivers prided herself on her independence, and I knew she wasn't bluffing about Pop's handgun. Woe to the intruder who'd mess with her.

"All clear," Dad said, jogging down the stairs.

"Thanks, Dad. You're the best." I showed him Granny's message, and he rolled his eyes.

"I'll drop by there before I go home to make sure every-thing's all right at the café and her place," he said.

"Better give her a heads-up before you do. She's liable to shoot first and ask questions later."

Dad chuckled. "True."

I gave him a peck on the cheek before turning back to the boiling water, pouring it over two herbal tea bags.

"How did you get to me so fast? Were you at the festival or something?"

Dad cleared his throat as I handed him a steaming mug.

"No, I was, uh, at Nyla's." He turned away to add honey to his tea, stirring an inordinately long time.

Well, that explained how he got downtown so quickly. Nyla lived just two blocks away from Main, on the police station side. Most of the time she walked to and from work.

"Nyla's? Why?" I asked.

"Because we're friends, that's why. And she, um, has been teaching me how to bake." The part of Dad's cheeks that wasn't covered with a heavy beard was mottled with red.

Dad was blushing. Interesting. *Play it cool, Lex.*

"Baking? Really?" I leaned against the counter and took a long sip of tea.

"Sure. You know I love sweets. Thought it was time I learned how to make some myself." He shrugged.

"Okaaay," I said, drawing out the word. "Maybe I can sample some of your work soon." I watched his reaction closely.

"Sure," Dad said, taking a towel from the rack and wiping up a stray wet spot on the counter. He changed the subject quickly, but I tucked the little morsel of information in my back pocket to revisit later.

Dad didn't have lady friends. At least, not ones that he spent evenings with *baking*, of all things. Or rather, he hadn't when I was growing up. It had been just the two of us for as long as I could remember. My mother, whom I not-so-affectionately referred to as the "uterus donor," had left us when I was three.

As we sipped our tea and chatted, I wondered if Dad had grown in his own way since I'd been gone. I wasn't entirely sure how I felt about that, but I'd have to sort it out later.

CHAPTER 8
PERSONALLY VICTIMIZED BY REGINA GEORGE

SOME PEOPLE CLAIM you are either a cook or a baker, but never both. The assumption is that cooks tend to be impulsive and imprecise, while bakers must be methodical and scientific.

Personally, I don't subscribe to this theory. Sure, I love cooking intuitively, adding a bit of this and that until a dish tastes just right. But I also enjoy baking, and relish putting my own twists on classic recipes.

After the events of last night, I'd been unable to calm down and go to bed at a decent hour. I called Georgia, since it was still early in California, and we'd chatted for a long while. I'd been missing my roommate, and she was eager to hear how things were going. She was shocked to hear of the murder and eager to know every detail.

It had been a less than relaxing conversation, but nonetheless, it was good to hear her voice and catch up.

Afterward, I'd turned the TV on for background noise and stress baked pan after pan of cookies while binging old episodes of *Psych*. Finally, that did the trick.

The quirky, familiar detective show I'd loved as a teen calmed me nearly as much as the copious number of cookies I'd sampled. I could almost hear the sidekick character talking about how his body craved buttery goodness. Because honestly, same.

This morning, as I stared at the mounds of cookies crowding my countertops while I guzzled coffee, I thought about Jessica and what Ravi had said about making more of an effort to be her friend.

Maybe she wasn't so bad. Ava and Tucker seemed to like her, and the drama club kids were eager to do her bidding.

Then again, I thought about all the snide comments and cutting remarks she'd made to me in high school. Passive aggression could be a powerful tool in the hands of an adolescent. It still wasn't easy to forget over a decade later.

I thought about how I'd changed in the last twelve years. Back then, I'd had an impulse control problem, raging hormones, and an inadequate dose of common sense. I had certainly not won any citizenship awards or been the easiest person to be around.

If I didn't want to be judged for my past mistakes, maybe I should give Jessica a chance, too. I picked up my phone and then set it back down again as though it were a hot potato.

I chewed on my lower lip, and Cap nudged me with his nose. We'd already been for our morning walk, but he'd been glued to my side since I'd come home the night before.

Finally, I grabbed my phone and texted Ravi, asking for Jessica's number. He sent it to me almost instantly, along with thumbs-up and several smiley face emojis.

Almost before I knew what was happening, I was in the car driving to the school to drop off a dozen apple cider cookies with cinnamon icing, along with an additional batch of pumpkin chocolate chip cookies. I'd brought both since I wasn't sure if Jessica was a fruity dessert person, or a rich chocolate lover.

She was probably more of a green smoothie and salad type of girl, if her figure was any indication. Still, she'd seemed happy to hear from me and delighted that I was bringing treats to her office.

The Emerald Bay High main office was decorated in the school colors of green and gold, and a paper pumpkin garland was strewn across the large front desk. A bouquet of fake yellow mums was set in a basket next to a visitor sign-in sheet. Ava waved to me from a little desk in the corner, where she was stapling stacks of paper together.

The large room was flanked by four office doors. I recognized one as the principal's office. We walked past two more, and the receptionist led me to the last door, labeled *Guidance Counselor.* At my brief knock, Jessica called, "Come in."

"Hi, Jessica. Or…Ms. Holliday?" I asked. The name felt strange on my tongue.

"Hi, Alex. Jessica's fine. Please, have a seat." She smiled tentatively, standing up to clear some space on her desk. She wore a burgundy sweater with a belted dalmatian print skirt and adorable black ankle boots with a chunky heel.

I glanced down at my sneakers and jeans. Generally speaking, I was happy with myself. I liked me. But something about Jessica always made me feel half-finished, like a slice of pumpkin pie without the whipped cream topping.

She turned to me expectantly.

"I brought you cookies," I blurted out, handing over the box I held in my hands. "I hope you like them."

"Thanks, Alex. That was really sweet of you." Jessica lifted the lid to peek at the treats. "Oh, wow, these look really good." She set the box on her desk and leaned against it in front of me.

"Thanks. I sampled one or five, and they're not bad, if I do say so myself," I babbled.

Jessica smiled gently. "I have to admit, I was kind of surprised to hear from you." Sincerity emanated from her, and I found it calmed my anxiety. I could do this.

"We haven't always gotten along, have we?" I asked.

"That's one way to put it." Jessica grinned sheepishly. I wondered which memory from our turbulent history brought that look to her face.

"The truth is, we're not kids anymore," I said. "And I thought the adult thing to do was start fresh...maybe even be friends?"

Jessica nodded. "I'd like that. But first, there's something I need to tell you." She hesitated. "I'm just afraid it's going to make you hate me more."

Huh. That wasn't what I expected.

"I don't hate you," I said. "And we should probably just get it over with and clear the air, right?" I asked. She bit her lip and nodded.

"Remember prom night?" Jessica asked. Like I could forget. I nodded.

"It...it was my fault you got blamed for the whole Bubblegate thing. I lied and told the principal that I'd seen you pouring soap into the fountain. Just you, not any of the guys, even though they were the ones I'd actually seen."

I felt as if I'd been slapped. I remembered the deafening silence that night after they'd cut the music and the dancing stopped. A math teacher had fallen into the fountain and several kids were sprawled out on the floor. I'd been called out in front of everyone and sent to the principal's office and made to wait. Deacon and the administrators had showed up minutes later, and we'd taken the punishment together.

"If it hadn't been for Deacon insisting that he had been the guilty party, not you, you would have been cleaning that gym alone. That was my plan, anyway. But even back then, even as a troublemaker, Deacon had a code of honor. And it didn't include throwing you or any of his friends under the bus."

"But...why?" I sputtered. All I could think of was how I'd berated Deacon, and all the while he'd tried to take responsibility.

"Why did I do anything back then?" Jessica said. "For the attention, because of jealousy, you name it. I had the biggest crush on Deacon, but he only had eyes for you. I wanted one night with you out of the way, thinking that maybe he'd finally see me." Jessica glanced up from the floor to gauge my reaction. My mouth hung open stupidly while I listened.

"Of course, it didn't work," she continued. "The principal didn't believe Deacon had acted alone, but he'd refused to name names. So, my plan backfired, throwing the two of you together anyway."

So much information to process. All those years I'd wasted being angry at Deacon.

"You liked him?" I asked.

"Who didn't?" Jessica smiled wryly.

He *had* been a total babe. Still was, to tell the truth.

"And now?" I asked. I had to know.

Jessica waved her hand dismissively. "He's a great guy and a good friend, but totally not my type. I see that now." Relief washed over me. I just couldn't see Deacon and Jessica as a couple.

"What, are you more into nerdy science teachers these days?" I couldn't resist asking, giving her the side eye and a wicked grin.

Jessica gaped at me, her mouth opening and closing, but no sound escaped. And suddenly, she laughed.

"Are you serious?" Jessica asked.

"Totally," I said, giggling. "You should think about that." I pointed my index finger at her, and she covered her face with her hands as her cheeks pinked.

"So, what now?" she asked, once we'd caught our breath.

I paused, thoughtful. Jessica had dropped some truth bombs, but did that change anything? The way I saw it, I had two choices. I could hold a grudge and continue punishing her, or I could accept her apology for what it was: acknowledgment that she'd made a stupid mistake as a teenager. Who hadn't?

"I'm really sorry for what I did that night. Believe me, I see my share of mean girls now, and sometimes I want to shake some sense into them. I wish someone had done that for me," Jessica said.

"Well, I wasn't ever very nice to you, either. And anyway, I *was* guilty. I was the one who started the prank war in the first place," I admitted. I took a deep breath.

"I think it's time to forgive and move on with our lives," I continued.

Jessica stood, waving a hand in the air dramatically. "Then it's all in the past. Friends?" she asked.

I nodded. "Friends."

She opened the box of cookies and offered me one. I chose an apple cider cookie, and she selected the chocolate chip.

"To starting over," she said, raising the confection as if making a toast. I grinned. She was just as much of a dork as I was.

"And burying the hatchet," I said, clinking my cookie with hers. "Cheers."

"Wow, this is amazing, Alex," Jessica said, chewing a tiny, dainty bite. I wouldn't know anything about that, as my cookie was already half gone.

Well, some things never changed.

"Thanks," I said. "And also, I wanted to tell you how sorry I am again about your uncle. How are you holding up?"

"Great-uncle," she corrected. "But thanks, I appreciate that. It's been a weird week, for sure, but I'm doing okay. I'm just sorry you had to be the one to find him. I totally would have freaked out."

"I kind of did." I shuddered. I would never forget those life-less eyes and the terrifying emotions that pierced straight to my bones.

A thoughtful look crossed Jessica's face.

"It's strange. You know, I don't really feel sad that he's gone. Maybe that makes me a terrible person, but you didn't know Uncle Alan. He was *not* a nice man. But I guess, in the end, his last thoughts were of my mom and me. I should be grateful for that."

I felt a little sorry for her. I'm sure it felt odd to take money from someone you disliked so much. Yet it didn't feel appropriate to just spill all the dirt I'd gathered on her uncle—I mean, great-uncle—in the last few days. In the end, I settled on an awkward pat on the arm.

"Well, I better get to the café. It'll be opening time before I know it," I said.

"Thanks for dropping by, Alex. It really means a lot. And for the cookies," Jessica said.

"No problem." I opened the door and exited to the office area. Jessica was on my heels, close enough that when I stopped short, she bumped into me.

Ravi led a miserable-looking teenage boy into the principal's office, and Deacon followed close behind. He was in his officer's uniform, so I assumed he was here on official police business.

I thought back to another time when he'd marched into that same principal's office, scowling, with his arms crossed over his tuxedo jacket. I'd been so angry with him that night. If only I'd known then that he'd had my back, like always.

Deacon noticed me standing there, and I mouthed, "What's going on?"

He waited until the other three disappeared into the office before whispering, "Found the missing snakeroot. Poor kid doesn't know how much trouble he's caused," he said, jerking his thumb toward the office. "Apparently it was some kind of dare. The stuff was in his locker."

"Oh, thank goodness," Jessica said. "I mean, not good for the student. But Ravi's been so worried, and honestly, so have I."

I glanced at Jessica, wondering if she was aware that the kid's stunt probably just cleared her name. Up until this point, she had both motive and access to the snakeroot. I caught Deacon's eye, and he quirked an eyebrow at me. I had the feeling he was thinking the same thing. He cleared his throat.

"Well, I'd better get in there. Time to scare the kid straight." He cracked both his neck and his knuckles and winked at me.

He was enjoying this entirely too much. I wondered if he and Ravi had practiced their good cop/bad cop routine.

I shook my head at him as he disappeared into the principal's office and shut the door behind him.

———

I rushed into the café, late after meeting with Jessica. I'd gotten stopped by two more people with nosy questions before I'd made it out of the school and to the blissful silence of my car.

Nyla and Granny bustled about the kitchen. Cinnamon, nutmeg, and clove tinged the air with spicy deliciousness. It was nearly time to flip the sign to "open."

"Why'd you send my son to check on me in the middle of the night?" Granny asked. She stopped vigorously wiping down the island to fix her glare on me. "I told you I was fine last night."

"It was before ten o'clock, Granny, not the middle of the night." I sighed. "And I was worried about you."

Granny Lu mumbled something about interrupted sleep and meddlesome youngsters as she made her way to the bar for another cup of coffee. I had forgotten how cranky she got without a full nine hours of sleep.

Nyla shook her head at Granny's retreating back, removing her apron and hanging it up on a hook.

"Don't worry about her; it was sweet of you to make sure everything was all right," she said, in a low voice to avoid Granny overhearing. "And I'm glad you were okay, too. Sounded like you had quite a scare," she said, slinging a toned arm over my shoulder and giving it a squeeze.

"Thanks…it was probably just the raccoons again, anyway," I mumbled.

It seemed we were going to downplay the fact that Dad had been at her house when I'd called. Okay, then. I could pretend everything was normal.

I gently ducked out of her arm and turned to my morning

tasks. "Sorry if she's been a bear about her lack of sleep this morning," I whispered, jerking my head at Granny.

"No worries," Nyla said, shrugging. "Her blustering about has never bothered me."

Cool as a cucumber, as always.

"Need anything else before I go?" Nyla asked, drying her hands on a towel. "The pastries are good to go, and the hot rolls are rising and will be ready to go into the oven at ten-thirty."

I'd forgotten she had an appointment for a haircut this morning and felt doubly guilty for my delayed arrival. "No, go ahead. I don't want to make you late."

"It's all good," she said, giving me a smile and a little wave before calling goodbye to Granny Lu and breezing out the door.

CHAPTER 9
COLONEL MUSTARD IN THE LIBRARY WITH A CANDLESTICK

I RELAXED into the smooth leather seat and breathed deeply of the cool wind blowing in my face. Cara sat at the helm, guiding the sleek boat out into the open water of the lake. Olive snuggled into my lap, her bulky life jacket scratching against my neck.

I had a rare morning off, and Cara had invited me to visit her folks at the retirement village. The community was situated at a country club on the lake a few miles from town and boasted its very own marina for the residents.

It had been Cara's idea to take her ski boat out on such a gorgeous autumn day, rather than driving the winding, hilly roads. She had worked with Tim designing the boat, and it was a streamlined craft of cool silver and cobalt blue that cut effortlessly through the glassy water.

I hadn't been out on the lake in years. As we passed the "no wake" zone, Cara accelerated, and I felt a thrill surge within me. The lake was nearly empty of other boats. It was too late in the season for most lake visitors, leaving only a handful of locals out on the water.

Windfall Lake was a deep basin with a rocky bottom, surrounded by steep, craggy hills rising around it. Thick trees with golden, orange, and brown leaves blanketed the hills, softening their sharp, rocky edges. We passed the cliffs we'd used for lake diving as teens. In the distance, I could make out the nearby tiny island we'd discovered and on which we'd picnicked many summer afternoons.

The beautiful scenery and crisp breeze did little to quiet my mind, though, as I went back to thoughts of Alan's murder.

I'd spent some time pondering possible suspects and my mind kept going back to Buddy Sikes, the portly man who'd had lunch at the café with Alan the day before he'd been killed. Coincidentally, Buddy was the manager of the country club golf course next to the retirement village. In fact, the residents had full access to the golf course, clubhouse and spa, so when Cara had asked me to come with her and Olive, I figured it was as good a time as any to take a look around.

Soon we had pulled up to the marina, and Cara docked the boat with practiced ease. A short bridge connected the dock to the winding, paved path. It was ADA compliant, so rather than stairs going straight up, the path zigzagged back and forth like tame switchbacks. Eventually, the path led up to an outdoor patio extending from a large stone building with a wall of glass overlooking the lake.

Olive insisted on walking, so it took an inordinately long time to make our way up to the clubhouse. When we finally arrived, we saw a few elderly couples seated at the café tables, enjoying a late breakfast on the patio.

The view was breathtaking up here. I stopped to admire the golden-leafed trees shivering in the breeze above the calm waters. The sky was a brilliant blue today, the air the perfect crispness of late October.

"Lex, are you coming?" Cara stood holding the door open, and I rushed to catch up, entering the clubhouse lobby behind her. We walked through a common area, with cozy sofas and chairs grouped together, along with an indoor dining area.

Signage pointed to the spa stretching out to one wing and offices and the fitness center to another.

"When I grow up, I want to live here," I whispered to Cara.

"I know. Mom and Dad love it."

Cara said hello to the concierge at the front desk. The woman looked to be a few years older than us and greeted us with a welcoming smile. At her direction, we exited out the front doors, where a curved drive was covered by a large awning. A parking lot lay directly in front of us, but Cara turned left, following another paved path toward the apartments.

The lush, unseasonably green golf course stretched out behind a cluster of single-story residences, flanked on the other side by the curving cliffs of the lake. I could see two more groups of apartments, and beyond that, a few large, single family homes lay scattered along the course.

Cara led us to the second apartment building and up the short sidewalk to the front door. A miniature scarecrow sat on a hay bale next to the stoop, surrounded by pumpkins and gourds. Cara's mom, Maggie, opened the door before we reached it, and Olive let go of her mom's hand, launching herself at her grandmother.

"Nana, Nana, Nana!" she exclaimed. Maggie laughed and tickled the little girl's stomach, calling over her shoulder to come in.

Soon we were chatting in the living room, situated in front of a large picture window overlooking the golf course and lake beyond.

"Where's Dad?" Cara asked, when there was a break in the conversation.

"He's out playing pickleball," Maggie said, taking a sip of coffee. "He should be back any minute. And when he gets here, I've got a surprise for you girls."

Right on cue, Cara's dad walked through the front door, whistling and removing his shoes.

"What kind of surprise?" I asked, after another round of greetings.

"I booked you both pedicures at the spa. I'll keep Olive and feed her lunch. You girls take the golf cart and skedaddle on over to the clubhouse. Your appointment is in twenty minutes."

"Mom, you're the best," Cara said, giving her mom a big hug. "I can't remember the last time I had a professional pedicure. Before our honeymoon, maybe?"

"Seriously, Maggie, thank you," I said. It had been a long while for me as well, and the thought of getting pampered sounded too tempting to pass up.

"Don't worry about it, girls." She waved us off. "It's a treat for me to have this little lady all to myself," Maggie said, hugging Olive close.

Moments later, Cara and I were back on the path, reaching the large carport to the side of the apartments where the residents parked their golf carts. Even if they didn't play the long game, the carts were handy for getting around the retirement community and adjoining country club.

Once we had checked into the spa and were seated in a comfortable waiting room, I took a deep breath and admired the surroundings. A water feature bubbled in the corner, a small fountain sending the liquid splashing over smooth black stones. Across from my chair, a blue gas-powered fire burned over black stones in a white marble fireplace.

Green plants were scattered throughout the area, lending a softness to the ultra-modern design, and an oil diffuser perfumed the air with the scents of lavender and orange. The receptionist brought us each a glass of water infused with cucumber and mint, which we sipped while we waited.

When our names were called, I was surprised to recognize one of our nail technicians. Lori Davenport sat on a stool in front of the small tub of sudsy water, carefully laying out instruments onto a towel. I hadn't seen her since the evening I'd delivered dinner to the trailer park, but when she looked up, she smiled and greeted me like an old friend.

"I wondered if you were the Alex Rivers on my schedule today. How are you, darlin'?" Her bushy blond hair was contained in a claw clip, but it trembled and shook as she spoke enthusiastically.

"Doing well, and you?" I replied.

"Fine, just fine. Well, we're just about ready here, but why don't you both have a look at our selection of polish colors and choose before we get started? And then we'll get you all pampered up!"

I smiled and thanked her, only wincing slightly at the sheer volume of her voice. Lori had the kind of enthusiasm and bright personality that took up a lot of space in the room. I appreciated her friendliness while admitting to myself that her energy was probably best served in small doses.

After we had chosen our nail polish colors—an olive green for Cara and a shimmery rust color for me—we settled into the thronelike chairs and slipped our toes into the warm, bubbling footbaths. *Heavenly.*

After our feet had a nice soak, Lori and the other technician, Beth, got to work massaging and filing, chatting with us as they did so.

"Alex, I didn't realize that *you* were the one to find Alan's body. Rusty told me he'd heard that, anyway. Was it just awful?" Lori asked. I groaned inwardly. Was there nowhere I could escape the town gossip?

"Yeah, it was…disturbing. Not an experience I'd want to repeat," I said.

"You're not kidding. Regardless of what I thought of that man, being poisoned and dying alone isn't something I'd wish on anyone," Lori said, shuddering.

"He was poisoned?" Beth asked, and the rest of us nodded. Word had gotten out around town, and it was now common knowledge. "Who would do such a thing?"

I shrugged.

"You never met the guy?" I asked Beth. She shook her head. "I live in Eagle Point," she said, referring to another nearby town.

"He wasn't exactly pleasant," Cara said. "I couldn't believe the way he made a scene yelling at my daughter and me. Still, it's a long leap from disliking someone to murdering them."

"That was the day he came into my café with Buddy Sikes... do you know him? I heard he works here. They seemed to be arguing about something," I said.

Beth and Lori exchanged a look.

"Sure, everyone around here knows Buddy," Lori said.

"I just wondered what kind of disagreement they could have had," I said.

"Well, Buddy's got his hands into everything. And there are always...rumors...about him," Beth said.

"What kind of rumors?" Cara asked, leaning forward.

"The kind that end marriages," Lori said abruptly, pausing to choose a new file. "But who knows if they're true or not. His wife is always around here, teaches yoga class, in fact. Buddy would be an idiot to do something like that right under her nose."

Buddy didn't exactly radiate intelligence to me, but I kept my opinion to myself.

"I wouldn't dismiss it so easily," Beth said, keeping her big brown eyes glued to Cara's feet.

"Why not?" I asked.

"Remember the company picnic we had over Memorial Day last year?" Beth asked Lori. She nodded.

"Well, at one point Buddy and I were alone at the drinks table. He said some inappropriate stuff to me, like maybe we should go somewhere private." Beth shuddered. "I just got out of there as fast as I could, before he could get handsy. And I've avoided him ever since."

"Why didn't you say anything?" Lori asked the younger

woman, pausing to touch her arm in sympathy. "You should have reported that creep and gotten him fired!"

"I'm so sorry," Cara said, and I nodded along with her. Why men like Buddy thought they could get away with things like that, I'd never understand.

"Why would anyone be interested in him, anyway?" I wondered aloud. "If there's truth to the rumors about him cheating on his wife. He's so sleazy."

"Some women find money very attractive," Beth said quietly.

"Oh yeah, he's loaded," Lori said. "Or I should say, his wife Melinda is. You know that mansion east of here, on the point?"

"The stone one with the turrets?" Cara asked.

"That's the one," Lori said. "That's where her parents live. And Melinda's the sole heir to all of it."

"So, Buddy married into money. What a catch," I said sarcastically, wrinkling my nose.

Our conversation drifted to other topics, and within the hour we were saying our goodbyes to the two nail technicians and promising to return soon. The two of us had gotten manicures as well, matching the colors of our toenail polish. I usually kept my nails trimmed short and didn't bother with polish—working in a kitchen with frequent handwashing tended to wreck my nails—but for once, I decided to splurge. And I had to admit, Lori had done a fantastic job, even working with my short nubs.

Since Cara and I hadn't planned on pedicures and it was a cool day, we had both worn boots for the short jaunt across the lake. The ladies had provided us with two flimsy pairs of one-size-fits-all flip-flops to wear while our nails dried, and we carried our boots in shopping bags advertising the spa.

The flip flops I wore were only about one size too large for me, but with Cara's petite frame and tiny feet, she looked like she was walking around wearing cross-country skis instead of shoes. We giggled about it as we made our way to the lobby.

I rolled my shoulders and sighed as we left the spa. "We

should make this a regular thing. I haven't felt this relaxed in a long time."

"Agreed. We could go for the massage next time, or maybe a facial," Cara said. "Do you want to get some lunch while we're here? We've got a little time, and it is past noon." She glanced at her watch.

I stopped in the lobby and looked down the hall that led to a few offices and exercise studios. "Yeah, we could do that," I said absently, wandering to the entrance of the long hallway.

"Where are you going, Alex? The café's that way," Cara said, pointing.

"Just wanted to see something," I said. She sighed and followed me.

I glanced back in the lobby and down the hall. Nobody was around—all gone to lunch, presumably. I could hear the murmured voice of a yoga instructor at the end of the hall, but nothing else. We passed two restrooms and a water fountain, and then I saw what I'd been looking for. A heavy mahogany door with a nameplate next to it showed this was the office of Buddy Sikes, Golf Course Manager.

With one last glance around to make sure no one was watching, I tried the door handle, certain it would be locked. To my surprise, it swung open with ease, not even a squeak on its well-oiled hinges. Before I could think too much about what I was doing, I slipped inside the office.

"What are you doing?" Cara whispered loudly, crowding in behind me.

I took in the office before me. A rich leather sofa was situated under a large window, with a heavy wooden desk opposite. One entire wall was a floor to ceiling bookcase, and the other three were decorated with vintage golf photographs and memorabilia.

"Investigating," I said, setting down my bag of shoes and hurrying over to the stack of papers on the desk.

"Did I miss Deacon deputizing you?" Cara asked dryly, rooted to the spot just inside the door. She crossed her arms.

"This is the police's job. Also, isn't this trespassing or something?"

"Gray area. The door was open." I shrugged.

I opened the small handbag I'd slung over my shoulder and pulled out two pairs of opaque food-safe gloves, the only thing I'd had on hand at the café that would prevent us from leaving prints. I'd stuffed a few pairs into my purse just in case such an opportunity presented itself. I mean, I've seen crime scene shows. I know how things are done.

I tossed the other pair to Cara, which she didn't even attempt to catch. The gloves smacked her crossed arms and flopped to the floor.

"Aren't you a *little* curious about what good ole Buddy's been up to?" I asked.

Cara looked at the gloves near her feet and back at me incredulously. "Seriously, Lex—who *are* you?"

I grinned at her sheepishly.

Cara sighed again, and then set her bag down beside mine and began putting the gloves on. "What exactly are we looking for?"

"I'm not sure. Some evidence that Buddy was hiding something…something Alan could have known about and been holding over him. Something like…dirty dealings or an affair. Doesn't it always come down to love or money?" I mused, thinking about the gossip between the two nail technicians.

Buddy kept neat files, and I didn't see anything out of the ordinary in the stacks of papers on the desk or in the drawers. I was fairly certain anything blackmail worthy wouldn't be kept out in the open. I spotted a file cabinet with a lock to the side of the desk.

"Bingo," I said. I tried both drawers and, as expected, they didn't give way.

"Quick, look for a key to this," I instructed Cara. She began searching the few knickknacks on the shelves while I checked the desk again.

"Found it," Cara said, lifting a small keyring out of a decorative bowl filled with old wooden golf tees. "Hidden in plain sight."

I quickly fit the key into the lock and the latch gave way. The first drawer slid smoothly out, and a cursory glance showed financial statements and tax information. Those files could potentially be important, but we didn't have the time needed to sift through them. I checked the second drawer, but it was mostly empty except a thick file of receipts.

"Look at this," Cara said. She'd pulled a book from the desk and held it open. Inside was a small piece of white paper, the size and shape of a bookmark. I leaned over to examine it, taking in the bright red imprint of a woman's lips on the paper.

"*Journeys end in lovers meeting*," I read. "It's signed 'S.'"

Cara jumped up and down, pointing at the bookmark. "That's a Shakespeare quote!"

"Since when are you a literature expert?" I asked.

"I'm not," she said, shaking her head. "I only know because Kate Winslet quotes it in that movie *The Holiday*."

"Oh, right. Well, this certainly looks...incriminating. And kind of gross," I said, holding the paper by the edge, careful not to touch the lipstick stain.

A familiar prickle ran over my arm, goosebumps following in its wake. Were we onto something? My sixth sense seemed to think so. I tried to quiet my mind and concentrate on the bookmark, but the strange feeling slipped away as quickly as it had come.

Huh. Disappointing.

A moment later, my heart rate picked up as I heard a feminine voice out in the hall, with a muffled reply further off. Cara's wide eyes met mine, and I could feel her alarm mirroring my own. The voices were close. Too close. We had stupidly forgotten to turn the lock behind us, and now the sound of it would be too noticeable.

I snapped the book shut, shoving it at Cara, who hastily put it back where she'd found it. I closed the file cabinet as quietly as I could and palmed the key.

"Quick, hide!" I whispered. Cara spun around in a circle. She looked ridiculous wearing the food handling gloves and flip flops that were at least three sizes too big, her unruly curls swirling around her face like a cloud.

"Where?" she asked. It was true, there weren't many places large enough for two adults to go unnoticed. If only there were a storage closet, but the room was devoid of any doors except the blocked exit to the hallway. And there wasn't time to unlatch the window.

"The desk," I said, turning to duck under it.

"Wait, our shoes!" Cara said, racing to grab the two bags we'd left near the door.

"Good thinking," I whispered. She glanced around and tossed the bags behind the large sofa as the voices grew nearer. The door handle turned, the woman on the other side pausing to answer her companion. I didn't stay to see who it was, wedging myself under the desk. Seconds later Cara was practically on top of me, pulling the desk chair as close to us as possible.

My knees were pushed up against my face, and Cara's elbow dug into my side. I concentrated on breathing slowly and hoped that nobody could hear my pounding heart. I had the insane urge to laugh hysterically, but I swallowed it the best I could.

The clack of heels sounded on the tile before they reached the thick Persian rug that covered most of the office floor. The person sat something down on the desk directly over our heads, and I cringed, expecting her to round the corner and discover us at any moment.

I risked a glance at Cara, but her eyes were shut tight, as though she were a child who thought closing one's eyes made her invisible. Or maybe she was just cursing our friendship and praying I'd disappear from her life. I wouldn't blame her.

A soft scraping sound came from the direction of the shelves, perhaps of a book being removed. Was it the same woman who'd left the lipstick message for Buddy?

Muffled footsteps came closer, and I, too, closed my eyes. This was it. She was going to find us. How would we explain ourselves, two grown adults hiding under a desk that clearly didn't belong to either of us?

The office door swung open suddenly, and the footsteps stopped.

"Toby, what's wrong?" the woman asked.

"Sophie, come quick. There's a fire," a young male voice said.

Cara's eyes popped open, and I mouthed, "Sophie?"

She nodded.

"A fire? Where?" Sophie asked.

"Buddy's house," he answered grimly. A soft thud sounded, and two pairs of feet rushed away, the door slamming behind them.

Cara and I waited a few moments before we began to extricate ourselves from underneath the desk. I was going to be sore tomorrow, but that was the least of my concerns.

"You okay?" I asked.

"I think so," Cara said, smoothing her tangled curls back into submission. I looked at the book that the woman, Sophie, had dropped on the carpet, but left it where it was.

"A fire, huh? You think that's a coincidence?" I asked, returning the file key to its original hiding place.

"Who's to say?" Cara shrugged. "Let's get out of here." She retrieved our shoes from their hiding place.

"Hang on," I said, eyeing the desk. I could see what Sophie had set down now. It was a cup of tea, so fresh it was still steaming hot. And the tea bag that was attached to the mug's handle was printed with *PT*. I pointed, and Cara rushed over to it. Without touching the cup, she bent down and sniffed.

"Spiced apple," she said. "Mine."

"That's what Buddy bought from me the day Alan died. And he said it was for his *wife*. Ha." I shook my head.

"What now?" Cara asked.

"We follow the smoke," I replied resolutely.

————

"I don't know how I let you talk me into this. What if we'd been caught? I can't be arrested—I'm a mom!" Cara was still slightly panicked over our cover nearly being blown, and she lumbered along the path in the golf cart a little too quickly, causing us to bump and jostle. "We should go straight back to Mom and Dad's," she said.

I wished I'd taken the keys and the driver's seat. I held on for dear life while attempting to calm her.

"You need to chill first. Your mom will take one look at your face and know something's up. Deep breaths, and let's just take a nice drive around the course first," I said. "If we happen to see something of interest, so be it."

Cara rolled her eyes at me, but she eased her foot off the accelerator a bit. Color returned to her hands as she unclenched the death grip she'd had on the steering wheel.

"You're right about one thing," she sighed. "The only thing worse than being arrested would be my mother discovering what we've been doing."

It didn't take long to figure out where Buddy lived. Past the retirement village apartments, smoke wafted in the air and a small crowd was gathered around a beautiful two-story brick and stone house near the fourth hole.

Both a fire truck and ambulance were parked outside, along with the county sheriff's SUV. The retirement village wasn't within the city limits of Emerald Bay, but I noticed a familiar police cruiser making its way up the drive. Cara and I parked the golf cart nearby and wandered to the edge of the onlookers.

The fire must have been put out quickly, because I didn't see any visible damage to the home's exterior. Buddy Sikes sat on a gurney behind the ambulance, breathing oxygen from a mask while a lady about his age, presumably his wife, held his hand.

I wasn't sure what Sophie looked like, but I did notice a woman who looked visibly upset at the edge of the crowd. As we drew closer, I recognized her as the concierge that greeted us when we'd first arrived at the clubhouse.

She wore high heels and an adorably chic outfit, her long strawberry blond hair cascading down her back. A male companion stood with her, his arm over her shoulder, and he seemed to be whispering words of comfort. I had seen him before, too. I recognized him as one of the hairdressers from the salon. Perhaps he'd been the one we'd heard warning her of the fire?

A car door slammed, and I ducked my head behind a tall guy as I watched Deacon exit his car. He began speaking with two firemen before they disappeared into the house.

"What happened?" I asked the woman nearest me.

"Fire, but nobody knows the details yet," she answered, craning her neck to see. "I heard someone say it originated in the fireplace but sparked onto something else and got out of control."

"Looks like the fire department got here before it did any significant damage," I said.

"Yes, it was lucky Melinda came home when she did," the woman said.

I wondered why Buddy was the one on oxygen, if Melinda had been the one to discover the fire. Had he been in the house when the blaze started? Had *he* started it?

Cara and I headed back to her parents' apartment, but my mind stayed busy with what this new development might mean. Was it really an accident, or was there more to the story?

———

I put in several hours of work after Cara and I returned to Emerald Bay, so by the time I came home that night, I was completely exhausted. After changing out of my café clothes and into leggings and a cozy oversized cardigan, I ate a late dinner of leftovers while watching TV with Cap.

I was about to go upstairs for the night when Cap whined at the back door. I let him out to do his business, and while I waited, I put the kettle on to boil for some soothing herbal tea. I hadn't tried Cara's lavender lemon yet, and it smelled aromatic and delicious as I poured the hot water over it. I finished it off by stirring in a generous spoonful of local honey.

Padding over to the sliding back door, I peered out into the darkness. Through the slats in the small fence that separated the duplex patios, I could see the glow of embers on Deacon's side. A flash of tail revealed that my dog had found him, too. He wasn't likely to hurry back inside.

Sighing, I slid the door open, and a blast of cool air breezed through my thin undershirt. Tugging the cardigan over my chest, I pulled the door shut behind me.

"Cap? Come on, boy," I called.

A small whimper answered.

"I think he likes me better," Deacon said. I walked around the partition to see Deacon parked in a deck chair, a nice bed of coals in a round fire pit, and my dog curled up next to it. Deacon held a drink lazily in his hand, and he gestured to the other chair.

"You're welcome to sit. Doesn't look like he's going anywhere soon," he said.

"But it's my bedtime, Cap," I said halfheartedly, patting his head. He looked pleadingly up at me, and I sighed, settling myself into the extra chair.

It was a beautiful night, and I supposed it wouldn't hurt to linger for a few minutes. I took a careful sip of steaming tea. Lemon wasn't ordinarily my favorite, but the addition of the lavender, honey, and a few other fragrant notes I couldn't identify rounded out the flavor nicely. I shivered in the cool evening air as the hot liquid slid down my throat.

Deacon leaned over to add a few small logs to the fire, the wood smoldering for a moment before catching and casting harsher light and shadows across his face. Tendrils of smoke rose, the pungent smell conjuring up cozy memories of past autumn evenings.

It was a clear night, and through the trees the stars shone brightly. It had been years since I'd sat under visible stars, unhindered by the ambient light of the city. There was a stillness to the air and a permeating quiet, only broken by the crackling of the fire, the wind in the trees, and the occasional hoot of a distant owl.

"Nice night," Deacon commented, leaning back in his chair and following my gaze to watch the stars twinkling overhead. I observed him quietly for a moment, his posture more relaxed than normal, the gentle firelight playing with his features.

Just because we hadn't kept in touch over the years didn't mean I was unaware of the path his life had taken. Cara and Tim had remained close to Deacon, and she'd mentioned updates here and there. I knew he'd gone to the police academy after getting his associate degree, becoming an officer in St. Louis. He'd made detective quickly, spending several years working homicide in the city before moving back to Emerald Bay.

"Why did you come home?" I asked, suddenly curious. "Was it your mom?"

Deacon's mother had fought a long, hard battle with cancer several years before. Last I'd heard, the treatment had been successful, and she was in remission.

"Partly," he said. "When she was diagnosed, we didn't know which way it was going to go for a while. I wanted to be here to support her and make the most of our time, in case the worst happened."

I nodded, completely understanding. If Dad went through something like that, I'd feel the same way.

"But it was more than that," he continued. "Being a detective could be very fulfilling, in a way. Catching bad guys and all that. But the toll it takes on you…" he trailed off, shuddering. "You could see it in some of the older guys on the force. A hollowness in their eyes from seeing too much, from putting the job before everything else; it's all consuming. My last case put me over the edge. I had to get out."

"What was your last case?" I asked.

Deacon pressed his lips together tightly, a muscle in his jaw spasming. "There were these kids…" His voice trailed off and he shook his head, looking away. "You don't want to know."

I swallowed hard, trying not to imagine what had been so horrible that he wouldn't even speak of it. He sighed, his eyes focusing on the darkness beyond the back yard.

"And then I came back to visit Mom one weekend, and she broke the news to me. Suddenly everything became crystal clear. Hard times will do that to you." He took another sip from his glass.

"There was an opening at the station, and it didn't matter that it was a lowly deputy position. It was a breath of fresh air, doing something good in this community. It's not all sunshine and rainbows, we've had a lot of cleanup to do. Like in a lot of small towns, drugs are a huge problem that we're constantly fighting, and all the issues that come with it. We're trying to be proactive, get involved in the community and with the kids before they get sucked into that world. But sometimes I still feel like I've failed, like I couldn't hack it in St. Louis. I think of the good I could be doing *there* if I had been tougher." He shook his head.

"But most of the time I'm grateful. I didn't expect this, didn't anticipate loving the job and this town again."

I nodded. "I get that."

"What about you?" he asked, turning his attention back to me. "I never thought I'd see your face in E.B. again."

I groaned. "I was eighteen and knew *everything*. Of course, I wasn't ever coming home."

Deacon laughed.

"I guess it was a combination of things," I said. "I felt like my career had stalled out; it was certainly nothing like I imagined it would be. Working at the restaurant, it was like being a machine on a factory line. There was no innovation, no creative license. Just the same recipes, night after exhausting night, always this frantic pressure to get the next order out. I had this dream to open my own restaurant, but it was almost impossible to save enough money. With the cost of living, I started to feel like I was in a pit and would never be able to dig myself out."

I paused before sharing the next bit. Deacon raised his eyebrows at me, nudging me to continue. I felt my next words spill out of me quickly and indiscriminately.

"And then there was a messy breakup with my boyfriend slash boss, and I quit my job that same day…anyway, right after that, Granny called. And it just felt like it was time."

I felt slightly breathless at the word vomit I'd just overshared.

Maybe Deacon wouldn't notice how suddenly flushed I'd become in the darkness. He took a sip of his drink before responding.

"Well. There's a lot to unpack there," he said slowly.

"You're telling me," I said, cracking a small smile.

"And were you right?" he asked. "Was it time?"

I nodded. "I think so. It's been a little weird coming back as an adult and feeling like everyone still sees you as some dumb kid, but there's a peacefulness about Emerald Bay that I needed. Of course, then we had our first murder in decades, so, maybe looks are deceiving." I shrugged.

"Good point. You come back to town, and it all goes to pot. That's it, I'm arresting you. You're clearly the common link here," Deacon teased.

"Shut up," I said, sipping my tea. "But, since you brought it up," I started.

Deacon flopped his head back in exasperation. "Ugh, seriously? I've got the night off here."

"Just one question," I said, leaning forward. "How did that fire start today?"

Deacon sighed, placing his drink on the small side table between us. He leaned forward and scrubbed his hands over his face. He watched me, thoughtfully, for a moment, and I fought the urge to squirm under his scrutiny. Maybe he was considering if he should be discussing the details with me, but a look of finality crossed his face and he spoke again.

"The thing is…we're not sure."

"Not sure?"

"We know it originated in the fireplace, of course. But Buddy denies starting it, and he was the only one home at the time."

"You're going to have to back up for me," I said.

"After Buddy was cleared by the medical team, we had he and his wife come to the station for questioning."

"Why?"

"Well, because there was evidence that connected Buddy to the Alan Harvey case. That's why the sheriff called me out to the golf course in the first place. Normally, it would be her jurisdiction."

My heart started to pound. I knew that Buddy had something to do with it! I contorted my face into what I hoped was a semblance of normalcy. It wouldn't do to look too eager.

"What kind of evidence?" I asked.

"Back when we searched Alan's house after his death, we found some files in his office. It appeared that someone had rifled through them, but we couldn't tell what, if anything, had been taken. We did find several folders containing material that could be used to blackmail people, arranged by name. Most of the files were several years old, and nothing that seemed like motive for murder."

I nodded. "A few people have mentioned to me that Alan

liked to find dirt on people and use it against them. But what does that have to do with the fire?" I asked.

"We found a file folder at the scene, half burned, just like the ones from Alan's house. However, the papers inside were charred beyond recognition. Buddy denies that he's ever seen the file and that he started the fire."

"What does he say happened?"

"Buddy claims that he went home for lunch, as he does every day. He said he was taking a short nap afterward, and the smoke detector woke him up. When he went out to the living room, he saw a throw blanket near the fireplace on fire, along with the curtains and part of the wall next to it. About that time, his wife came downstairs. She claimed she had come home while he was napping. She saw Buddy attempting to put out the blaze himself with another blanket, unsuccessfully. That's when she called 9-1-1 and got them both out of the house."

"So that's why he was on oxygen," I said. "He breathed in the smoke while he tried to put out the fire."

"Wait, you were there?" Deacon sat up straight and looked at me accusingly.

Whoops.

"Um, maybe?" I said.

"And what exactly were you doing there?" he asked.

"Just visiting Cara's parents. And we had an appointment at the spa."

"How convenient." Deacon leaned back in his chair and looked me up and down before taking another sip of his drink.

"Whatever," I said. "I might have a clue as to what was in that file, though."

"I don't want to know how, but…go on."

"I have reason to believe Buddy was having an affair, with Sophie, the concierge at the clubhouse."

"Do you have any proof?"

"I don't *not* have any proof," I said, widening my eyes.

Deacon threw his arms up in exasperation.

"What does that even mean?" he asked, gruffness edging into his tone.

"It means that you ought to interview the staff at the spa and country club. I'd start with Beth and Toby at the spa, personally. And Sophie, of course. So, is Buddy your lead suspect in Alan's murder, then?"

"He's only a person of interest right now. He doesn't have an alibi for the estimated time of death, and we know he'd argued with Alan earlier in the day. If Alan was blackmailing Buddy, that would give him motive. And yet, there was enough suspicion that someone else had been in Buddy's house and started the fire themselves that I'm questioning that line of thought."

"Did you find evidence that someone had broken in?"

"No, but Buddy claimed he'd left the back door unlocked when he came inside. The main evidence we found was a lighter dropped in the grass, a unique one. It was engraved, from the town's centennial celebration back in 1978. Buddy lived here then, so it could belong to him, but he denied that it was his. He would have been young in the seventies, though."

"I remember seeing those; Pops had one. It was an old-style, refillable metal lighter, right?" I asked.

Deacon nodded.

"Pops said they gave them out to adults that attended the celebration that year. Have you checked it for fingerprints?"

"We got some partial prints, but no hits on it yet. Could be someone who isn't in the system."

"Hmm," I said, finishing off my tea. I didn't care for Buddy, but the notion that someone even worse could be setting him up to take the fall for Alan's murder was certainly troubling.

CHAPTER 10
BURN NOTICE

I STIRRED the simmering vat of vegetable beef stew slowly, appreciating the hearty aroma that filled the café kitchen. My secret was to use a slow cooked beef roast, which I made the day before with onions, spices, and a generous pour of red wine over the top. It was a lengthy process, but the result was totally worth it.

The meat was falling-apart tender in the pot, swimming in a savory broth with lots of veggies. It would pair perfectly with the mountains of homemade hot rolls Nyla had just finished, especially since the weather had turned nasty and a cold drizzle fell steadily outside. Folks would be looking for a filling, hot meal today.

I was alone in the kitchen, humming to myself and half-listening to Granny and Nyla chat with the Vets. The group of men played cards in a booth, while the women drank coffee at the bar, halfway turned around to face them. Jasmine rolled silverware at another booth and joined the conversation here and there.

It was the lull right before the lunch crowd came, and no other customers were in the café. A rare calm had settled over the place before the frenetic energy of our busy time, nothing filling the air but amiable banter and delectable aromas.

I cleaned the kitchen island and washed my hands, checking the fridge to confirm the salad and side dish prep had been completed. Granny entered the kitchen, still chuckling at whatever story Ike had been telling. She dabbed her eyes with a hankie and poured herself another coffee.

"You've been a million miles away lately, just lost in your thoughts. Anything you need to talk about?" Granny asked, leaning back against the countertop to eye me. She had a certain look that pierced right through me, and as a child I'd been convinced she could read my thoughts.

I shrugged. "I've just had a lot going on, I guess. Moving and getting used to things here, and then everything that happened with Mr. Harvey. I can't stop thinking about it." I twisted a bar mop towel in my hands, winding and unwinding it anxiously.

Granny nodded. "Yes, I'd imagine finding someone like that makes you want to find some sort of closure, so what you're experiencing seems very natural." She took another sip of her coffee, hesitating like she wanted to say something else. I tossed the towel onto the countertop and crossed my arms.

"If you've got something to say, spit it out, Granny," I said, tempering my sharp words with a faint smile.

"It's just that, well, we're not ordinary, you and I. You know this." My stomach twisted at her words. Here it came. Granny moved closer, setting her coffee down. She gathered my hands into her weathered ones, and inexplicably, sense of calm stole over me.

"I gather that returning here has made you remember just how special you are," she continued. "And I just wondered, are you listening to yourself? Really *listening* and tapping into your intuition?"

I blinked for a moment. I didn't really want to get into the woo-woo stuff with Granny just now, but she was right. Coming home *had* brought an onslaught of, well, whatever my ability was.

"Sometimes I feel like I'm cursed," I whispered. Experiencing the emotional ambush of others all day long was exhausting. "I can't control it. I don't *want* to feel it."

"Oh, Alex," Granny said, letting go of my hands and gently holding my upper arms. "You have a wonderful gift. But you must stop fighting it. I know it's hard for you to be different, to struggle with things that others simply don't understand. But it's part of who you are, and the good you will do in this world."

She pulled me into a fierce embrace, and a sense of wellbeing surrounded me, even as her puffy white hair tickled my nose. I wondered how far Granny's gift went, and if she was purposely sharing her tranquility with me. She pulled back and looked into my eyes, fierce love and understanding radiating from her.

"Accept yourself as you are. Learn to clear your mind and welcome the revelations when you receive them. Only then will you be able to hone your abilities."

I sighed. "At this point, I'll try anything," I said. "How do I 'clear the mind,' exactly?"

"Well, it varies from person to person. Personally, I find long walks in nature to be particularly soothing. If I'm not able to do that, I enjoy burning candles, listening to soft music, saying a prayer." She waved her hand in the air. "But wherever you can find peace and quiet, away from the noise and emotions of others; that's the key. An animal companion doesn't hurt, either," Granny said, smiling. "I don't think it's a coincidence that dog found his way to you."

"I'll keep that in mind," I said.

I had been so busy that I'd been cutting my daily walk with Cap short, but I resolved to rectify that immediately. We both felt better after a good, brisk walk in the cold air. It couldn't hurt to give it a try.

My phone buzzed, and I turned to answer it after a quick pat on the cheek from Granny. It was my dad.

"Hey, Dad."

"Hi, kiddo. Sorry to bother you at work," he said.

"No problem, we're not busy right now. What's up?"

"Well, I was wondering if you could help your old Dad this afternoon. A couple of our volunteers at the food pantry are sick, and we could use an extra pair of hands to pack boxes."

I thought about my to do list for the day. I was ahead on dinner prep, so I'd have a little extra time after the café closed for the day and before I needed to start cooking again for our evening orders.

"I'll check with Granny, but I think I could come down for an hour, maybe a little longer, around two?"

"That sounds perfect. Thanks, hon."

I checked with Granny Lu, who agreed. I confirmed the plan with Dad and then we disconnected.

The next two hours flew by when, as expected, people flocked into the café to warm up with a hearty meal. By the time two o'clock rolled around, I was ready to collapse. I usually took a short break between closing and dinner prep; sometimes I ran home for about half an hour, and other times I simply relaxed in one of the booths with a cup of hot tea or a late lunch.

Instead, today I made myself a cup of strong iced coffee in a travel mug and set off down the sidewalk to the food pantry. Thank goodness I had worn my most comfortable shoes today. The food pantry was a few blocks away, and, keeping in mind Granny's advice, I figured the walk would do me good.

The sky was still overcast, but thankfully the drizzle had ceased, and the brisk walk had a calming effect after the busyness of the cafe.

When I arrived at the food pantry, the large garage door at the back of the building was open. Crates of produce were stacked haphazardly on long folding tables, and I saw Dad and two other volunteers arranging empty boxes. Dad introduced me to the two women, and after quickly instructing me on the process, we all got to work filling each box.

"Where does all this come from?" I asked, while adding bags of pears, potatoes, and apples to a box.

"Donations mostly," one of the ladies replied. "This shipment came from a grocery store that had an excess they wouldn't be able to sell quickly enough. We have agreements with several stores. Sometimes we don't know it's coming until the day it arrives, so we must be able to pack quickly and get the word out to the community."

"And anyone can come get it?"

"Yes, we have some programs that are need-based, but with the produce boxes it's first come, first served. We have a pickup time this evening, and what isn't claimed we'll take to the school tomorrow to be distributed."

"Sounds like a great deal," I said, stacking another full box on the table.

"Sorry I'm late," a familiar voice said, and I looked up to see Deacon rushing in the door, shedding his jacket along the way and placing it on an empty chair. "It's been busy down at the station."

"We're just glad you could make it, Chief Lane. We know you're busy doing important work," one of the ladies gushed, and I bit my lip to keep from giggling. She was probably thirty years his senior and gazing at him with doe eyes. He sent her a cordial smile and took his place next to me.

"Friend of yours?" I teased.

Deacon grinned. "What can I say? The ladies love me."

"I figured you'd be busy following up on leads today."

"I am, but I could use the break, clear my head for a bit."

"And did you discover anything new?" I asked.

"As a matter of fact, we did," he answered, ignoring me while he packed a crate, making sure to put delicate food on the top so it wouldn't get smashed.

"And?" I prompted.

"And…it's not looking good for Buddy Sikes."

"Really?" I asked. Deacon glanced over at me for a moment, catching my eye.

"He doesn't have an alibi for the night of the murder, for one thing. Says he was at home, but his wife was out of town and can't corroborate it," he said. "For another, Buddy's not being very forthcoming. He's acting cagey. And something else…I've been looking into Alan's financials. He came into quite a lot of money from the casino a couple of weeks before he died."

I paused my packing to listen more carefully. This was news to me.

"Alan made a large cash deposit the day he died…untrace-able because it wasn't in the form of a check or bank transfer," Deacon continued. "This was a separate transaction from the casino winnings deposit. Now, Buddy's not admitting anything, but we were able to get ahold of *his* bank statement, and it looks like he made a large withdrawal just hours before Alan made his deposit. So, either that's a huge coincidence, or Buddy paid Alan off for some reason."

"Was it the same amount of money?" I asked.

"No, the deposit Alan made was larger than Buddy's with-drawal. I'm just speculating, but Buddy could have had cash on hand at home, or maybe Alan was blackmailing more than one person."

"You know, I was talking to a contractor buddy of mine. You remember Phil?" Dad chimed in at my shoulder. Deacon and I both jumped, not having realized he'd joined us and been listening to our conversation. *Oops,* I mouthed, and Deacon shrugged in response. It couldn't be helped now. Besides, I think we were both curious about what Dad might have to say.

"Go on," Deacon said, nodding.

"Phil said that Alan called him at the beginning of that week to rehire him for his renovation project at the lake cottage. Obvi-ously, when Alan had run into problems with the bank earlier this year, the contractor had moved on to his next job. But he said when Alan called, he was excited about paying off his loans and ready to start the next phase on the renovation. Alan told Phil he had cash and could pay upfront."

"Interesting," Deacon said. "Did the contractor start work on it?"

"No, he was in the middle of a job. He'd planned to start in a couple of weeks, after he'd seen proof that Alan really did have the money. He didn't want to get burned again."

"I've seen his bank account. He did have the cash, although where it all came from is still a mystery," Deacon said.

"And now it's going to Brenda and Jessica," I pointed out. "They were very excited to relieve some of their financial burden."

"That's true. I hope it stays that way," Deacon said.

Huh. I hadn't thought about what might happen if the inheritance was gotten through illegal means. What a tangled mess.

———

The crisp autumn air caressed my skin as I strode along briskly behind Captain on our morning walk. I'd taken my favorite route today: down the hill, through the park, and alongside the lake. The sun was out, and it was already looking to be much better weather than the drizzly day before.

The haunted hayride was scheduled for this evening. I'd promised Cara I'd attend as part of her girls' night out, and I was very relieved that it wouldn't be a wet, miserable evening.

I slowed as I entered Alan Harvey's neighborhood. Both his house and the rental he'd been renovating were dark and deserted. I stopped in front of his house, peering at the drawn shades in the upstairs windows. *What secrets were you hiding?* I wondered.

Something niggled at the back of my mind. Even though all the evidence currently pointed to Buddy Sikes as the most likely suspect, I still felt like I was missing something important.

The sound of a sprinkler system powering up made me

jump, and seconds later water blasted my ankles, soaking my leggings in seconds. I pulled at Cap's leash and ran a few steps up the sidewalk to a dry patch. Mrs. Crawford's sprinklers hummed along merrily, water raining down on cheerful blooms.

Droplets ran down my legs, moistening my socks and shoes. I thought about turning back and heading home, but I was nearly to the halfway point in our walk. It would take just as long to turn around as it would to finish the route.

"Come on, Cap, let's get a move on." My dog was reluctant to leave the fascinating sprays of water, but with a little coaxing I managed to get him to move. His fur had gotten wet, but he seemed happy about that fact, his tongue lolling out as he trotted next to me.

The smell of woodsmoke greeted my nose as we approached the trailer park, and I saw several bonfires smoldering in the open space. Rusty Davenport carried two heaving trash bags to the collection of cans near the entrance.

"Morning," he greeted around a lit cigarette dangling out of his mouth. I waved back and called hello, but Cap pulled away from me and toward Rusty.

"Sorry, fella," Rusty said, dropping one of the bags and petting Cap. He sucked back on the cigarette, holding it with two fingers in one hand as he gave my dog a good scratch around the ears. "No breakfast scraps today."

"You don't need them anyway, Cap," I said, turning away. "Have a good one, Rusty."

Rusty nodded, adjusting his baseball cap before picking up the garbage bag he'd dropped. He'd only taken one step when the bag busted. Beer bottles and soda cans spilled onto the ground, rattling as they hit the gravel. Rusty swore as he reached down to keep the rest of the bag's contents from falling out.

"Here, let me help," I said. I dropped Cap's leash, trusting that he'd stay near, and jogged back to Rusty to pick up the stray cans.

"Thanks," Rusty said, carrying the offending bag to a large

bin before coming back to gather the rest. Cap followed me, sniffing at the ground where the garbage had fallen and trying to lap up a puddle of orange soda.

"Y'all have another party last night?" I asked.

Rusty nodded. "Someone's always got a fire going on these fall nights, and people start gathering around. One thing leads to another, ya know."

I nodded, tossing the last of the trash into the bin. One can had been half full, and my hands were wet and sticky. I shook my fingers absentmindedly, trying to rid them of the liquid.

"Sorry about that," Rusty said, gesturing toward my hands. "You want to wash up?"

"Uh, sure. That would be great." Tacky hands were one of my top ten ick factors.

I called to Cap, who happily followed us across the common space and to Rusty's trailer.

"Down the hall, first door on the right," Rusty said. He gestured at the house but didn't follow me. Rusty plopped into a red and blue lawn chair while Cap waited in front of him, nosing around his lap.

"Well look at that, Cap. You did find something. The last of my beef jerky." Rusty pulled out a dried piece of meat from his pocket. Cap eagerly took it off his hands and gobbled it up, wagging his tail at Rusty while sniffing around for more.

Shaking my head as I walked up the steps to the house, I wondered if Rusty regularly stuffed dried meat in his pockets to save for later. If so, that was kind of gross. What if it got all linty? Cap didn't seem to mind, though.

Pocket meat shot up on my ick factor list. I hadn't ever thought of that before.

When I opened Rusty's front door, the faint aroma of cigarette smoke hung in the air. As I moved down the hall it mingled with the unmistakable scents of hair spray and women's perfume. I found the bathroom and made quick work of washing up, hoping the smell of smoke wasn't clinging to my hair.

I made my way back to the front door, pausing as I glanced around the tidy living room. A large family photo hung over the faux fireplace. In it, Rusty and Lori sat on a checkered blanket against the stunning backdrop of a lake sunset.

A little blond boy, the spitting image of her, leaned back against them with a mischievous grin. I recognized him as one of the kids that had been running around the trailer park, but hadn't put two and two together. I thought about what Lori had said, that Alan liked to pick on her boy. The thought made me frown with discomfort.

Moments later, I was back in the fresh air and picking up Cap's leash where it had fallen among the gravel and dead leaves.

"Thanks, Rusty. Tell Lori hello for me. She did a great job on my nails yesterday." I waved them in the air, the deep color shimmering. They really did look pretty awesome.

"Will do," he nodded. He pushed his sleeves up as he stood. "I better get to work myself." My eyes flitted to an angry red mark along his forearm, where it disappeared under his shirt-sleeve. My own arms prickled in response.

"That looks painful," I commented.

"Nah, I've had worse," he said, folding up his chair and tucking it next to his front porch steps.

"How'd you do it?" My voice was even, but I twisted Cap's leash in my hands nervously, *You really need to work on hiding your tells*, I thought to myself, forcing my fingers to still.

"Welding," he shrugged. "It happens sometimes."

I nodded. "Well, we better get going. Cap." I jerked my head at the dog, and after one last forlorn look at Rusty, he trotted to my side.

"Y'all have a good day, now," Rusty said.

"You too," I replied, turning and walking briskly back

toward the path. My brain raced ahead, and my pulse quickened.

Rusty, obsessed with bonfires. Rusty, a smoker. And Rusty, with a freshly burned arm two days after the fire at Buddy Sike's.

Curious. *Very* curious.

———

"Okay, that's the last of it." I carefully situated the final takeout order in Tucker's car. It was growing dark where he idled in the alley. "You want a hard copy of the list?" I asked.

"Nah, I've got all the order details on my phone. See?" He waved the screen in front of my face to prove it.

"Good. I'm going to make sure Granny's got everything ready inside for the folks picking up, and then I'm heading to the Haunted Hayride."

"The Haunted Hayride, really? That's kind of lame, isn't it?" Tucker asked, leaning against the open door of his car.

"Oh, we can't all be as cool as you, Tuck. Besides, Cara promised it was going to be good this year."

He grinned. "If you say so. See you later, boss."

If the Forest of Fear was aimed primarily at teens, the Haunted Hayride was geared toward a slightly older crowd. One that still enjoyed a good scare, but preferred to experience it while sitting down.

I hadn't ever gone to the Haunted Hayride as a kid, as it was something parents were into. Like Tucker, I'd thought it must be boring. Honestly, I wasn't yet convinced otherwise, but Cara had been pestering me to join her monthly girls' night out group for weeks now.

"There's no one from high school in the group," Cara had said. "They won't have any preconceived ideas about you, and it's very casual. You'll like them, promise."

This was the first time I'd make it to an event, and I couldn't decide how I felt about it. Generally, I enjoyed meeting new people and being social. But ever since I'd moved back and my glitchy sixth sense had decided to rear its ugly head, I struggled to keep my emotions regulated around others.

After leaving Granny Lu to finish up the evening's orders, I drove outside the city limits, to the old Beckman farm, where the hayride would take place. Although it was officially a Harvest Festival activity, town streets weren't very conducive to a hayride, so it was staged in the nearby countryside.

The roadways outside of Emerald Bay were winding and hilly, choked with dense foliage on either side and rocky outcroppings where the road had been carved from the side of the hill. If I drove far enough, it would eventually lead to a large, open interstate that connected with major cities.

But tonight, civilization felt very distant, and I leaned into the eeriness that can only be felt in lonely places, in which help might be far off. I let my imagination run wild with thoughts of what kinds of spooky things might lurk in the shadows of the forest. By the time I arrived at the farm, I had sufficiently creeped myself out and was prepared for a haunting good time.

A narrow, tree-lined drive opened to a field which served as a haphazard parking lot. I edged onto the grass to the right as a steady stream of cars exited the lot. The Haunted Hayride had started at dusk, and one of the groups must have just finished.

I recognized a compact car that turned from the field toward me, and as my lights shone on it, I made out two people seated inside. In the driver's seat, as expected, I saw Nyla's silhouette. But next to her, a familiar full head of hair and broad shoulders filled the passenger seat, looking too large for the tiny vehicle. The figures were turned toward one another, seemingly oblivious to me as they passed by.

I turned my car stiffly into the field and made my way to an empty space, but I stayed frozen in my seat once I'd killed the engine.

Dad and Nyla, again? Sure, I knew he'd been spending time

with her. They were friends. But something about their body language, the way they'd been attuned to one another, made it seem more like a date.

I wasn't sure how I felt about that. I mean, it wasn't like Dad needed my permission, but he also wasn't in the habit of keeping secrets from me.

A small voice reminded me that Dad was an adult, and so was I. It wasn't like I'd ever been under the illusion that my parents would reunite, and he didn't owe me any explanation of his social life. I still found that it hurt, though.

Dad rarely spoke of my mother, and I had very few memories of her. They'd married young and had me in quick succession. By the time I was born, it had become clear their relationship was too immature to start a family, yet there I was. A blanket-wrapped, tangible reminder that they weren't kids anymore.

Dad said he felt a much deeper love holding me that first time than the thin, fleeting thing he'd had with my mom. Sill, he'd tried to make it work, but she was like a caged bird, finally leaving town for good before I turned three.

We didn't keep in touch. She sent a birthday card with money inside every year until I turned eighteen, which I'd promptly tossed into the garbage.

Dad was the hero, the one who stayed and built a stable life for me, surrounded by Granny Lu, Pops, and our chosen family and friends.

I don't know if I'd expected Dad to go on being alone forever, but this thing with Nyla left me feeling unsettled. I'd known her for years—we both had—and we'd always gotten along well. Nyla treated me like an equal in the kitchen, which had been a boost of confidence when I'd first returned to town and had been worried everyone would still see me as a wayward kid.

If I liked her and she made Dad happy, what exactly was my problem?

Thunk! Something slammed against my driver's side window, and I jumped, my heart in my throat. Thoughts of Dad and Nyla flew out of my head just as quickly as they were replaced by my monstrous musings from the drive out here.

"Are you coming, or are you just going to sit there all night?" Cara's muffled voice reached my ears through the window, her face obscured by a beanie and the large scarf around her neck.

I opened my door, zipping my keys into my coat pocket for safekeeping and pulling on a pair of warm gloves.

"You scared the crap out of me!" I said, exiting the car while clutching one hand to my chest.

"Sorry," Cara said. "You were totally spaced out there. Everything okay?"

I hesitated. Cara would be a sympathetic listener, but that was just it, wasn't it? She couldn't really empathize with what was going on. Her parents had been happily married for over thirty years. And I wasn't sure I had the energy to deep dive into my familial issues now, anyway. Wrong time and place for it.

"I'm fine," I answered. "Just tired and have a lot on my mind."

That was the truth. In addition to discovering my dad might be dating again, I'd also been thinking about Alan's murder and whether Buddy Sikes really could have done it, or if my suspicions about Rusty Davenport had any merit. Was one of them the dark figure I had spotted lurking around Alan's house?

I hadn't talked to Deacon today, but I was itching to pick his brain on the subject. This whole case felt like one big knot that was impossible to untangle.

I pushed all those thoughts aside, though, as Cara looped her arm through mine. We made our way through the field and to an open barn that served as a gathering area for those of us waiting for our turn on the hayride.

Edison lights were strung across the ceiling, and electric warmers were placed throughout the barn. Cozy groupings of cushy patio furniture were arranged throughout the place, and people chatted while indulging in the drinks and appetizers included in the ticket price.

"Okay, this is seriously cool," I said, taking the paper plate Cara offered while trying to decide if I wanted the bacon-wrapped chicken bites or jalapeño poppers that were piled on a serving table, along with several other appetizers. Spoiler alert: I picked both, and then some.

Cara led me to an L-shaped sofa and introduced me to two of her friends. Both had moved to town while I was in San Francisco. Callista, Cara's friend that also had two small children, was sophisticated and polished. She seemed perfectly nice, but I found myself pulling back from the type-A anxiety that rolled off her.

The other woman, Maisie, had a bit of a rumpled appearance but a calmer aura to which I gravitated.

"I'm such a sucker for all this local history stuff," Maisie said, pushing her teal, plastic-rimmed glassed back up her nose. I liked her immediately.

Maisie worked at the city library, and I happily let her gush about how excited she was to go on her first Haunted Hayride while my mind drifted.

After about twenty minutes of chatting and stuffing our faces with appetizers and sparkling water, a bell rang, announcing that it was time to load up on the trailer. Soon we were tucked in like sardines, seated on quilt-covered hay bales.

I'd only ever been on hayrides pulled by tractors, but this one was led by a team of beautiful horses. I assumed it was so we would be able to better hear our guide, who was to narrate the hayride, as well as add to the authenticity of the experience. A man stood at the front of the trailer going over safety precautions, and soon we were on our way.

We had started out in the open field, but quickly the trees closed in around us, with only dim lantern light illuminating the path ahead. The clip-clop of the horses' hooves transported us back in time. As we slowly made our way down a narrow country lane, the guide began to tell of local legends and myths from our area.

Our first stop was in front of a gaping, black-mouthed cave. These hills were full of them, and I felt goosebumps rise on the back of my neck as the guide spoke of the outlaws that used them as hideouts for their nefarious activities.

We continued, being deliciously scared at the night sounds that only complimented the talented storyteller.

"This is so great," Maisie said.

"Yeah, I definitely needed this," Callista echoed, sipping from a paper cup of apple cider.

Cara smirked at me in an *I told you so* kind of way. I didn't mind.

When we returned to the barn and carefully stepped down from the wagon, we spent a few minutes reliving the spooky stories the guide had told us.

"My favorite part was the story about the girl who went missing in the eighties," Maisie said. "I'm going to have to research that." She pushed her glasses back up the bridge of her nose again.

"Remember how we used to dare each other to go into the woods where she was last seen and call for her ghost?" I asked Cara.

She shuddered. "That was nightmare fuel at *many* sleep-overs," Cara said.

"And they never found her body?" Callista asked.

"Nope." I shook my head. "It's a cold case now."

After a few more minutes, we said goodnight and went our separate ways to our cars.

"That wasn't so bad, was it?" Cara asked, falling into step with me.

"No, actually, it was perfect. I'm glad you made me come," I replied.

"And next time you can meet the rest of the group," Cara said. I'd almost forgotten, there were a couple of women that had canceled tonight, so I hadn't met all of Cara's friends yet.

"Okay, deal," I said, unlocking my car and waving as she

walked the last few steps to her SUV. It had been nice to meet new people, and the evening's activities had taken my mind off Alan Harvey's case for a while.

But as I slowly drove down the country road back to town, my mind quickly buzzed back to life, going over the details once more. Ugh. I was going to have to talk to Deacon again.

CHAPTER 11
CALL THE BRUTE SQUAD

AS IT TURNED OUT, I didn't get a chance to speak with Deacon until the next day. His house had been dark when I'd come home, and the cruiser was gone. Must have been working late again.

The café was abuzz with gossip this morning. Word had spread about Buddy being questioned by the police. They didn't have enough to formally charge him, but he was definitely a person of interest, and it seemed that every table I passed had their own theory about his involvement. Frankly, it was getting to be a bit exhausting, and I was only too happy to escape to the kitchen as our lunch rush picked up.

Nyla had slipped out the back door before I made my way back to the kitchen. She'd acted completely normal, and I certainly wasn't going to bring up her outing with my dad. Not until I'd talked to him, at least. I wondered if he'd say anything to me at all, or if I should broach the subject.

After most of the crowd had left and only a few diners lingered, I brewed a fresh pot of coffee and made a lap around the place, asking if anyone needed a refill.

"Oh, yes, dear. I'd love a cup," Myra Crawford said. Her dining companion had already left, but she lingered in the window booth with a generous slice of berry crisp. I noticed the hardback novel she'd placed on the table when I'd stopped with my carafe.

"Preparing for book club Friday night?" I asked, pouring steaming coffee into a clean white mug.

"Yes, I've been busy and now I'm catching up on my reading for the week. Janet would have my head if I showed up unprepared. I usually read in the evenings, but I've found it difficult to concentrate the last few days, between thinking of poor Alan being gone next door and our noisy neighbors on the other side."

"What noisy neighbors?" I asked. I knew perfectly well she meant Rusty and his friends, but I was curious what she'd have to say.

"Those hooligans at the trailer park," Mrs. Crawford said, shaking her head. "Now, Alan was never very neighborly to them, but at least he knew how to get them to be quiet."

"Really? He didn't get along with the Shady Glen folks?"

"Not at all," she said, stirring a bit of milk into her coffee and taking a dainty sip. "He and Rusty had an ongoing feud. In fact, they had a shouting match that weekend before Alan was killed."

"Do you know what it was about?" I asked. She shook her head.

"I couldn't quite make out the words, but Alan and Rusty fought like cats and dogs about everything under the sun. Alan was always trying to get his hands on that land, but Rusty was adamant he'd never sell, *especially* not to Alan. Alan thought it would be a fine location for a new development of vacation properties, one that would be, shall we say…a bit more desirable than a trailer park."

"I see," I said. It didn't come as a surprise that the former first lady of Emerald Bay was a bit snobby, but I couldn't help but feel sorry for her. Her neighbor had been murdered, and the poor woman just wanted a little peace and quiet.

"Anyway, since Alan's been gone, they've been obnoxiously loud at night."

"Rusty seems like a reasonable man," I said, even as doubt niggled at the back of my mind. "I'm sure if you had a friendly chat with him and Lori, they'd tone it down."

"I'm sure you're right, dear." She patted my hand. "I should speak to them, and Lord knows I'll be a sight more polite about it than Alan was."

I smiled at the old woman. "Well, I'd better get back to work," I said. "Enjoy your book, and let Jasmine know if you'd like anything else."

I left Mrs. Crawford to her novel and returned to finish cleaning up from lunch. Now I really needed to talk to Deacon.

———

"Hey, Donny, is the chief in?" I asked. I'd walked over on my break with a dozen cinnamon rolls to butter up...er...bless my favorite law enforcement officers.

"Sorry, you just missed him," Donny said, glancing up from a mountain of paperwork. The station seemed busier than usual, with nearly every desk occupied and several officers standing together in the break room, mainlining coffee.

I squinted, trying to read the whiteboard they were examining, but I couldn't make out anything. I supposed it was all-hands-on-deck until the Alan Harvey case was solved.

"Oh, well, I'll leave these with you, then. Looks like y'all could do with some sustenance."

"You're a godsend, Alex," Donny said, taking the box off my hands. "It's been a crazy day, what with Buddy's alibi coming through, after all."

He opened the box, pulled out a roll and took a generous bite.

"His alibi?" I asked. "I thought he didn't have one."

"He didn't want to fess up to it," Donny said, talking around a mouthful of cinnamon roll. He swallowed. "But his…um… mistress walked in here first thing this morning and gave an official statement. He was with her the night of Alan's murder. Photos and timestamps on her phone confirmed it, along with the restaurant thirty miles away where the two of them had dinner."

"Wow," I said. "So, he definitely couldn't have killed Alan?"

"Highly unlikely. The timelines don't match up."

As much as I wanted Buddy to be guilty so the case could be wrapped up in a neat bow, I found myself unsurprised that it hadn't turned out to be that simple. I sighed.

"Back to square one, then?" I asked.

"Yep. That's why Chief Lane headed back to Mr. Harvey's house. Said he needed to clear his head and retrace his steps from the beginning."

"I see. Well, I'd better let you get back to work. Good luck, Donny."

Officer Swanson thanked me, and as I left, I heard him call out, "Hey guys, cinnamon rolls from Lulu's!" A swarm of officers quickly obscured him from view, and I chuckled despite the bad news I'd learned. Granny would be pleased to know how popular the café was with the local law enforcement.

I paused on the sidewalk, glancing across the street at Lulu's in indecision. I checked my watch. I had about an hour to kill until I had to be back at work to prep for the evening. Glancing down at my leggings and tennis shoes, I crossed the street and skirted around the patio seating, heading for the lakeside path of Wayfinder Trail.

Ten minutes later, I emerged out of the trees into Alan's neighborhood. As expected, Deacon's police cruiser was parked in the driveway. I stopped in front of the house, the cool breeze tickling the pesky hairs around my face. The curtains were drawn tightly. I tucked the strays behind my ears and jogged up the front steps.

I knocked on the door, but nobody answered. Maybe he was

around back. I let myself in the side gate, the dead grass crunching softly under my shoes. As I rounded the corner, I heard the screened back door slam and a glimpse of a uniform disappearing inside.

Rather than retrace my steps back to the front porch, I followed whoever had gone inside, opening the back door.

"Hello? Deacon?" I called.

The sound of a gun cocking made me stop short in the doorway with my hands up. Deacon stood across the room, at the entrance to the kitchen, his pistol locked on my chest and his dark eyes hard and flinty.

"It's just me," I said, my voice coming out a little shaky. I'd never seen him in full cop mode, and it was a bit terrifying. He'd certainly scare me straight if I were a criminal.

A curse escaped his mouth as he lowered the weapon, tucking it into its holster. His eyes lost their venom, replaced by a familiar annoyance.

"Don't ever sneak up on me like that again. Lex, you can't just walk into a victim's house during an active investigation. What do you think you're doing?"

"Um, I was on a walk, and I saw your car?" It came out as a question rather than the statement I'd intended.

"I did knock, but nobody answered. That's when I came to the backyard and followed you inside," I said.

"Look, I'd like to *not* shoot you today, so why don't you go back outside and continue your walk? I've got work to do." Deacon ran his hands through his hair, pulling upward until the unruly locks stood on end.

"I heard about Buddy's alibi. Tough break," I said, folding my arms and leaning against the doorjamb.

"How—" Deacon began.

"Doesn't matter," I said. Donny didn't deserve the chief's wrath for slipping up and telling me about the developments. "The point is, I know you must be frustrated."

"I really thought we had him. Now it's like starting over,"

Deacon said. "I feel like I've gone over this place a thousand times and I'm not coming up with any new angle. Nothing makes sense."

I walked a slow circle through the dining room and into the kitchen. "Why don't you walk me through it? Maybe it will help to say it all out loud."

Deacon sighed, and though I knew he didn't want me there, he could see that I had a point.

"Okay, a lot of what we found was taken as evidence, but I'll go over it again. When we came to search the house, we first saw partial muddy footprints here at the back door, see? Men's boots, judging from the size. You remember it was rainy the day Alan died. The prints led over here to the office, where we found a file drawer ajar and a few papers on the desk, as though the perp had been looking for something very quickly. And sloppily."

I nodded. I knew about the files, but the boot prints were news to me. "Was anything else missing?"

"Not that we could tell. The living room and upstairs bedrooms all appeared normal. Alan had a safe in his room, but he'd made a large deposit at the bank earlier in the day. There was only a small amount of cash inside. The safe seemed secure, and there were no disturbances upstairs."

"All right. What about the kitchen? What you've just told me sounds like someone searching down here when Alan wasn't home, like maybe when he'd left for his evening walk. What about earlier in the day? Could someone have come over and poisoned his tea before he went on the walk?"

Deacon led the way into the small kitchen. The cabinets were darkly stained wood, and a single window over the sink let in a scant amount of natural light. He flipped a switch and illuminated the space.

"There was a teacup in the sink, emptied, and it tested positive for the victim's DNA. We couldn't determine if it contained snakeroot as well, though. There was another cup and spoon in the dish drainer that had been washed, so that was a dead end."

"That could have been the murderer's," I said.

"Maybe, or it could just be another cup that Alan had used and washed himself. The trash had recently been taken out, but there was packaging from a bag of store-bought cookies in the garbage. And a pot on the stove that appears to have been used for boiling water. It's possible that whoever poisoned Alan did so right here."

"What about fingerprints?" I asked.

"We found several that didn't belong to Alan, but nothing that got a hit on our system."

I chewed on my bottom lip for a moment, thinking.

"Do you know anything about the route Alan took on his walk? And why he was in the maze in the first place?" I asked.

"We spoke to a few neighbors. They said that Alan usually walked the lake path and to the park in the evenings. As to why he was in the maze, I'm not sure. We visited with his doctor, who believed that Alan simply got disoriented, wandered into the maze, and couldn't find his way back out. At that point, the poison would have been affecting his heart rate, vision, and muscle movements, so I'm inclined to believe that theory. I walked through the maze again before I came here and didn't find anything significant. Only the disturbances that we noticed the first time around, which line up with the doctor's assumption that Alan was lost and confused."

That made sense. How terrified poor Alan must have felt. Yes, he was kind of a garbage human, but even so, he'd been met with a harsh fate.

"But nobody else saw him on his walk?"

"Nobody that's come forward, anyway," Deacon said.

"Have you spoken to Rusty Davenport? I heard he got into an argument with Alan before he was killed," I said, trying a different angle.

"We were told they had an ongoing feud, but Rusty has an alibi the evening of the murder."

"What's the alibi?"

"He worked until five, and then his wife said they were at home all evening."

"Is that credible though? A spouse's alibi?" I asked. I had no idea how these things worked.

Deacon lifted one shoulder in a shrug. "We can't discount it simply because they're married, but we also weren't looking closely at Rusty before. What makes you think he had something to do with it?"

I recounted the conversations I'd had with the Davenports about the tensions with Alan, as well as what Mrs. Crawford had said.

"He could have easily stopped by Alan's house on his way home from work," I said. "Oh, and get this: when I saw Rusty this morning, he had burn marks on his arm," I finished triumphantly.

"So? He's a welder."

"Yeah, I know, but what about the fire at Buddy's house? He could have done that to throw suspicion off himself."

"Hmm. It's thin, but I can look into it," Deacon said.

"Good." It was all I could ask for. I looked around the kitchen again. "Did you find any tea bags in the trash? And was there a sponge or wash cloth in the sink?"

"Settle down, Nancy Drew. No, the tea bags were missing, but Deputy Swanson insisted there was a slight smell of spiced apple tea in that cup in the sink. And whatever was used to wash up the other mug disappeared as well. Too bad. We might have been able to collect DNA from it otherwise."

I made my way back to the office, reaching for the file cabinet. "Did Rusty have a file in here?" I asked. "I'm sure Alan would have gathered any dirt he could find on the neighbor he despised. Sounds like he wanted that land badly."

Deacon grabbed my hand before I pulled the cabinet open. "Don't touch anything," he reminded me, releasing my fingers once I nodded. "No. That's not to say there wasn't one, but whoever rifled around in here might have taken it."

I tapped my foot impatiently, wishing I could get my hands on something concrete. All we had were a handful of clues that made zero sense.

"There is one inconsistency that's bothering me," Deacon said.

"What is it?" I asked.

"The property two doors down, the one Alan was renovating...we checked it out after he died. It seemed to be a place he was mostly using for storage while he renovated one area at a time. Nothing suspicious, a few pieces of old furniture and tools, things like that."

"Okay, so what's the problem?"

"I scoped it out again today, and there were some...disturbances. A few things were moved around, and there was a broken railing on the landing."

"Hmm, that is weird," I said. "Do you think it could have been an animal or kids, something like that?"

"It's possible. The windows are old, and some of the locks are broken. It would be easy for someone to get inside."

"But who would want to?" I wondered aloud. The silence stretched between us, neither of us coming up with anything profound.

"Is Cap with you?" Deacon asked suddenly.

"No, the walk was a...spur of the moment thing," I replied.

"Uh-huh," Deacon said, quirking an eyebrow. "Well, how about I give you a ride back to Lulu's? I need to go to the station, and under the circumstances, I don't think you should be taking any more walks alone. At least take your dog with you next time. And maybe skip going by Rusty's place for the time being. Just this whole area, really," he said, glancing toward the renovation house.

I placed my hand over my heart in mock sincerity.

"Why D, it warms my heart to know how much you care."

Deacon rolled his eyes. "More like I can't afford the time suck it would be keeping you out of trouble."

"Nice," I said, scowling.

We exited the front door and while Deacon locked up, I eyed the cruiser.

"Shotgun?" I asked.

"Uh, sorry. You'll have to ride in the back," Deacon said, looking apologetic.

"Seriously, in the back, with the partition and everything? Like a criminal?"

"Afraid so. No ride-alongs. Department policy."

I wrinkled my nose.

"I'll just walk and take my chances with the murderer, thanks." I marched down the steps and to the sidewalk.

I could only imagine the gossip it would conjure, me riding in the perp section of the chief's car. Deacon always parked right across the street from the café, and I could hear the tongues wagging already.

Deacon hurried to catch up with me, grabbing my arm and whirling me around. His dark eyes crinkled at the corners in amusement and his lip twitched.

"Relax, Lex. I was just kidding. You can ride up front. *If* you promise not to touch anything, of course."

"I wouldn't dream of it," I said, purposely knocking into him with my shoulder as I pushed past him to get to the car. His answering chuckle dug at my nerves, but not quite enough for me to set out on foot.

———

"Ouch!" I yelped, glaring at the offending needle in my hand. A tiny drop of blood appeared on my index finger, and I viciously stabbed the needle back into the fabric. I left it there while I grabbed a tissue from the end table and applied direct pressure to the bleeding.

"Cookies, as promised," Cara said, appearing with a plate full of treats and setting them down on the coffee table. Her canvas apron was splattered with paint and dusted with flour, and a paintbrush had been wound and stabbed through her hair, holding back her unruly curls. A few stray ringlets had sprung free and danced around her face.

"I don't know why you recruited me to help with this. Seventh grade home economics did not prepare me for Pinterest-level sewing projects," I said.

"Me either. I barely passed that class, and only these chocolate chip cookies saved me. Anyway, as my best friend, you're morally obligated to help in my time of need." Cara wafted a cookie under my nose. "And in return, I promise to ply you with desserts."

"Fine. But I'm taking the biggest one," I grumbled, grabbing a cookie with my free hand and taking a giant bite.

She was right. Even though I wasn't the best at sewing, Cara had been atrocious, odd because she was such a talented artist in other areas. I was confused as to why she had wanted to make homemade costumes in the first place. I was guessing it was a mom thing, although I knew for a fact Arthur and Olive would have been just as happy picking out something in the costume section of the supermarket.

Cara had called me in a panic this morning, having put off the costumes until the last minute. They were supposed to dress up the next day, Friday, for the kiddie Halloween parade.

I eyed the beige fleece pajamas in my hands, to which I was adding fur trim around the sleeves and hood. I had squandered most of my patience attaching rounded ears to the hood, and what was left was wearing thin.

Maybe Cara had bit off more than she could chew with the circus-themed family costume idea, but I had to admit, Olive was going to be the most adorable lion. If I could pull off some passable sewing and my stitches didn't unravel before she got a chance to wear the costume.

"Did you finish the weights?" I asked, polishing off the

cookie. Arthur was going as a strong man, and Cara had been painting craft foam and wooden dowel rods in the kitchen.

"Yes, just waiting for the black paint to dry now. I've moved onto the popcorn box." Cara was finishing up the paint work on Tim's popcorn seller costume, while I got the raw deal of trimming Olive's lion costume and Cara's ringmaster ensemble. She'd bought a red jacket and black top hat at the thrift store, and I was tasked with adding sparkly gold embellishments to both.

I picked up my needle and fur and proceeded to stab myself two more times.

"Son of a biscuit!" I yelled, narrowing my eyes at the costume and letting out a heavy sigh. "New plan. Do you have a hot glue gun around here?"

"Yeah, I think so," Cara replied from the kitchen. "Do you want me to go dig for it?"

"Yes, please. I'm about done with the fur, but I think I can glue the gold trim onto your jacket. It's either that or I'm going to lose a finger today."

Forcing myself to slow down, I carefully finished my stitches and tied the thread off, hoping it would hold up well enough to last both the Halloween parade and trick-or-treating. Olive was going to wear brown fur boots with it, and Cara planned to paint a nose and whiskers on her face. Olive was going to be the cutest little lion in town, if I had anything to say about it.

I stood up to stretch, walking to the big windows overlooking the yard. Cara rustled loudly in the craft closet she kept off the dining room. I heard a container of beads hit the floor and saw a roll of tulle tumble down the hallway as she rifled through her supplies.

"Need any help in there?" I called.

"I'm good. Almost have it!" Cara yelled, her voice muffled in the depths of the closet.

I turned back to the window. If only I'd thought before to

open the curtains to let in more light, maybe I my fingers wouldn't be riddled with holes. *Work smarter, not harder, Lex.*

I pulled back the drapes and was surprised to see a wooden monstrosity in the back yard, setting squarely atop Tim's boat trailer. It stood about ten feet high and was triangular shaped with one long wooden arm hanging from the highest point down to the lowest. I couldn't tell what it was supposed to be, but it looked like a medieval torture device. Like "the machine" in *The Princess Bride.*

"What the heck is that?" I asked, as Cara walked back into the room. I gestured to the thing out the window. Out of breath, she absently blew hair out of her eyes, handing over a hot glue gun that had seen better days along with a few rubbery sticks of glue. It would have to do.

"That's the trebuchet," she answered, in the same nonchalant manner as one might say, "That's the new swing set," or, "I did some landscaping; do you like it?"

"The trebu-what?" I asked, unable to tear my eyes away from the machine.

"Trebuchet. You know, for launching cannons in the Middle Ages. Or, in this case, launching pumpkins."

I rolled my eyes. Of course, Tim the engineer would build an ancient war device for the pumpkin launching competition scheduled for the weekend.

I guess you just never know when you might need to storm the castle.

"But…why?" I asked.

Cara shrugged. "I stopped asking myself why men do the things they do years ago. Apparently, he's 'always wanted to build one' after we saw a replica on that trip to Europe. Deacon thought it was a great idea, and they were off and running."

"Deacon helped build this?"

"A little. Since he's so busy with the case, Tim and another guy from the marina have done most of the construction, but he was in on the planning."

"Huh. Well, that's…pretty impressive, actually. Does it work?"

"They're going to test it out this evening, I believe. I wouldn't let them do it this close to the house. I don't need to lose a window over this, you know? They'll hook it up to the truck and do trial launches from the overlook, into the lake."

I let the curtain fall back into place and shook my head. Boy, with both the murder investigation and weird Harvest Festival competitions ratcheting up in intensity this week, the town was starting to feel slightly unhinged. We were one "charming" quirk or mishap away from becoming a bizarre human-interest story. I could see the headline now: *Emerald Bay, the Bermuda Triangle of the Ozarks.*

The afternoon passed quickly, and before I knew it, the Wheelers had a completed set of four circus costumes. They didn't look terrible, and I was excited to see Arthur and Olive in the parade. Cara thanked me profusely, and me and my now bandaged *and* burned fingers drove home.

CHAPTER 12
THE UPSIDE DOWN

I HADN'T EVEN REACHED the back door to the café before the tantalizing aroma of Granny's chicken pot pie assailed me. My stomach grumbled. I had a personal guideline to not cook on an either empty *or* overly full stomach. However, Cara's chocolate chip cookies were a distant memory, and I hadn't taken time to eat when I'd gone home to let Cap out.

"It smells amazing in here, Granny," I said, closing the door against the cool outside air and entering the warm kitchen.

Pie tins with freshly rolled crust were lined up neatly on the big island, waiting to be filled, topped and baked. Granny Lu stirred a huge pot at the stove, and I could smell the fresh thyme and minced garlic mingling with vegetables and tender chicken. My mouth watered in anticipation.

"I can't remember the last time I had your pot pie. I don't suppose you need a taste-tester, do you?" I asked, coming up behind her and squeezing her squishy middle. Her gray hair, tucked into a bun, tickled my nose.

"I tested the first batch; the leftovers are on the counter. Help yourself, but be quick about it, because I need you to make broccoli salad."

"Yes, ma'am," I said, already at the small pan on the countertop with a plate and fork. Three-fourths of the pie had already been eaten, I noticed. Granny was pro-indulgence, but even so, tended to eat birdlike portions. I knew she hadn't eaten it all herself.

"Has Tucker been here?" I asked, slicing the remaining piece in half and sliding it onto a plate. Creamy, saucy chicken and vegetables spilled out, and I gathered them up with my fork, along with a flaky piece of crust.

"Guilty," Tucker said, appearing in the bar window with a mop. "But only because she made me," he said, pointing at Granny with the end of the mop. He grinned, placing earbuds in each ear before wandering off to finish cleaning. He bobbed his head along to the music, occasionally spinning and dipping the mop like a dance partner.

"He's a growing boy," Granny said. "I insisted on an afternoon snack."

I took my first bite of pie, and it did not disappoint. The rich, earthy flavors of herbs balanced the savory filling and slightly sweet crust perfectly. I finished off the plate with embarrassing speed, stopping myself short of licking it clean. I'm not a total barbarian.

"Two enthusiastic thumbs-up for you," I said to Granny as I rummaged in the fridge for broccoli salad ingredients. "The pot pie is perfection."

"Psh, of course it is," Granny preened, her cheeks pinking slightly with pride.

Granny Lu and I chatted while I chopped vegetables and she filled the pie tins. It seemed that there was always someone else in the café kitchen with us lately—Nyla doing her baking in the morning, the servers bustling about at lunch time, and Ava or Tucker in the afternoons. But today, it was just the two of us.

For a fleeting moment I was transported back in time, to my childhood learning at Granny's knee.

In those simpler days, I'd stand at the island on a step stool, dressed in my favorite apron. It was red-and-white striped with a happy cherry print. Inevitably, I would be covered in flour as Granny patiently showed me the steps, letting me mix and stir to my heart's content, but always to her exacting standards.

She didn't have to give me instructions these days (although, sometimes she did anyway), but the kitchen still held the same warmth and camaraderie that was uniquely Granny.

"Hand me that egg wash, will you, dear?" Granny asked, breaking me out of my daydream. The tins of pot pies were all filled now, and she had placed a thick crust on top of each one, fluting the edges around the pan with practiced ease. The egg wash she spread on top was purely for aesthetic reasons, giving each crust a pretty sheen as it baked.

As for me, I'd finished a sweet, homemade dressing and carefully stirred it in the giant metal bowl filled with broccoli, shredded carrots, sunflower seeds, bacon, and dried cranberries. I then portioned out the salads into portable containers, giving the flavors just enough time to marinate in the fridge while the pies baked.

Once all the orders were assembled, Tucker left to make deliveries and Granny, too, went home for the evening. Although we'd already cleaned up the kitchen, I stayed behind to get a head start on the next day's work. Fridays were always busy, but this one would be especially so.

We planned to open an hour early in the morning to accommodate the festival crowd. It was sure to be busy all through lunch, and the kiddie Halloween parade was set for two o'clock. We would be open Friday evening for dinner, complete with the Silver Vixens book club in the private room.

We anticipated a larger crowd than normal, with the festivities launching into the big Halloween weekend. I took some time to check our stock to make sure we'd have plenty of ingredients on hand. Our supplier would arrive early in the morning, as he did every Friday, and we'd ordered extra in preparation.

Nyla was set to make cinnamon rolls, pumpkin muffins and cranberry orange scones, along with the usual hot rolls for lunch.

I was making three types of quiches in the morning, and had planned two soup specials for lunch instead of the usual one.

My head was inside the refrigerator, counting eggs, when I heard my phone ring on the other side of the room. I jogged across the kitchen to answer it before it went to voicemail. Tucker's name flashed across the screen, and I frowned. Generally, I only heard from him if there was a problem with an order, and I really didn't have time for an irate customer tonight.

"Hey, Tucker," I answered. "What's up?"

"Yeah, boss...something weird is going down at your bestie's." Tucker's voice sounded odd. Tighter than normal.

"What?" I asked.

"I just dropped off the order at the Wheelers' house, and the cops are there. Not just the chief, like a friendly visit, but the lights were flashing on the cars, and there were two other officers with him."

Cara had said the guys were going to be testing the trebuchet tonight, but it sounded like something else was going on. Had there been an accident? Alarm slammed through my body, and I felt my fingers and toes jolt from the adrenaline.

"Is Cara okay? Tim and the kids?"

"I don't think anybody's hurt," Tucker said slowly, in his lazy way. I mentally willed him to talk faster. "But Mr. Wheeler looked like he might punch a wall any minute, and your girl's eyes were all red like she'd been crying. You know, like full mascara tragedy on her face."

"Okay...did you ask any questions?" I couldn't fathom what had happened to warrant such a reaction.

"Naw. The chief ushered me out of there real quick. But I figured you'd want to know."

"Thank you, Tucker. I appreciate it. I'm going to head over there right now."

———

Cara didn't answer her phone or the frenzied text I sent before locking up at Lulu's. I hopped in my car and called Tim, but it went straight to voicemail. I slammed my hand against the steering wheel in frustration as I peeled out of the alley.

My thoughts went to Cara's parents. Had something happened to them? I couldn't imagine that three police officers would be at their house on a Thursday evening with *good* news. It had to be something terrible.

Or maybe it was the kids? Had they escaped out of the yard fence and fallen off the dock? My mind was racing with all the terrible scenarios that were possible.

It felt like an eternity until I was pulling into the gravel driveway at Cara's house. Two police cars were parked outside, lights flashing just as Tucker had said. I threw the car in park and ran up the steps, flying through the front door.

As I ran through the foyer and into the living room, I saw with great relief that Olive and Arthur were sharing a bowl of fish-shaped crackers and watching cartoons. I stopped, with my hand over my heart, while Arthur looked at me curiously.

"Auntie Alex, I didn't know there was going to be a party tonight," he said, shifting his body to turn and look at me. I heard crackers crunch into the sofa fabric, but he didn't seem to notice. He pointed at the kitchen.

"Lots of people are here," he said. "And Daddy said we can watch all the shows we want while we wait for Nana to come pick us up."

"That sounds...exciting, buddy." I worked to keep my tone even, but I couldn't help walking into the room and giving Arthur a big bear hug.

"Can't see," Olive complained, pushing at me with a chubby arm. I wrapped her in my arms as well, but she squirmed out of them. Shaking my head, I looked up to find Deacon at the kitchen doorway, watching us.

"What are you doing here?" he demanded.

"Um, that's what I came to ask you. What's going on?" I stood up and rounded the sofa.

Deacon shook his head, his lips tight. "You shouldn't be here."

"The heck I shouldn't. Where's Cara?" I asked, pushing past him into the breakfast nook.

Cara sat at the table, her eyes red-rimmed and swollen. Tim stood behind her, with his hands on her shoulders, and two uniformed officers sat on each side of Cara at the table. I recognized Donny Swanson, but the other cop, a woman with her hair in a tight bun, was unfamiliar. Half empty cups of coffee littered the table, and a platter of this afternoon's cookies sat untouched in the middle.

I marched over to my best friend, kneeling down and pulling her into a fierce hug.

"Are you okay? What happened?" Cara shuddered into my shoulder and sucked in a deep breath.

"We had an anonymous tip," Donny began.

"Swanson," Deacon said, a warning edge to his tone. Cara pulled away from me.

"No, it's okay," she spoke up, her voice shaky. "Alex should know. Someone called the station this afternoon. They-they said that I was in the woods. Picking strange flowers."

"Huh?" I asked.

"White snakeroot," Tim said, massaging at the back of his neck with one hand. "They said she was picking white snakeroot."

"But that's ridiculous," I began, turning to Deacon. "Besides, I was here all afternoon with Cara. We were making Halloween costumes."

I gestured to the four circus costumes that still hung across the upper trim of the doorway, where we'd admired our handi-work earlier. The bright, cheerful colors contrasted sharply with the somber mood of the room.

"We can't just ignore a tip," Deacon said gently. "We're

required to follow up on calls like that, so the three of us came over here, and Tim and Cara voluntarily let us search the place."

"So, what's the big deal? Of course, you didn't find anything," I began. My eyes locked with Cara's, and the desperate look in them quieted me. My stomach twisted into an anxious knot.

"We found this," the female officer said, holding up a clear evidence bag. Even I could see it was filled with tiny white flowers. "In Mrs. Wheeler's shed."

My gaze swung to look out the window. It was dark outside, but I knew past the kids' play set was Cara's "she shed," which she used for drying the herbs and spices for her teas.

"Someone's setting you up," I said, my eyes going back to Cara's.

"We can't speculate," the female officer said. "The evidence is right here, and it's pretty incriminating."

I glared at her.

"That's a load of—" I began, but Deacon cut me off.

"We are looking into *all* explanations," he said, his hands out as if placating us.

"Cara doesn't have a motive," I said. "And she's been here all day anyway, right?"

Tim and Cara glanced at one another.

"What?" I asked, exasperated.

"I went for a run this afternoon," Cara whispered. "After you left, and Tim came home. I went out for a run on the trail."

"So, someone is spying on you *and* trying to frame you for Alan's murder?" I asked. "You guys could be in danger." Cara's breath came in short gasps, and her eyes welled up again.

"What about your security cameras?" I asked, turning to Tim. They'd had a home alarm system since the kids were born.

"We checked already, and they didn't catch anything. They're trained on the front and back doors." He coughed uncomfortably. "And the, um, boat dock. I never thought the shed would need surveillance."

I rolled my eyes. "Aces, Timmy. Great job. At least the boats are safe."

"Okay, that's enough. Can I speak to you?" Deacon asked, pulling on my arm toward the formal dining room. I guess he wasn't going to wait for an answer. He led me to the foyer and out the front door.

"What?" I asked, yanking my arm away once we'd reached the porch. The wizard hat decorations danced merrily over our heads, and I wanted to pull them down in frustration.

"I need you to take a deep breath, for one thing," Deacon said. "Winding everyone up in there isn't helping matters."

"You can't seriously think that Cara had anything to do with this."

"You're right, I don't. But I still have a job to do, and if someone is trying to throw us off, then I need to be on top of everything. Leave no stone unturned. I can't have any accusations of bias or not following protocol. Why do you think I brought not just one, but two extra officers?"

"Fine, then. But are they safe here?" I jerked my head toward the house.

Deacon bit his lip. "Probably, since we've already collected the evidence, but...it's possible they could be in danger. That's why we're staying with them until Cara's parents can take the kids to their place, then we'll all go down to the station to finish questions and take official statements. Cara and Tim will then be free to either come home or get a hotel room, but they'll need to stay in town until this is resolved."

I sighed, pinching the bridge of my nose. It was all too much. "Who would do this?"

"I don't know. But you can be sure I'm going to find out." He looked exhausted, but there was a glint of determination in his eyes. "Meanwhile, you've got to stop serving and selling Cara's tea at the café, just to be safe. We don't need any more 'accidents.'"

"Copy that," I said, nodding. It sucked, and the gossip would be flying tomorrow, but we couldn't afford to give the killer an opportunity to strike again.

"And one more thing," Deacon said, sighing wearily. "Let me do my job."

I opened my mouth to protest, but he silenced me again.

"I know you love Cara and Tim like family, but so do I. I'm going to find out who did this, and I'm going to make them pay."

———

Something fuzzy tickled at my nose as I worked my way toward consciousness the next morning. I pawed at it, squinting. Was it fur? Hair? I was too out of it to tell. I rolled away from it, only to feel something cold and wet press against my hand.

I blinked sleepily, my eyes feeling dry as sandpaper. Cap blinked back at me, moving closer until his big doggy eyes were just inches from my face. His wagging tail hit the bed with a heavy *thunk, thunk, thunk.* His wet nose assailed me again, this time against my cheek, and I winced.

The long night came back to me suddenly, and I turned in the dim light to see Cara's sleeping form. Her back was to me, puffy hair wildly splayed across my pillow. Ah, the source of the tickling.

She appeared to be out cold, finally. I don't think either of us had slept much, discussing our worries long into the night.

After they'd finished at the station, Tim and Cara had shown up at my door. Cara had wanted to go home, but Tim insisted that they stay somewhere else for the night. He'd taken the sofa downstairs while Cara bunked with me.

I glanced at my phone, and I groaned when I saw the time. I should have been up half an hour ago. I rolled out of bed, grabbing some clothes and dressing quietly in the bathroom. Tiptoeing downstairs, I slipped on my shoes and grabbed Cap's harness. Tim snored softly from the sofa, his long legs dangling off the edge. It looked uncomfortable.

Cap and I slipped out the door quietly. The early morning was still and silent, but the low-lying fog that blanketed the sidewalk didn't do anything to ease my anxiety. Considering yesterday's events, I decided to skip Wayfinder Trail completely, opting for a quick jaunt through my neighborhood instead. My eyes darted side to side for anything suspicious, but nothing appeared out of the ordinary.

By the time I returned home, I was no more awake than I had been when I rolled out of bed. I fed and watered Cap and jumped in the shower, hoping the scalding hot water would do something to clear the cobwebs from my brain.

Cara was in the kitchen when I came back downstairs. Tim was awake, too, although he hadn't made it off the couch yet. He sat with his elbows resting on his knees, staring blankly into space with his mouth hanging open. I understood the feeling.

"Where are my pants?" he asked groggily, running a hand through his messy hair. He scanned the living room and ducked his head under the sofa.

A knock at the back door made me jump, but my heart rate settled when I saw that it was only Deacon peeking through the glass.

"I brought donuts," Deacon said, when I opened the door. He balanced a box on his right hand, holding it up for my inspection.

"Really leaning into that cop stereotype, aren't you?" I said, resting my shoulder against the doorjamb. Deacon pressed his lips together, his eyes narrowing slightly.

I scrubbed at my face with my hands. "Sorry, sorry." I sighed. "I didn't get much sleep last night."

Deacon held up his left hand this time, revealing a cardboard drink carrier. "I brought coffee, too."

That perked me up a little, and I straightened my back. "What I meant to say, was 'please come inside,'" I amended, holding the door wide and moving out of the way. He grinned crookedly at me.

"Yeah, that's what I thought," he said.

I was relieved to see that Tim had found his clothes, and Cara eagerly took a coffee from Deacon.

"Thanks, man," Tim said, snagging a donut from the box Deacon set on the counter.

"Did y'all get any rest?" Deacon asked.

"Not much," Cara answered, guzzling her coffee like she'd just been handed a post-marathon bottle of water.

"Isn't that hot?" I asked, taking a cautious sip.

She nodded, gasping and coughing. "I think I just scalded my esophageal lining," she said, clutching at her throat. "But this day will not beat me." She punched her fist into the air while I rushed to fill a glass of water for her.

"Thanks," Cara said, taking a swig. "I mean it, though. I'm ready for whatever comes at us today." She had mom determination in her eye, and I wouldn't want to mess with her.

Her meaning became abundantly clear after we'd all packed up and went our separate ways. The café was bustling that morning as soon as we opened, the whole town excited for the Halloween weekend to begin. Between cooking and preparing orders, I caught snatches of gossip here and there. It was not helped by the fact that Jasmine had to tell several customers that we were unable to serve Cara's tea.

When I got a moment to catch my breath, Granny Lu agreed that I should run to the store to buy supplies for apple cider and hot cocoa, which we didn't usually serve. Perhaps it would take the focus off our unavailable menu items. We'd call it a Harvest Fest special.

Ordinarily, we planned our menus weekly and placed a large order through our supplier, who gave us better rates to purchase in bulk. But occasionally, we miscalculated and had to make a quick run to the Emerald Bay Market to bolster our supplies, and this was one case that qualified.

I slipped out the back door, planning to be back to the café within fifteen minutes. Unfortunately, who should I run into in the baking aisle but Phyllis Goat.

She stood in front a display of s'more supplies, her back turned to me. I felt my body stiffen, an involuntary reaction I'd had to the woman since I was a child. I had the odd desire for the wall of marshmallow bags to come tumbling down on top of her.

I turned my head while I plucked a large can of cocoa powder off the shelf and set it gently into my shopping cart. If I didn't clang, maybe she wouldn't notice me. I'd just grab a bag of sugar quickly, and then I could turn around and be on my way.

"Good morning, Alex." Phyllis's shrill voice pierced through my skull. My hand froze halfway to the granulated sugar. No such luck, then. Taking a deep breath, I lifted the bag of sugar into my cart. As I turned around, I arranged my face into what I hoped looked like a smile.

"Hello, Mrs. Goat." I met her cold blue eyes for a moment before dropping my own to her basket. It was filled to the brim with all manner of instant pudding mixes and nothing else. That is, besides a single bunch of asparagus placed precariously on top of the pudding pile. It was a peculiar sight, and my frazzled brain fixated on it.

"Are you…making some dessert today?" I asked lamely. "You must really love pudding."

What did one do with that amount of pudding? Did she plan to eat it all herself? As it was, it appeared she could ration one box of pudding a day for the foreseeable future.

"No," she answered. "I don't particularly care for pudding." Her tone managed to convey what an imbecile she thought I was. "There was a sale. I always stock up when there's a good sale." She gestured to the now-empty shelf on which the puddings had been, next to a red handmade sign declaring, "Two-for-One Sale!"

All that was left was the pistachio. I nodded vaguely.

"These days, the world's heading south. You never know when it's all going to fall to pieces around us," she continued. "Best to be prepared."

"Sure, sure," I said, pushing my cart past her. "Well, I'd better be on my way."

"I heard about that nasty business with the Wheelers," Phyllis called after me. The wheels on my cart squeaked as I pulled to a stop.

"What do you mean?" I asked, turning back around.

"Oh, just that Cara was taken in for questioning last night. Something about the police finding something suspicious in her possession. I do hope you're not serving her tea anymore, dear. Didn't I warn you about that?"

Was she threatening me? I shouldn't have been surprised that the rumor mill had been churning out gossip so quickly, but I was. My teeth ground together, and I forcibly unclenched my jaw.

"Cara hasn't done anything wrong," I managed to get out. "Once this investigation is over, she'll be proven innocent."

"We'll see." Phyllis sniffed.

"Yes, we will," I said. "Now, if you'll excuse me, I have a café to run, and I need to get back."

"I have a busy day ahead of me, too. See you tonight, Alex."

I hope everything in your cart is expired, I thought uncharitably. But I was a professional, so I took a deep breath and said, "Book club tonight, of course. See you then."

Phyllis and her pudding walked briskly down the aisle, as though in a hurry to ruin someone else's day.

CHAPTER 13
SMOKING GUN OR SMOKE AND MIRRORS

THE HUM of conversation mingled with the vintage country music that played from Granny's old radio in the café kitchen. I'd tried to encourage her to use the Bluetooth speakers I bought, but she was adamant that FM was good enough for her.

I supposed that there was something special about Patsy Cline's crooning, and I hummed along to *Crazy* as I ladled out soup and prepped plates. The radio crackled with static and interference, but it somehow added to the charm.

We were in the lunch rush and even busier than normal, with the last days of the festival in full swing and the parade set to begin in less than two hours. All hands were on deck in the kitchen and in the eating area, but our servers were struggling to keep up.

"Be right back," I said to Granny, who was occupied with assembling ham and Swiss croissants and swaying her hips in time to the music.

"Here you go, ladies," I said, smiling at Diane Frasier and another woman I didn't recognize.

"Oh, Alex, this looks absolutely delicious," Diane said, unwrapping her napkin and eyeing her chicken stew hungrily.

"We could have waited for Jasmine to bring it out; I know you're swamped today. I've never seen the place so packed."

She glanced at the entryway, where several people stood waiting for a table. There wasn't an empty seat in the house.

"It's no trouble," I said. "Hope you enjoy it."

"Didn't I tell you? Lulu's has the best service in town," Diane said to her companion. I beamed. Granny would be pleased to hear her reputation still held up.

"Alex, have you met my sister?" Diane asked as I started to turn away.

"No, I don't believe so," I said. Now that she mentioned it, there was a familial resemblance around the eyes.

"She's in town visiting for the weekend."

"Very nice to meet you," I said.

"You too, hon. Oh, your nails are gorgeous! Where did you get them done? Diane, do you think we'd have time to squeeze in nail appointment?"

Now that the other woman was talking without so much as taking a breath between questions, I could see the eyes were not the only resemblance to Diane.

"I'm not sure we'd be able to on such short notice," Diane said. "But we can certainly try. My husband is out of town, and we're having a girls-only weekend," she said, turning back to me.

"How fun," I said. "Lori Davenport, over at the country club spa, did my nails a few days ago. She must have worked some magic, because my hands are in and out of hot water all day and the color hasn't chipped yet."

I held my nails out and inspected the glossy sheen. I was surprised it had lasted this long.

Diane wrinkled her nose. "I'm not sure we'd want to go there, Sis."

"Whyever not?" the other woman asked, stirring her stew with a spoon.

I had started to back away again, but now I was interested in

Diane's answer. I stepped toward the table and took it upon myself to clear their empty salad plates.

"Well, you know I don't like to speak out of turn, but let's just say that I don't believe a leopard can change its spots."

"You know I don't like when you speak in riddles, Di. What exactly do you mean?" her sister asked.

Diane glanced around the café, before speaking in a hushed tone.

"Lori Davenport has priors. Assault charges, in fact. Back when she worked at the casino, she was always getting into trouble."

"How do you know that?" I couldn't help asking.

"Honey, when you've been around as long as I have, you see the ugly things people do to one another. My niece on my husband's side worked with her for a short time, and she came home one night with a black eye. Courtesy of Lori Davenport." Diane took a bite of a hot roll, as if to punctuate this news.

Diane's sister gasped and held a hand to her chest.

"Did this happen recently?" I asked.

"Oh no, this was years ago. Maybe ten or fifteen?" Diane waved a hand in the air. "It was before Lori had her son and took up with Rusty."

Diane took a large bite of stew and moaned in appreciation. "Sis, try your soup. It's to die for." Her sister took a bite, and the two of them made a chorus of *Mmm*s as they dug into their meal.

It looked like gossip time was over.

What a strange interaction, I thought, as I excused myself back to the kitchen. Granny scowled at me as I reentered, and though I felt bad leaving her in a lurch, I wondered if my detour had been worth it for the information I'd learned in the last five minutes.

———

"Hey, I've been thinking. Do you know who called in that anonymous tip?" I whispered to Deacon, sliding next to him as he leaned up against his cruiser. I'd made a beeline for him when I'd seen him parked right in front of the police station.

The parade had just started, and several law enforcement officials and City Hall personnel had come out to wave to the kids and watch the festivities.

"It's called anonymous for a reason," he said, lifting one eyebrow and smirking.

"I'm not an idiot, jerk face. But this is a small town. Did you recognize the voice?"

"I didn't take the call. But no, I doubt the officer knew who was speaking." He looked past me, his face splitting into a grin. He gave a thumbs-up to a little boy who was dressed as a policeman.

I blew out a breath and cocked my head. "Okay, let me ask you this: was the tipster a man or woman?"

Deacon finally peeled his attention away from the parade, his eyes flitting over my face.

"A woman," he replied. My pulse quickened. "But I don't see how that's relevant."

"It's relevant if it was a fake tip, to throw off suspicion," I countered.

"And who do you think is trying to throw us off?"

I chewed on my lip. Might as well just come out with it.

"Okay, you know how I was thinking Rusty could have had something to do with Alan's murder? What if I was just a little off, and it was his wife, Lori, instead? Or they could be working together. I mean, they *are* one another's alibi."

"Lori…" Deacon frowned as he tried to place her. "Lori, the hairdresser?" He didn't look like he was buying it.

"Nail technician," I corrected. "We know Alan had a problem with both her husband and kid, which could be motivation enough for some women," I said. "And get this: she has assault priors."

"Where are you getting this information? She's lived here since her kid was two and I've never seen her booked."

"My source is not the point," I hedged, knowing he wouldn't find Diane's gossip reliable. "Even if it was a long time ago, it proves she's capable of violence."

Deacon rolled his eyes.

"All it proves is that she had some wild younger days. Kind of like a couple people I know." He gestured back and forth at himself and me.

I did my best to ignore his logic.

"She also does all the landscaping at the trailer park *and* is a member of the Garden Club."

"Ooh, I'll get my cuffs right now. You want to ride shotgun?" Deacon asked sarcastically, arching that eyebrow at me again before turning his attention back to the parade.

"Hello!" I socked Deacon on the arm, and he scowled at me while rubbing the spot.

"That proves that she knows her plants. Whoever called in the tip and framed Cara had to know enough about botany to find the snakeroot and plant it in her shed."

"Or has access to the internet," Deacon said.

I glared at him. Was I the only one taking this investigation seriously?

Deacon heaved a world-weary sigh. "I'll take it under advisement, okay? Now, will you stop harassing the law enforcement in public?"

"That's all I'm asking," I said, holding my hands up in surrender. I shifted my eyes back to the parade, and I saw the Wheelers walking with Arthur's preschool class. The garish circus colors were hard to miss. Both kids looked adorable and waved enthusiastically when they spotted Deacon and me. Arthur's comically large muscles wobbled atop his skinny arms as he lifted the fake weights over his head.

Cara had a smile plastered on her face and held her head

high, but I could see the tension she carried in her shoulders. We needed to fix this, and quickly.

"Did you find out anything about whoever was messing with the renovation house?" I asked.

"No. Nobody's seen or heard anything suspicious. Still working on it," he said.

I glanced across the street and found Granny eyeing me at the café's front window.

"I've got to get back to Lulu's. Let me know what you find out, and I'll keep my ears open for any more information," I said.

"You ever wonder how I did my job before you came back to town?" Deacon shot back at me as I waited for a break in the parade of kids and families. I turned around and stuck my tongue out at him, before dashing across the street.

"Jaywalker!" he yelled.

I didn't turn around or let him see my grin as I slipped back into the café. Despite all the mayhem surrounding us, why was annoying the chief the highlight of my day?

———

The Silver Vixens book club was in high spirits that evening, and though I winced at the raucous laughter coming from the party room, it was preferable to Phyllis and Janet arguing about the merits and faults of cliffhanger endings. I thought I was going to have to escort them outside after the last meeting concluded with the two of them in a shouting match.

It felt like days ago that Cara and Tim had stayed the night at my house, yet it had only been hours. I was dead on my feet, and I rubbed at my aching lower back in between sautéing vegetables at the cooktop.

They planned to stay at Cara's parents house tonight, not wanting to leave the kids for the second night in a row. As one or both kids tended to join them in bed halfway through most nights, I couldn't say I was sorry we weren't having a slumber party at my house.

Still, I worried about them and wondered if Deacon was any closer to a lead on who could be framing Cara. I hadn't seen him since the parade, and he hadn't popped into the café or texted me. I craned my neck to see if the cruiser was still parked at the station, but it had begun to rain, and the street lamps glaring off the water droplets made it impossible to see.

The crowd had thinned considerably throughout the evening. The festival had closed early due to weather, and everyone seemed eager to be warm and dry at home. As our customers trickled out, I instructed Ava to start closing duties.

I wouldn't rush the book club, but we just might get to leave ahead of schedule if everything else was taken care of besides the party room. A hot bubble bath and my pajamas sounded heavenly.

Janet finally adjourned the meeting, and I wished the women goodnight and locked the door behind the last one, sighing with relief. Ava and I bussed the table while Jasmine began stacking chairs so she could sweep and mop.

"Someone left their book," Ava said, holding up a hardcover volume.

"I think that's Mrs. Crawford's," I said. "Everyone else had a paperback, except Brenda." She preferred an e-reader, a choice of which Janet staunchly disapproved. I knew because Janet had given me an earful about it when she had arrived early to set up.

"I'll take it," I said to Ava. "I can drop it by her house."

We rushed through the rest of our closing duties, leaving the café sparkling clean to start our Saturday morning smoothly. The three of us walked out together, and after making sure everyone got to their cars safely, I started my own. I was looking forward to snuggles with Cap and a relaxing evening.

———

I had barely begun to inch my way out of the parking space, when a flash of red and blue lights in the rearview mirror caught my eye. Two cruisers pulled in front of the station, sirens off but lights flashing.

I put the car in park and swiveled in my seat, trying to get a better look.

Deacon and another officer exited one car, and another pair of officers emerged from the other. One of the cops opened the back door, and a man shuffled out.

I squinted, knowing he looked familiar but taking a moment to place him. The scruffy outfit was the same, but he was missing his hat, and the limp was new. It was the musician from the festival, the one I'd stopped to listen to that night I'd met Ravi for chai.

The man was flanked on both sides by officers as they escorted him into the station. I jumped out of my car, calling to Deacon before he, too, could disappear inside. He spoke briefly to the other officer, and she followed the group into the station while the chief turned to me.

"Is that the guy? Did you get him?" I asked breathlessly.

"I hope so," Deacon said. The worry lines on his forehead had faded a bit, and he smiled at me. "Ravi overheard some students talking and encouraged them to speak to us. They were in the park the night of Alan's murder and I.D.'ed this guy. They said he was running after Alan, calling his name, and that Alan had disappeared into the maze to get away from him."

"Did he follow Alan into the maze?"

"The witnesses said that he did, and that he came running out moments later. They didn't think much of it at the time," Deacon said, shrugging.

"Is their word enough to go on?" I asked.

"It's enough to bring him in for questioning. Unfortunately for him, when our guys stopped by his place, he was enjoying some…illegal substances. So, now he's under arrest, and we'll see where the rest of the trail leads."

"Drugs. Awesome. This story just gets better and better," I said. "Do you think he's guilty?"

Deacon's eyes shifted toward the bright station, the light catching his face. "He admitted to breaking into Alan's rental house, but he's adamant he had nothing to do with his death."

"Why would he break into the house?" I wondered.

"I'm about to go find out," Deacon said. He shook his head. "He wasn't making much sense, but said Alan had something that belonged to him. He was trying to get it back, when he broke the rickety railing and fell off the landing, hurting his leg. He was afraid someone heard, so he abandoned his search and fled the house."

"I've seen him around," I said. "His music was actually really great at the festival. He was staying at one of the cottages in Alan's neighborhood, right?"

Deacon nodded. I thought of the shadowy figure I'd seen skulking around last week and said as much to Deacon.

"Exactly what I was thinking about. Listen, Lex, I've got to get inside and see this through. I'll let you know something when I can."

Deacon waited until I drove away before disappearing into the station. I desperately wished I could be a fly on the wall, but at this point, there wasn't much I could do except wait.

After I arrived home, I lost track of how many times I checked my phone for a call or text from Deacon. It was ridiculous; I knew he needed time to interview the man and put the pieces together, but that didn't stop me pacing in front of the windows and looking for Deacon's cruiser every few minutes.

Who was this guy, and what did he want with Alan? Belatedly, I remembered the poster I'd seen advertising his show, which was supposed to happen tomorrow evening. I hadn't paid much attention to his name, and I wrinkled my brow, trying to remember. Something…Jennings. I remembered because he had the same surname as Waylon Jennings, another of Granny's favorite classic country singers.

But what had his first name been? It was a common one that started with a "C." Was is Charlie? Or Chris?

I grabbed my phone and pulled up one of my social media apps. Yes, I was going to stalk the guy.

I didn't hit anything earthshattering with Charlie, but after sifting through about fifteen Chris Jennings profiles, I found him. Hometown: Emerald Bay. He had even listed his graduating year, which was eleven years prior to my own. His profile was public, most likely because it appeared he used it primarily as a marketing tool for his music.

Chris's most recent posts had to do with his appearance at the festival, and the older ones were photos and short videos of him playing at various events. He was currently living in Tennessee, trying to make it in the music business.

How did he know Alan? What could Alan possibly have that belonged to him, and was it motivation enough to kill? I thought about what Deacon had told me, that the kids in the park had seen the musician chase after Alan, and then race out of the maze only moments later.

The night stretched on, and my eyelids grew heavy. I finally texted Deacon before going to bed.

Deacon: Still sorting things out so I can't talk, but this guy's acting shady. Could be the drugs making him seem suspicious...still waiting for him to sober up. Gonna be a long night here.

Unfortunately, that did nothing to satisfy my curiosity. I finally collapsed into bed with more questions than answers.

CHAPTER 14
I FALL TO PIECES

"THANK you for bringing it by, dear, but that wasn't necessary," Myra said, when I arrived on her front porch the next morning. It was bright and clear after yesterday's rain, and I'd elected to go for a long walk with Cap.

I planned to circle back through Alan's neighborhood, avoiding the trailer park on the way home. Even though the musician was in custody, I was still suspicious of Rusty and Lori. I had paused in front of the rental cottage where I had seen the musician out strumming his guitar just days ago, but the house was quiet and dark. It didn't seem as though anyone else was staying there with him.

Deacon's cruiser had been parked in our driveway when I'd gone out, but, unsure of how late it had been when he got home, I knew better than to go knocking on his door demanding answers. I would just have to practice a little patience, something that didn't come naturally to me.

But, as Granny would say, there was always room to better oneself through discipline. So, I had forced myself away from Deacon's front door and resisted the urge to shoot him yet another text.

"It's no problem," I replied, bringing myself back to the

present with Myra. The delicious scents of cinnamon and orange wafted out of the open doorway. "It smells wonderful in here. Are you baking?"

"Oh no, that's my new essential oil diffuser. A gift from my granddaughter. Actually, I'm a terrible cook," she said, giving a little shrug as if to convey that she'd made her peace with it. "I much prefer the outdoors. But, I can manage to make a decent pot of tea. Would you like to come in for a cup before you walk back?"

Goosebumps prickled on my arms, and I had a feeling that it wasn't only from the cool breeze. Unfortunately, my sixth sense didn't come with a user guide, so I had no idea what it meant. Was it telling me to go inside?

"Sure. That sounds nice," I said, smiling. Cap whined at my side, looking forlornly to the trail and whatever he had been sniffing at while we walked here.

"Would you prefer I leave my dog on the porch?" I asked. People could be finicky about pets indoors, and I didn't want to be presumptuous. Cap turned to me, and if a dog could glare, he was nailing the expression.

"You'll be fine," I whispered to him. "You like it outside."

"He's welcome to come in, so long as he can behave himself and stay off the furniture," Myra said, moving back to allow us to enter.

"Thank you," I said, wiping both my shoes and Cap's paws on the mat before we went inside. The path had been full of puddles, but luckily, Cap had avoided the mud.

A few pairs of shoes and rubber boots were arranged neatly on a bristly rug by the door. I noted that the floors were hardwood, not carpet, so I felt better about letting Cap come in with me.

"Be good," I hissed. He looked insulted.

Myra led us through the small entryway and into a cozy living room. I instructed Cap to lay down, and he obeyed. I peered at a collection of black and white photographs on the wall above the floral sofa.

"Wow, these are great," I said. "Your family?"

"Yes, there's my husband Gerald and me with our boys. This one is of my parents. And our engagement photograph is right here."

She pointed at the picture of a much-younger version of herself and the former mayor. He wore a brown suit with a thin tie, while she wore an avocado green dress with a high neck and cat's eyeglasses. Her hair was arranged in a bouffant style, with one long, single curl resting over her shoulder.

"You look so glamorous," I said.

"Such a long time ago, yet it feels like yesterday." Myra caressed the frame with a wistful look in her eyes.

"What's this one?" I asked. It was a photo of Myra and Gerald, who looked to be about in their thirties or forties. The city park was in the background, and they stood under a balloon arch.

"Oh, that was Emerald Bay's Centennial Celebration. Back in seventy-eight, I think it was. You know, my husband's ancestors were one of the founding families of the town. It was established just over a decade after the Civil War ended, by a group of families looking to rebuild in a peaceful place, surrounded by Missouri's natural beauty." She stroked the photograph's frame lovingly. "Anyway, we had a weeklong festival to commemorate it. What times those were," she said, shaking her head and chuckling, more to herself than to me.

"Ah, here's a picture of Gerald's great-grandparents. They are older here, of course, as this was taken around the turn of the century, but can you imagine what it must have been like to build this whole town out of nothing but dreams and determination?"

"It is pretty amazing," I said, my eyes flitting across the photographs that spanned over a hundred years.

"Listen to me, prattling on." Myra shook her head. "I'll go get that tea. Have a seat." She gestured to the couch.

"Can I help you?" I asked.

Mrs. Crawford waved me away.

I turned back to the wall of photographs while I waited, examining them closely instead of sitting on the sofa as she'd suggested. Myra certainly had a way of speaking that had me caught up in the magic of yesteryear.

Suddenly, a wave of nausea rushed over me, leaving a trail of dizziness in its wake. My arms and hands tingled, goosebumps popping up all over my skin. I felt like I was going to be sick.

I swayed, sitting down on the couch quickly. Closing my eyes, I put my head between my knees and took a few deep breaths. What was happening to me?

Cap came forward and whined, pushing his head against mine, which oddly alleviated my panic a bit. After a few more deep breaths, the nausea faded away as quickly as it had come.

"Thanks, boy," I said weakly, stroking his head and while I waited for my heart rate to return to normal. Was I now going to have to add panic attacks to my list of conditions?

Cap turned slightly away from me and began sniffing at the couch.

"Cap, no," I said, pushing his head away. He ignored me, continuing to snuffle and paw at the fabric. Ugh, he was going to stain it and I would be in big trouble with Mrs. Crawford.

"What are you doing? Come on, get out of there," I said, standing up and trying to pull him back. In an uncharacteristic show of defiance, he resisted me, now with his nose practically shoved under the couch cushion. I gave up, gently moving his head out of the way while I tucked my hand under the soft fabric, feeling around. My fingers caught on something sharp, and I grasped it and pulled.

Two plain, brown file folders came out. The label of the top one read *Rusty Davenport*. The missing file! But even more intriguing was the folder underneath, labeled *Gerald Crawford.* Why did Myra have a file on her late husband?

I tiptoed to the doorway and saw Myra's back to me, still in the kitchen fussing with a kettle.

Quietly, I opened Gerald's file and began to read. Photocopies, receipts, and pages of transactions stared back at me. It took me a moment to figure out what I was seeing, but then it finally clicked.

This was another blackmail file, and it contained incriminating evidence that Mr. Crawford, our former mayor, had embezzled city funds. For years, if the dates were accurate. And I'd just bet it was Alan Harvey who had collected this evidence.

I swallowed hard. Could Alan have been using this information against Myra? I thought of the look on her face whenever she spoke of her late husband. She clearly loved him and was proud of his legacy as a pillar of the community.

Was I just being paranoid? Maybe the panic attack I'd just had was clouding my judgment. *What about the musician?* a tiny voice reminded me. *You know he broke into Alan's rental house, and he was seen running after Alan the night he died.* Perhaps Mrs. Crawford had taken the file simply so Alan couldn't hold it over her head anymore. Either way, I felt that the chief needed to see it.

Quietly, I took my phone out of the pocket of my yoga pants and snapped a few pictures of the files. The sudden slam of a door nearly made me jump out of my skin, but it came from the back of the house. Myra must have stepped out into the backyard for a moment, but still, my time was limited. Rather than taking more photos, I quickly sent a text to Deacon.

At Myra Crawford's. Missing blackmail file from Alan's house? I sent the pictures I'd taken. I needed to get out of here, but I didn't even have a purse with me, just my key looped around my wrist with my pepper spray. The backdoor closed again. There was no way I could sneak the files out before Myra came back into the room.

I should have run out the front door with the folders as soon as I'd discovered them, but there was no time now. I could hear Myra's footsteps coming closer. Hurriedly, I shoved both files back under the couch just before she appeared in the doorway with a fancy silver tea tray.

"Here we are," she said brightly, placing the tray on the coffee table. She was wearing her gardening gloves, oddly enough. She must have forgotten to take them off when she returned inside. I wondered if her memory was starting to go, as sometimes happened with age.

Myra sat down next to me and poured tea into one of the dainty floral cups. A beautiful bouquet of deep bluish-purple blooms rested in a vase in the middle of the serving tray. I had seen those flowers before, but I couldn't remember where.

"Thank you," I said, taking the cup. It didn't escape my notice that the tea she'd kept for herself had already been poured before she entered the room. I held the cup in my hands, letting its warmth seep into my clammy fingers.

"Mrs. Crawford, you forgot to take off your gloves," I said.

"Oh, no I didn't, my dear," she said, calm as could be.

I wrinkled my brow at her puzzling response.

"You're wondering why I'm still wearing my gardening gloves, and, well, I'm wondering why you've been sticking your nose where it shouldn't be."

Myra maintained eye contact while she took a deep sip of tea. A shiver ran down my spine as malice rolled off her in waves, unmistakable now.

Fine time for my sixth sense to start working properly.

Still, it took a moment for my brain to catch up, while I just sat there gaping at Myra like a trout.

She would do anything to protect her late husband's good name. The realization exploded into my head, physically sending shockwaves through my body. As my eyes locked with Mrs. Crawford's shrewd gaze, I realized how true it was.

I went back over the evidence in my mind. The missing

blackmail files, the muddy footprint. My eyes shot to the rubber boots by the front door, too large to be Myra's. Gerald's old ones, perhaps?

The method of poisoning itself—Myra had extensive knowledge of gardening and local flora; she would have known poisonous plants from benign ones.

Then there was the Centennial lighter, the one that had been dropped in the grass at Buddy Sikes' house. Myra had been there with her husband all those years ago. Buddy Sikes was the most obvious suspect, and it would have benefitted Myra greatly to cast suspicion his way.

I swallowed hard, but my mouth felt dry.

It fits, I thought. *Oh, crap on a cracker; it fits!*

"I...I don't know what you mean, Mrs. Crawford," I said, trying to keep my voice steady.

She shook her head. "Just like your grandmother, think you're something special, do you?"

"No, ma'am."

"Don't lie to me." Her sudden sharp tone jolted through me. It was such a drastic change from the docile old lady who'd welcomed me inside.

"You've been snooping all around town trying to solve Alan's murder. When I checked on you, sure enough, you were reading the files you found under the couch there. It's why I had to go out back and retrieve my little helpers," she said.

"Helpers?" I asked. Good grief, this woman was off her rocker. How had I been so wrong about her? In the handful of times I'd interacted with Myra, I had mostly detected a sad aura coming from her.

What was that old saying? Hurt people hurt people?

Myra stroked a gloved finger across the violet blooms rising from the vase. "Monkshood. Every part of the plant is poisonous. Just a taste can cause nausea and vomiting, hallucinations, irregular heart rate, and delirium. So beautiful, so deadly, so...underestimated. Quite like a woman, don't you think?"

She turned and pierced me with her gaze, a small smile on her lips.

"Mrs. Crawford, you didn't have anything to do with Alan Harvey's death, did you?" I asked, my voice coming out in a whisper.

She waved her hand in the air. "Not purposely, my dear. That was a happy little accident. I only wanted to send dear old Alan a message that *I* wouldn't be taken advantage of anymore. Who was I to know that he had a heart condition that was aggravated by the snakeroot I put into his tea? Whoopsie daisies," she said, shrugging. "I must say, it all worked out so well. Until you started poking around, that is. Drink your tea, dear."

"I'm good," I answered, scooting to the edge of the couch so I'd be prepared to run if I needed to. How exactly did one deal with a homicidal psychopath?

Number one: don't provoke them. Pretend you understand. At least, that was the logic I was going with. Improvisation was the name of the game now.

"You know, I had a run-in with Mr. Harvey myself," I began. I wrinkled my nose. "Horrible, unpleasant man. I can see why you did what you did. He was blackmailing you, too, wasn't he?"

Myra nodded, raising her chin a bit. "My husband was a good and decent man, the kind of leader this town needed. He put us on the map, I tell you. I couldn't let the likes of Alan Harvey soil the good Crawford name."

"Of course not," I said.

"I've been paying off Alan for years to keep quiet, ever since I moved into this rental property, and he showed me the files. Well, no more." She made a sweeping motion with her hand.

"Like you said, it was an accident and Alan had been taking advantage of you. I'm sure the police would understand if you told them the truth," I began.

"No. No police," Myra said, her sharp eyes flashing. "You're not going to cause any trouble now, are you, Alex?"

"N-no, no trouble, honest," I said. Ugh, how was I going to get out of here? I leaned back as Myra loomed closer, invading my space.

Cap, for all his snooping around, had been quite oblivious to both of us up to this point. But he finally seemed to sense my unease, sitting up straighter and letting out a low, warning rumble from his chest.

"Control that dog of yours," Myra warned.

"Easy, boy," I said softly.

My phone chose that moment to let out a cheerful ding that meant I had an incoming text. I had stupidly placed it on the coffee table. I reached for it, but Myra snatched the phone before I could get to it.

"Deacon Lane," she read. "Well, well, well, look who's been conspiring with the chief of police," Myra sneered.

"It's not what you think," I began.

"You know, I was prepared to come to an arrangement with you. But now I can see that you're going to be a problem."

"Calm down, Mrs. Crawford," I said, but she already had her hands at my cup. Before I realized what she was doing, she splashed the tea into my face and then lunged for the tray, fixing her gloved grip around the bouquet of monkshood. I fell back into the sofa, the overly soft cushions preventing me from jumping up quickly.

A burning sensation skittered over my face where the hot liquid dripped, and I spat out a small amount that had landed in my mouth. I wiped at my eyes with the sleeve of my shirt. My tongue was already tingling with numbness, but I didn't have time to think about the poison I'd possibly ingested. The crazy old shrew was coming at me again.

I fumbled with the pepper spray at my wrist, my finger sliding it into the unlocked position. I closed my eyes and sprayed, praying that the nozzle was pointed her way and not my own. Angry wails let me know I'd hit the target, and I kicked out my feet while she floundered in front of me. My feet connected with her stomach, and she stumbled backward, falling over the coffee table and onto the floor.

The tray crashed to the ground beside her and the teapot shattered, scattering porcelain shards in all directions. Cap ran over to Myra, barking loudly as she sat up, still wielding the flowers like a weapon. Which, as it turned out, I guess they were.

I stood up shakily, but my head felt woozy, and I could feel my heart beating erratically between my ears. Cap turned to me once and whined, before climbing on top of Myra's body and barking again.

"Get off me, you stupid dog!" Myra shrieked.

I stumbled around the coffee table, my sights on the front door, but my vision blurred, and the room tilted precariously. I belatedly wondered if there was an antidote to monkshood poisoning, or if this was the beginning of the end.

Something like a claw grabbed my ankle and I fell to the floor, pain shooting through my wrists as they broke my fall. I sensed a struggle behind me and realized it must have been Myra's gloved hand that held me fast. I tried to shake it off, but I felt limp as a rag doll and her grip was unyielding, surprisingly firm for such an elderly woman.

Cap's barks mingled with the curses she shouted at me, their discordance echoing through my head. The wood floor was cool against my cheek, and I had the bizarre thought that I'd like to bury my face into it. It seemed a peaceful reprieve from my current situation.

Another pained scream reached my ears, sharper this time, and the grip on my ankle finally released. I couldn't make my body turn over to see what had happened, but the commotion had subsided.

I stared at Myra's couch, the edge of the offending file sticking out. The floral pattern tipped and swayed, as though moved by a breeze, and I felt annoyed that the ugly fabric would be the last thing I ever saw.

A crash from the vicinity of the front door sounded, and footsteps echoed through the floor and into my aching head.

"Alex! Lex, are you okay?" Deacon's booming voice pierced my ears painfully, and I lifted my head a fraction off the floor. All I could see were his shoes.

"I'm…not so good, Chief," I slurred.

Strong hands rolled me over to my back, and his eyes met mine. I was surprised to see raw, open fear in them. I felt his fingers at my pulsating neck. It was awfully hard to focus with two Deacons looking at me, both of them asking rapid-fire questions.

"What happened? Lex? Answer me!"

"Poison…tea. The flowers," I croaked out. "On…her gloves… too." My brain and mouth both felt stuffed with cotton.

"Mrs. Crawford, stay where you are," he said firmly.

Past Deacon I could see that she was lying on the floor. Cap stood with his front paws on her chest, growling. My vision blurred, but I saw something deep red dripping from the arm she clutched tightly to her chest.

Did he bite her? *Good boy,* I thought. I hoped he wasn't hurt, too.

"This is Chief Lane at 505 Morningside Drive requesting back up and an ambulance," Deacon spoke into his radio. "Suspect and victim are both injured."

A strong hand squeezed my limp one. "You're going to be okay, Lex. I'm here now, and help is on the way. Just hold on." He looked over his shoulder briefly, and watching the movement caused a wave of nausea to sweep over me.

"Cap! Over here, boy. Good dog. Stay with her."

A furry head nestled into my side, and I slung a shaky arm over his body lying next to mine. I felt cold all over, and Cap's body heat drew me in. I heard the metal clink of handcuffs and Myra's muffled sobs.

Deacon said something, returning to my side, but his words were lost in the pounding of my own heartbeat. Black spots clouded my vision, and I fought to stay awake. The last thing I remember was the wail of sirens and Cap's whines before I succumbed to the blissful, quiet darkness.

———

The clinical beep of machinery woke me from a dreamless sleep, and I scrunched my eyes closed, as if it could silence the annoying sound. My head was pounding, and I wanted nothing more than to slip back into the cozy embrace of oblivion.

"Her fluid's empty. I'll change this bag right quick," a chipper voice said. It was entirely too loud.

Snatches of memories drifted back to me. Had Myra Crawford really tried to kill me, or was that all some bizarre dream? My entire body felt sore, and now that I was coming to, I realized the skin on my face burned. Meanwhile, my brain was something like scrambled eggs, my thoughts jumbled and chaotic.

I felt as though I was swimming underwater, everything foggy and muffled. I struggled toward a faint light overhead. Suddenly, I surfaced, gasping with clarity as my eyes popped open. The room was far too bright, causing the pain in my head to sharpen. I blinked, squinting slightly to diffuse the light.

Dad was perched on the edge of the hospital bed, while Granny Lu and Cara sat in chairs upholstered with blue vinyl. Everyone stood and rushed to me while I attempted to sit up.

"Easy now, just lean back," a nurse said, turning away from the IV pole. "Welcome back, sleepyhead. How are you feeling?"

"Tired," I said. "And my head hurts."

"All very normal," the nurse replied. She made quick work of checking my vitals while everyone stared at me with tentative smiles. I was too tired to say much, but I felt like I was being inspected under a microscope.

"Your body's been through a lot today. You just rest, and I'll let the doctor know you're awake," the nurse said.

"Thank you," Dad said, as she slipped out the door. When she moved, I saw that Deacon stood near the doorway, still in his uniform. When our eyes met, a big smile lit up his face and he stepped forward.

"You gave us quite a scare, Alex," Granny said sternly.

"Sorry, Granny," I said.

"You don't have anything to apologize for," Dad said. "You did good, kid. Real good." His rough hand patted mine, careful to avoid the huge IV in my left one.

"Thank goodness Deacon showed up when he did," Cara said. "Who would have thought little old Mrs. Crawford was so...diabolical?"

"Where is she now?" I asked, my eyes turning to Deacon. He stood at the end of the bed.

"After she had her wounds dressed, she was taken down to the station. I'd imagine she's sitting in the holding cell by now."

"You didn't take her yourself?" I didn't know why, but I felt uncomfortable knowing that Deacon hadn't actually seen her locked up with his own eyes. Not that I thought she'd escape, but still. The rational part of my brain had been crowded out by survival instincts.

"No, I stayed with you. But don't worry, I've been in contact with my officers. They're taking care of it."

"He rode in the ambulance with you," Dad said. I nodded, wondering at the strange softening I felt realizing that Deacon had stayed to make sure I was all right.

"What about Captain? Is he okay?" I asked.

"Probably eating day old donuts right about now and dreaming of a glorious K-9 career. They wouldn't let him ride in the ambulance, so Donny took him back to the station and promised to look after him," Deacon said.

"Okay," I said. "His services are not for sale, you know," I added.

"I was just kidding, Lex," he said gently. "But Cap's a hero, all the same. Who knows what would have happened if he hadn't stopped Myra? The two of you did quite a number on her, between the pepper spray, kicking and biting."

Dad chuckled. "That's my girl."

"We make a good team," I said, my eyes connecting with Granny's. She gave an approving nod.

"I mean, normally I wouldn't condone beating up an old lady, but she was asking for it," Cara agreed.

"She's just lucky there are iron bars between her and me," Granny said. "If I could just get my hands on her, oh what I wouldn't do!" Her mouth pressed into a thin line and she clenched her arthritic fists.

"Okay, easy, tiger," Dad said. "Why don't we go grab a coffee, Mom? And you can check in with things at the café." Turning to me, he asked, "Will you be all right for a bit?"

"Yeah, I'm good," I said. He pressed a kiss to my forehead and Granny gave me a tight hug.

"Don't you go doing anything like that ever again, you hear?" she said, and I nodded. After they left the room, Cara turned to me, leaning her elbow on the bed and squeezing my hand.

"I'm so glad you're okay. What an absolutely terrifying experience."

I shuddered. She wasn't kidding, and I felt a stinging sensation behind my eyes. I blinked back the tears and looked at Deacon.

"What will happen now?" I asked.

"Myra's already been formally charged and has confessed, so things should move along nicely. I'm not sure where she'll ultimately end up, but she'll be transferred to the county jail until sentencing," Deacon replied.

"Good. I don't even want to think about being in the same town as her," Cara said.

"How did she do it?" I asked. "I mean, she claimed that killing Alan was an accident."

"You already knew that Alan had been blackmailing her for

several years. Apparently, the morning he was killed, he stopped by her house, demanding more money. They had an argument, but Myra reluctantly paid him the requested amount and he left. Later, he met Buddy at the café with the same demands. I guess Myra heard about their altercation, and that's when she came up with her plan.

"Late in the afternoon, she stopped by his house with a package of cookies and the box of tea, pretending to make nice to get on his good side. They had tea there, and then she made him another cup in his travel mug, dosing him twice with the poison. She claims she only wanted to teach him a lesson, thinking that the worst that would happen was that he'd get sick, or feel weak for a day or two. Anyway, she took the rest of the tea home, along with the bags she'd already used, and waited for him to leave. He always went for an evening walk just before dark. Once he'd left, she slipped into his house and raided his files. She looked for the cash she'd given him earlier in the day, but he had already deposited it at the bank."

"How did she get in?" Cara asked.

"They were neighbors, and she knew where his key was hidden. That's why there was no sign of forced entry. But there were those little clues that someone had been in there. You remember it had been a wet day, and she'd left a couple muddy boot prints on the carpet."

"Her husband's old boots?" I asked.

Deacon nodded. "She must have been distracted, forgetting to take them off. And she left a file drawer ajar. Then there was the extra teacup in the dish drainer. She had the foresight to wash it, but didn't realize Alan had thrown her cookies away. All seemingly unconnected, but now it makes perfect sense."

"What about the fire at Buddy's? Was she behind that, too?" I asked.

"She was. It was no secret that Buddy went home for lunch and a nap at the same time each day. Myra made an appearance at a fitness class, but left early and went to his house. Once he'd gone to bed, she slipped in the unlocked back door and set up the file she'd found on him snooping through Alan's office. She wanted to make it look like he was destroying evidence that connected them, but she hadn't counted on Melinda coming home. When she heard someone coming in the front door, she set the curtains on fire and raced out of there.

"Myra was so rattled, she dropped the lighter in the backyard. And since Melinda went straight upstairs, not to the living room, she didn't see the fire until the smoke alarms started blaring. That's why Buddy suffered from smoke inhalation. He was napping in the guest room, nearest to the fire. He tried to put it out, but Melinda called the fire department and convinced him to get outside."

"What was her plan exactly? Breaking into his house and starting a fire sounds...chaotic," I said.

"She planned to set the fire, escape, and then call the fire department," Deacon said.

And leave Buddy to either die before they got there or set him up. Yikes.

"What did she have against Buddy? Other than he's kind of an awful person?" Cara asked.

"Sometimes criminals have their own moral code, and apparently marital faithfulness is pretty high on Myra Crawford's list. She'd been friendly with Melinda on various committees. The fact that Buddy had cheated on her, multiple times, in fact, was more than she could stomach, making him her perfect fall guy."

"Mom said that Melinda has thrown Buddy out of the house, by the way. He moved into his office, but since the country club wasn't too keen on that, he's staying at a hotel for the time being," Cara said.

"So she 'accidentally' killed Alan, panicked, and then set up Buddy to take the fall. But she didn't count on Sophie coming through with his alibi," I said.

"Right. Or your snooping around," Deacon said.

"So, when you showed up at her house, Lex, and pieced

everything together, the old bat just came completely unhinged," Cara finished.

"Up to that point Myra's plans had been calculated, if not a little reckless, but with you, she had to improvise," Deacon said.

We all sat in silence for a few moments, and I thought about Myra coming at me with the monkshood. I didn't think I'd ever forget her crazy eyes, so different from the meek old lady I thought I knew.

"You know, I almost feel sorry for her," I said.

"Are you serious?" Cara said. "She tried to kill you!"

"I know, but you should have seen her face when she talked about her husband. She *really* loved him. And Alan was blackmailing her for years, holding that information over her head. It couldn't have been easy to realize the man she'd loved for a lifetime did something so wrong. And then she felt like it was her job to protect his memory," I said.

"Well, the truth has a way of coming to light, in the end. All her efforts were in vain," Deacon said.

I supposed he was right. I didn't excuse her actions, far from it. But the whole situation still left me feeling somewhat melancholy.

"Wait, what happened with the musician?" I asked.

"Chris Jennings? Minor drug charges," Deacon replied. "The guy's got an interesting story, and so far, the details check out."

"What's his story?" I asked.

"Chris grew up in the house Alan Harvey was renovating. When he was a kid, he cut a hole in the plank floor of his room to hide things in. At some point, his grandfather gave him a medal he had earned in the Korean War and he hid it in there. Chris grew up, moved out, and had basically forgotten about it until his parents sold the house to Alan. They relocated to be near that same grandfather, who is in poor health. So, when our musician friend came back to town, he visited Alan to ask if he could access the house to find it. Alan refused, and when Chris saw him in the park that night, he was trying to catch up with him and ask again. By the time he found Alan in the maze, he had collapsed, and Chris panicked and left."

"Yikes. He didn't call for help or anything?" Cara asked.

Deacon shook his head. "He was under the influence and not thinking clearly. Legally, a person is not under any obligation to render aid, with a few exceptions. It sounds harsh, and I believe most people would have stayed to help an unconscious man, but in all likelihood, Alan was beyond help by that time."

"Wow," I said. "What about him breaking into the house?"

"When he broke in, he fell off the landing and sprained an ankle. He was too disoriented to do anything besides get out and back to his rental home. As you know, Brenda and Jessica Holliday own the house now, and they're not pressing charges. In fact, they plan to let him look for the medal when he's released, and Jessica is hoping to connect him with a twelve-step program she knows about. They just want to put the whole mess behind them and move on."

"Can't say I blame them," I said.

Cara's phone buzzed and she glanced at the screen. "Shoot, I'm going to have to go. I didn't realize how late it's gotten, and we promised to take the kids to the hay maze."

"It's reopened?" I asked.

"Yes," Deacon said. "The Forest of Fear's been such a hit that the drama club didn't want to move locations again, so some volunteers turned it into a less spooky, fun maze for the little ones. There's even a scavenger hunt inside."

"Nice," I said. I didn't think I'd personally want to go back in the maze, but I was glad it was going to be used, after all.

Cara gave me a gentle hug. "I'll see you later, okay? We've got the pumpkin launch this evening, but I'll come check on you after."

I had forgotten about that.

I nodded, and then Deacon and I were alone again. He sat in the chair Granny Lu had left, closest to me. The silence stretched between us, and I was suddenly aware of the drab hospital gown

I wore. I wondered where my clothes had ended up. I supposed that as they'd been covered in monkshood poison, I didn't want them back. I pulled the scratchy blanket up a little higher and cleared my throat.

"I guess I should say thank you," I began, staring at my hands. "If you hadn't come when you did...well, it could have been a lot worse. So...thanks." I met his gaze, surprised that despite how he'd changed over the years, his eyes still held the same kindness.

However, the tinge of mischief I normally saw was replaced with something else. Worry, perhaps? He scrubbed his hands over his face and through his hair, making the dark locks stick out erratically. He rested his elbows on his knees, fisting his hands under his chin before looking at me again.

"I was so scared when I got your message. I lost track of the laws I broke flying to Myra's house, but I was sure I'd be too late..." he trailed off. He gave me a wry smile. "Anyway, I'm glad I wasn't."

"Me too," I said softly. His dark brown eyes held mine, and I couldn't look away.

A sharp rap on the door shattered the unexpected intimacy of the moment, and we both sat up a little straighter as the doctor entered the room.

"How are we doing now, Alex?" he asked. "Quite an exciting day you've had, from what I hear."

"That's one way to put it," I said drily. "I'm feeling okay. I'm tired and sore, and I have a headache, but I suppose it could be worse."

"Indeed," the doctor said. "Sorry, officer, could you step out for just a moment while I visit with my patient?"

"Oh, it's okay. He can stay," I said. "He's a...friend." I realized at that moment just how true it was. Our eyes met briefly, and Deacon gave me a crooked, knowing smile.

"All right," the doctor continued. "Well, as you know, you were exposed to the toxins of the monkshood plant. Thankfully, you're young and healthy and it was only a small amount. Fluids and rest are my recommendations, but you shouldn't be any worse for wear after a few days."

"That's a relief. When can I go home?"

"Well, if you're able to get up and walk around this afternoon, use the bathroom, and keep some food down, I don't see a problem with releasing you by this evening. So long as you promise to rest at home, no working or going out and getting crazy tomorrow night."

I had almost forgotten, tomorrow was Sunday. Halloween.

"I think I can handle that. Thank you, doctor."

"You betcha. I'll have hospitality come around with a menu. Take care, now."

Dad and Granny Lu came back in as the doctor was leaving, so I caught them up on what he'd said. They held paper coffee cups, and I'd guessed that they hadn't wanted to let me out of their sight for long.

"I'd better be going," Deacon said, as my family settled back into the chairs. "I've got a mountain of paperwork and a pumpkin-launching trebuchet to oversee."

I rolled my eyes and he grinned, mischievous look firmly back in place.

"I'll take a video and send it to you. I know you're bummed to miss it." He winked at me. "See you soon, Lex."

"Bye, D," I said as he slipped out the door.

CHAPTER 15
JUST A BUNCH OF HOCUS POCUS

I KNOW the doctor had said I needed to rest, but I was feeling so good the next morning that I didn't see any harm in going down to the festival for the Monster Run. I planned to sit in a lawn chair and watch the festivities, rather than participate as originally intended. So really, it was no different than sitting on my couch binge watching TV. Except I'd have to put on real pants, unfortunately.

Cap stayed close while I was getting ready. Granny Lu had gotten him from the station last night before taking me home, and we'd had quite a tearful reunion in the hospital parking lot...on my end, anyway. But since then, he'd seemed afraid to let me out of his sight. I imagined he'd made it his personal mission to keep me out of trouble.

Dad's truck lumbered into the driveway just as I was grabbing my keys. Busted.

"What are you doing here?" I asked, when I opened the front door.

"Good morning to you, too." He gave me a big bear hug. "How are you feeling?"

"Much better," I said.

"Planning on going somewhere?" He eyed the keys in my hand.

"Well, I was feeling so good, I didn't think there would be any harm in watching the race. On the sidelines, promise."

"That's what I figured. Come on, I'll drive you in the truck. Cap can come, too."

"I can drive myself, Dad."

"I know, kiddo, but I'm going down there anyway. Let me take care of you, for once."

Well. There were worse things in life than being fussed over by your loved ones. Dad held the door open while Cap and I exited the house. I doubled checked the lock before hopping into the truck.

"Are you going to watch Nyla run?" I asked, sneaking a glance at Dad as he drove through the neighborhood and down the hill to the park. I watched, fascinated, as a blush crept up his neck and into his cheeks. He kept his eyes to the road.

"Is she a victim or a monster?" I asked, when he ignored my question.

The annual Monster Run is always held on Halloween morning, with participants following a predetermined course. The "victims" in the race run through a series of obstacles along the racecourse, wearing touch football flags around their waists. Costumed monsters are stationed throughout the course to chase the victims, and if they grab a victim's flag, that racer is disqualified.

"She's going as a victim," Dad finally replied. He glanced at me, looking so unsure of himself that I couldn't help but feel a little sorry for him. *Maybe I should be a grown up and not give him a hard time about this*, I thought.

"It's okay, you know," I said quietly. The events of the past twenty-four hours had really put things into perspective for me. "If you like Nyla, you should go for it. Honest."

Dad blew out a breath he'd been holding. "I do like her. I really do," he said, a tentative smile on his lips. "I don't know how it happened, but one day, I just started to look at her… differently. You know the last thing in the world I'd want to do is hurt you, though…"

"Dad, this is not about me, okay? I'm happy for you. And *you're* allowed to be happy, too. After all this time, you deserve it." He reached out and I squeezed his hand.

"She's so great," he gushed, his face breaking into a huge grin. "We're taking things slowly, but I love spending time with her. It doesn't even matter what we do. I just want to be with her."

His face looked ten years younger as he talked about Nyla. Maybe he couldn't see it yet, but he acted like he was truly falling for her. It was weird, thinking of Nyla in that context. Although surprisingly, not unwelcome.

"I love Nyla as much as the next person, but you're a catch, Dad. *She's* the lucky one."

"Thanks, kid."

———

It seemed like the whole town had turned out for the final day of the festival. It took an inordinate amount of time for Dad and me to find a place to park our lawn chairs. The news about Myra Crawford had spread like wildfire, and it seemed that each person we passed wanted to have their own say, with plenty of well wishes for me and everyone singing Deacon's praises.

"I never liked that woman," Phyllis Goat said. "Deep down, I just *knew* something was off about her. But it wasn't very smart of you to go to her house alone, was it?"

"Pshh," Diane scoffed. "You sat next to her at book club not two days ago. The two of you even shared a dessert! She had us all fooled."

Diane turned back to me. "I can't believe I never saw this side of her, after all the years I've known her. I mean, I always knew she had a bit of a temper, but I never would have thought she'd be capable of what she did. I'm just glad you're all right, hon."

Diane gave me a hug, and my arms reached all the way around her tiny frame while Phyllis made some sort of acquiescing grunt next to her.

"Chief Lane was certainly heroic," Phyllis admitted, determined to not give me any credit. I shrugged it off. Not even Phyllis could ruin this beautiful morning.

We finally found a place next to Cara's parents, and after hugs all around, we settled into our chairs. The kids, Arthur and Olive, had a blanket spread on the ground with toys, but they seemed more interested in playing tag with the other little ones running around while we waited for the race to begin.

"Tim told me he's going to be hiding in that tent right there," Maggie pointed out. "Five bucks says that he'll get Cara when she runs by."

"Nope, my money's on our girl. She's still fast," Cara's dad said.

"We'll see, old man." Maggie giggled.

We heard the starting gun go off in the distance, and a cheer from the crowd. A few minutes later, the first victims began to race toward our area.

By the end of the race, my sides were hurting from laughter. I had the satisfaction of watching Tim take down Deacon, who was running as a victim. They missed the "flag football" memo. Instead, the two of them went full tilt with tackle rules and a side of wrestling thrown into the mix.

They rolled around on the grass like schoolboys until Tim triumphantly pulled off Deacon's flag. Only a handful of runners made it to the end, and Cara's dad did indeed win his five dollars for his daughter's triumph over Tim. He was right, she was too fast for him.

After the race, Jessica Holliday ran over to me, in the same zombie prom outfit I'd seen her wear at the Forest of Fear. This time, she wore running shoes and a first-place sash around her torso. I had to admit, I was impressed with her athletic skills. Not many people would be able to dodge monsters in a prom dress and win first prize, to boot. And she was barely winded.

"Alex, I'm so glad you're okay," she said, throwing her arms around me. I patted her back awkwardly. A few days ago, we had barely been friendly acquaintances, and now we were hugging.

"What a horrible thing for you to go through." Her blue eyes were round with sincerity.

I couldn't help the involuntary shudder that went thorough me.

"It was awful, but I'm feeling much better now," I said.

"You let me know if you need anything, okay?"

"Got it. Thanks, Jessica."

Ravi made his way over to us. I'd already spoken with him earlier in the day, and after saying our goodbyes, the two of them walked away to finish planning the Forest of Fear grand finale tonight. And for the first time, Jessica looked at him with a glimmer of the admiration with which he looked at her. Maybe the prom queen had changed, after all.

———

The sky was darkening outside, and I poured bags of candy into a huge bowl in anticipation of the trick-or-treaters soon to be knocking on my door. Several folks had reminded me that our neighborhood was a hot spot, and Cara and Tim had promised to bring the kids by. The circus costumes had held up during the parade and were ready to go for the evening.

My phone dinged, and I saw it was a message from Cara. I'd already received video clips from Deacon and Tim of the pumpkin-launching trebuchet, and now my best friend was sending her footage.

I had to laugh at that ridiculously monstrous contraption the guys had built. They hadn't had a chance to make sure it worked before the pumpkin launch competition, and they were ecstatic to see that it could, indeed, hurl a pumpkin into the lake. They whooped and high-fived and fist-bumped one another and anyone else within reach.

Unfortunately, they had been bested by a group of physics students with a pumpkin cannon. Ravi had claimed bragging rights for being the kids' "faculty advisor."

Even so, Tim and Deacon were pleased with second prize and already planning on improvements for next year, much to Cara's chagrin.

Cara: I'm chopping that thing up for firewood as soon as Tim's back is turned.

I sent a laughing emoji response to her text and set my phone on the counter. Checking that my outside light was switched on, I grabbed a lighter for the jack-o-lantern on my small porch. Dad had brought me his goofy pumpkin from the carving competition a few days ago, adding it to my porch decorations.

As I went outside, the scraping of a lawn chair alerted me to Deacon's presence on his own stoop.

"Hey, neighbor," I said. "You ready for this?"

"Yeah, it's such a nice night that I'm going to set up out here, rather than answer the door a million times," he said, unfolding the chair in front of his garage and setting up a card table next to it. "You want to join me?"

Well…why not? It was chilly, but not freezing, and suddenly my own house seemed all too quiet and lonely.

"Um, sure. Just give me a few minutes," I said, ducking back inside. I layered on some warmer clothes and grabbed a folding chair from the closet. Then, I had an idea.

Deacon wasn't a big tea fan, but he'd never been able to resist Granny's caramel hot chocolate. I'd perfected the recipe years ago, and I had homemade caramel sauce in the fridge. I quickly grabbed the rest of the ingredients to whip up a batch.

Soon I was pouring steamy, creamy hot chocolate into two

large mugs. I topped our drinks with a generous dollop of whipped cream and caramel drizzle.

"Did you get lost inside?" Deacon asked, when I finally returned. I raised my eyebrows and the mugs in his direction. Cap trotted after me, not wanting to be left out. He looked perfectly adorable in his new doggie-sized Captain America costume.

"Hey, thanks," Deacon said, taking them off my hands and setting them on the table next to a basket of fun-sized candy. I grabbed my chair and a lap blanket and quickly fixed myself a place next to Deacon. I settled Cap's dog bed near my feet. He circled a few times and then finally snuggled down. Deacon gave Cap a good rub on his belly, chuckling at his Halloween costume.

Cap had already proven he was a superhero, so his doggie Captain America costume was perfect.

"Not all heroes wear capes, sometimes they just need a vibranium shield. Right, boy?" Deacon said to him. Cap wagged his tail in agreement while Deacon settled into his chair with the hot cocoa.

"I thought we could use something to warm us up," I said, taking my own mug into my hands and relishing the heat seeping into my cold fingers.

"Looks delicious," Deacon said. "Granny Lu's recipe, right?"

I nodded. He took a sip and rolled his eyes heavenward.

"Perfection," he said, grinning. "This is going to send me into a sugar coma."

"Either this or the candy will, if we don't get some trick or treaters soon," I said, unwrapping a miniature chocolate bar and popping it into my mouth.

"It's all about pacing yourself," Deacon replied. "And cutting the sugar with some salt," he said, pulling out a bowl of buttery popcorn from the other side of his chair.

"I underestimated you," I said, grabbing a handful. "You got wise in your old age."

Soon, we didn't have much time to chat because a steady stream of kids kept us busy handing out candy. I loved seeing all the costumes, from the adorable little ones in their fluffy outfits, all the way up to a few teenagers with their trendy pop culture costumes.

When we finally had a lull, I went inside and refilled our hot chocolate mugs before settling back under my warm blanket. The silence stretched between us, but it was a comfortable, peaceful quiet, only broken by the shouts of delighted children throughout the neighborhood.

"So, how did you do it?" I asked Deacon, blowing on my steaming cup before taking a careful sip.

"Do what?" he asked.

"Weasel your way back into the hearts of everyone in town? I swear, everyone I saw at the festival was singing your praises today. Face it, this town loves you. It's like they've completely forgotten your wayward past," I teased.

"They said the same things about you, actually," he said quietly.

"They did not. Everyone thinks I go looking for trouble." I set my cup on the table.

"To be fair, you kind of do."

"Whatever," I said, crossing my arms.

"You really want to know? How I got back into everyone's good graces?" Deacon asked.

"I really do."

"Okay, come here. It's a secret," he said. I sighed, scooting forward in my chair, and he leaned in close to my ear. His breath tickled the hairs against my neck as he spoke.

"Bingo," he whispered.

"Huh?" I pulled away, socking his arm with my fist. "That doesn't tell me anything."

Deacon leaned back in his chair with a smile.

"No, literally. Bingo. I play once a month down at the community center. I'm telling you, you get the old folks on your side, and everyone else follows." He made a sweeping motion with his hand.

I felt unchecked laughter bubbling up inside me, and before I could stop it, a string of giggles escaped. Deacon had grown up a little, sure. But he hadn't lost his boyish charm.

I envisioned Deacon sandwiched between the Silver Vixens book club ladies, checking his bingo card, and an undignified snort escaped my mouth. He began to chuckle at me, and soon, we were both laughing uncontrollably.

"Does Phyllis let you cheat?" I asked, through my giggles. He looked at me incredulously.

"How did you know?" he asked. "The bad thing is, she's the caller!" he howled. "I have to pretend I don't hear her to avoid winning every round."

I wiped the tears from my eyes. "I'm crying here!"

The stress of the last few weeks had finally broken, leaving me feeling spectacularly giddy.

"Oh, that's good stuff," he said, letting out one last laugh. It took several moments for us to catch our breath.

Deacon watched me carefully as we quieted, his huge smile fading. His eyes turned thoughtful, and his head cocked slightly to one side.

"What? Something wrong?" I asked.

"No, not at all," he answered, leaning forward again. "I was just thinking how glad I am that you came home, Lex. It's been too long since we laughed together."

"Me, too," I said. "I'm glad I don't hate you anymore," I added cheekily.

He narrowed his eyes at me, but I didn't miss the way he fought the corners of his mouth quirking upward.

He lifted his mug. "To friends," he said. "And justice," he added, winking at me. I clinked my cup with his.

"To friends," I echoed. Our eyes connected as I smiled softly at him, and a lazy grin lit his face. I felt the goosebumps trail all the way up my spine and down my arms, but it had nothing to do with the cold breeze that ruffled my hair and stung my cheeks.

This time, I welcomed the sixth sense that perceived the warmth and joy radiating from Deacon, and I tried to catch and hold onto whatever it was that was blooming between us. It felt fragile and tenuous, but also something like a new beginning. I couldn't wait to see what would happen next.

THE END

RECIPES

HEARTBREAK SOUP (CREAMY TOMATO BASIL)

Ingredients:
- ½ onion, diced
- 2 garlic cloves, minced
- 1 Tbsp. olive oil
- 2 cans diced tomatoes
- 6 oz. can tomato paste
- 2 (8 oz.) cans tomato sauce
- 2 cups chicken broth
- ½ stick butter
- 1 Tbsp. sugar
- 1 cup heavy whipping cream
- 2-3 tsp. dried basil
- 1 tsp. dried oregano
- shredded parmesan cheese (optional)

Directions:
Sauté onions in olive oil until translucent. Add garlic and cook a minute or two. Add all tomatoes, sauce, and chicken broth. Bring to a boil, reduce heat and simmer ten minutes. Turn to low and add butter, sugar, cream, basil, and oregano. Remove

from heat once mixed. (At this point I like to use an immersion blender to create a uniform texture, but it's not necessary if you prefer a chunky tomato soup.) Add salt and pepper to taste. Ladle into bowls and top with shredded parmesan cheese.

JALAPEÑO POPPER DEVILED EGGS

Ingredients:
Dozen boiled eggs, peeled
¼ cup mayonnaise
¼ cup cream cheese, softened
1 Tbsp. mustard
10 small slices bacon, crumbled
3 Tbsp. chopped pickled jalapeños + 1 Tbsp. for topping (optional)
2 Tbsp. jalapeno brine
Salt, pepper, cayenne pepper, chili powder, paprika to taste
Directions:
Cut eggs in half, separate yolks into bowl and put whites on serving tray or platter. Mix yolks with all ingredients and spices. Fill egg whites with yolk mixture. Top with more paprika, cayenne, and extra jalapeños if desired. Chill in refrigerator and serve.

SPICED APPLE CIDER

Ingredients:
Gallon apple juice
¼ cup brown sugar
4 cinnamon sticks
1 heaping tsp. whole allspice
1 heaping tsp. whole cloves
2 star anise
2 pinches ground nutmeg
Peel of one orange (use vegetable peeler)

Directions:

Combine all ingredients into pot on stove, simmer on low for about half an hour (Longer is fine. Your home will smell heavenly!). Use a fine mesh sieve to strain the spices and peel, pour into mugs and serve. This will also keep in the refrigerator to heat and serve later.

SLOW COOKER ROAST BEEF

Ingredients:

Chuck, arm or rump roast

Onion

1/8- 1/4 cup Worcestershire sauce

1/4 cup dry red wine, such as cabernet sauvignon

1 cup water or beef broth

Seasoned salt

Cracked black pepper

Directions:

Chop onions and place in bottom of slow cooker (you can easily skip this step and use onion powder with your spices). Pour in water or beef broth. Cut roast into 4-5 chunks, sprinkle liberally with seasoned salt and pepper, and place on top of onions. Pour Worcestershire sauce and wine on top of roast. Cook on low for 8-10 hours. Serve or save for vegetable beef soup.

ACKNOWLEDGMENTS

First of all, thank you, reader, for choosing to read my book! There are so many wonderful books in the world, and I consider it a true honor anytime someone picks up something I've written. I had so much fun diving into this quirky story, and I hope you enjoyed the world and characters of Emerald Bay as much as I did creating them. You haven't heard the last of Alex and the gang!

If you enjoyed this book, please consider leaving an honest review. Reviews help indie authors gain exposure and reach new readers! If you'd like to connect online, please follow my Instagram @cozykatewrites for updates, bookish things, and all things cozy.

Huge thanks to my family for putting up with Mama getting lost in another world from time to time. Kids, you're the absolute best and I love you bigger than the sky. Keep imagining, stay wild, and never lose your wonder of the world around you. Clint, thank you for your continual support and love, and for answering all my bizarre questions for "book research." I love when we get uninterrupted moments and the way you focus in and listen to all the random stuff that makes my weird brain tick. Love love love you.

Taressa, thank you for being my constant sounding board and always listening to my ideas, from tiny seedlings to fully fleshed out books. Anthony, see your dedication at the beginning of the book, haha. Love you guys so very much.

Lindsey, thank you for always being there, whether it's to

vent about frustrations or to celebrate the wins. I appreciate you putting fresh eyes on this when I simply couldn't do another read-through!

To my extended family and local community, your continued support means the world to me. Your excitement for each story I write fuels me and fills me with joy.

And finally, to the ultimate Creator of it all, thank you for the ability to create something of beauty and humor and love and forgiveness and justice, tiny though it is. Thank you for writing the ultimate Story of impossibilities, with the unlikeliest of heroes, and making a way to right all wrongs and bring us out of the shadowlands and into the true light.

Made in the USA
Las Vegas, NV
29 September 2023